Twisted Mind

6 Science Fiction Stories
by D. Michael Martindale

Worldsmith Stories
Salt Lake City, Utah

ISBN: 978-1-970065-00-8

Published by
Worldsmith Stories
1042 Ft. Union Blvd. #109
Midvale UT 84047

info@worldsmithstories.com
http://worldsmithstories.com

Artwork courtesy of **Pixabay**
pixabay.com

What readers have said about D. Michael's novels

"I found Martindale's writing exciting and compelling. He created a world of nations, customs, and peoples that blends magic with the gods of the lands. It's an exciting read, carefully constructed with sequences and twists to sustain a series. I'm looking forward to the second book of the series."

— Doug Gibson, writer, blogger

"Exciting, clever, and action packed. A great story and a great ending. This is going to be such a hit!"

— Sharon Dodge, database administrator

"The story drew me in right from the beginning. I was so engrossed in the first chapters when I read them that I knew I wouldn't be able to put the book down again."

— Karen Crapo, caretaker

"Jack London once made my heart pound, but Michael Martindale is the first writer to rock me back in my chair in wide-eyed amazement."

— Preston McConkie, journalist

"Like Stephen King, Martindale captures the earthy rhythms of daily life as the characters get caught up in bizarre, harrowing events."

— Christopher Kimball Bigelow, author and editor

"Outrageous, provocative, insightful, courageous and thoughtful. Michael Martindale reminded me of the sensitivities of Orson Scott Card in his novel *Saints*."

— Eugene Kovalenko, blogger

"Martindale's frank sensuality...is not salacious; it's simply a matter of fact. A lesser book would have found a way to ignore it completely. It is frustrating when people, in life and in fiction, say what they think should be said instead of what they feel. In that light, Martindale's relative profundity is refreshing."

— Sam Vicchrilli , In Utah This Week Magazine

"Martindale...paints a scenario at once believable and shudderingly delusional."

— Kim Madsen, readers group coordinator

"The story still lingers in my mind. It was a real page-turner!"

—Eileen Stringer, reader

"Reading this fast-paced and quickly changing story is like embarking on a river rafting trip that starts out in placid shallows, never suspecting that around the next corner whitewater rapids wait, anxious to engulf you. The ride never slows down until the last few pages."

—Jonathan Neville, writer

"One of the things that a novelist, especially one who writes fantasy fiction, is required to do, is get the reader to suspend disbelief, and then sustain that suspension... This is where Martindale succeeds hands down."

— David Birley, reader

"His captivating storytelling keeps the plot moving without being predictable or trite. His descriptions ring true."

— Wife of reader

"Skillfully written, creating a realistic, complex, difficult world where everything is not as it initially seems. It's a page-turner, a real heavy weight."

—Mahonri Stewart, playwright

"D. Michael has an incredible talent for writing. I was utterly wowed by his characters' inner thoughts."

— Brian Sheets, digital media specialist

"I had a hard time putting it down, and as a result I read it surprisingly quickly. I had to know how the whole mess was going to end. It's deep, well thought out, and opens up some interesting and thought-provoking ideas."

—Lee Penrod, systems programmer

TABLE OF CONTENTS

BOOKS BY D. MICHAEL MARTINDALE

Celeste & the White Dragon
Brother Brigham

Twisted Stories series
Twisted Mind
Twisted Soul

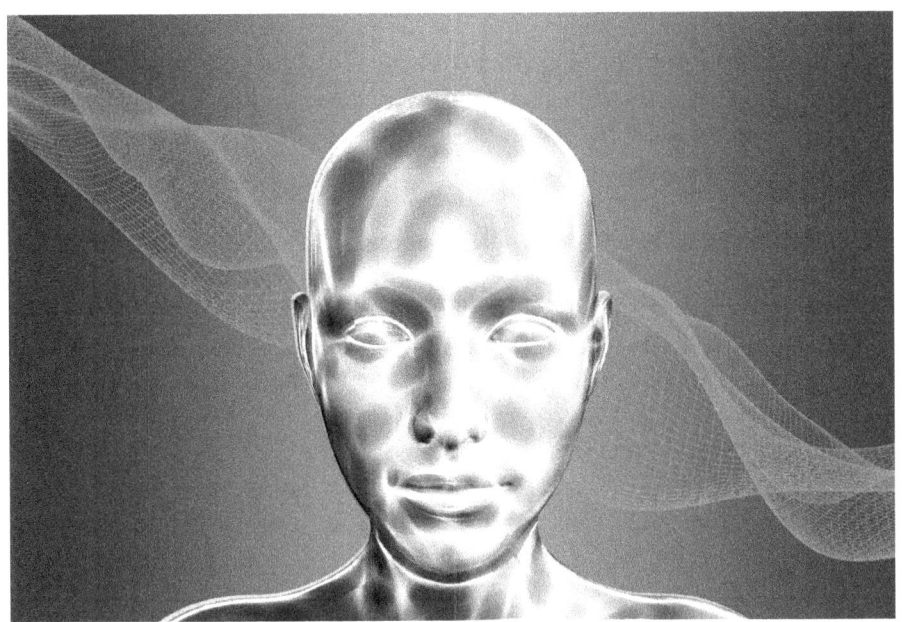

A Growth in the Backyard

Phil fidgeted with a blade of grass between two fingers as he stared at Emily's crossed legs. Barefoot and with shorts on, her creamy legs shone sensuously in the bright sunlight. Occasionally the pleasant breeze threw a whiff of her his way. He loved that.

"You're sure quiet this morning," she said in her tiny elfen voice. It was a voice that rendered most people incapable of taking her seriously, in spite of her sharp intelligence and determined ambition. She used it to her advantage, shocking people with unexpected zings from the little-girl voice, throwing them off-guard. It was one of the things he loved about her.

As his fingers combed through the grass, the tip of his thumb brushed a sharp rock hidden under the blades. "I was just thinking about the meteor shower last night," he finally said, suppressing the self-disgust he felt putting the question off one more time he'd been trying to ask for days. He fondled the rock absently. It must have been half-buried in the ground because it didn't budge.

"Are you still fretting over that?" Emily smirked in a way that made him love being teased. "You couldn't help that we didn't see it. Are you so arrogant that you think you're responsible for an overcast sky?"

He smiled bashfully as he glanced up at her. Her golden blonde hair—another piece of the mosaic that caused people to underestimate her—glowed with backlighting from the sun. Her face was lost in a murky silhouette, but he knew its features and its expressions well enough to fill in the details with his imagination, right down to the half-smile she'd be smiling right now, and the crinkles at the corner of her left eye that squinted a hair's breadth tighter than her right when she was amused.

Phil felt a bit of grittiness as he rubbed his thumb and forefinger together. He looked at them and found a fine, graphite-colored powder on their tips. Strange rock! He brushed the powder off against his pants thigh.

"But that's not what you're really thinking, is it?" she challenged.

He shook his head. It still amazed him how transparent he was to her. It made him feel exposed, naked, but in a way he loved. He didn't want any secrets for her to discover after...

But there'd be no "after" if he didn't work up the nerve to ask.

Her hands trembled in her lap. Trembling hands were not a common feature on Emily. He realized she anticipated his question and was nervous about it herself. That gave him the courage he needed to overcome his hesitation.

"Emily, will you marry me?"

Damn the sun! He couldn't see her face well enough to read her expression. This was one time he couldn't fill in the details, because he didn't know what her reaction would be. She peered at him silently for many seconds. Was she going to refuse him after all and couldn't bring herself to say it?

A glittering jewel of a tear dripped from her cheek and landed on her trembling hand. Phil's heart jumped. A tear of joy or sorrow? The suspense was unendurable.

She lunged forward and grabbed his hands in hers, pulling them into her chest so he nearly toppled over. "Oh, Phil, yes, I'll marry you!"

Suddenly she let go and stared at her fingers. "What's that?" She rubbed her hands together.

"What?"

"Some kind of powder."

He looked at his fingers. The powder was back on the tips. But he'd rubbed it off!

"What *is* that?" she cried louder, pointing at his thigh.

Where he'd rubbed was a patch of grey sheen. Sunlight splashed rainbow colors on it like a reflection on oily water. He looked at his hand again. The patch was already larger and thicker.

"What is this?" She rubbed her hands together violently. "I can't get it off."

"Stop!" he shouted, causing her to freeze in mid-rub, eyes wide. "Don't rub it anymore."

She let her hands hang limply before her. "What's going on?"

"I don't know." He scrambled to his knees and bent over the spot in the grass where he'd felt the rock. He parted the blades and found a rock like no rock he'd ever seen. A perfectly shaped hexagonal column sprouting from the ground, about a quarter inch in diameter and a half inch tall. Dull graphite grey. He parted the grass wide so she could see. "It came from this."

She peered over it, the hair of her bangs brushing his forehead. "What is that?"

"I don't know, but we'd better find out. This stuff seems to be growing."

A disturbed look crossed Emily's face. "How does rock grow?"

Phil gaped at her, then looked at his fingers. He rubbed them hard against the grass, then held them out. The powder was gone.

They stared at his fingers. Before a minute could pass, more powder formed as if it were a slow dissolve in a movie.

"My fingers are tingling," he said.

She held up her palms. The fine powder dusted both of them. "My hands too." Suddenly she gasped. "Look at your pants."

Where the shimmering patch had been was a ragged hole in his jeans. The patch was dull grey like the column and fastened to his skin. He could feel the slight tingling there too.

"We gotta get this stuff off of us fast. Come on!" He reached his hand out to help her up.

"I don't think we better touch each other."

"Or anything else," he added. "Let's call for an ambulance."

He reached for his phone in his pocket with his good hand, only to find dust forming on that one too. They gaped at each other, and she held her hands up in desperation, showing the layer of dust.

Finally he spat, "Hell!" and grabbed the phone, leaving fingerprints of dust as he dialed 911, reported the address, and said, "We've got some kind of chemical on us that keeps spreading—fast. We don't know what it is. Please hurry."

Her eyes floated in tears as she held her hands out. The powder had become so thick, wisps of it billowed into the air.

"Oh God," Phil said, "we're probably breathing that stuff."

He leaped to his feet and stepped back. As each footstep hit grass, a cloud of dust billowed up. Dull flat tops of hundreds of tiny columns littered the lawn.

"Phil, they're everywhere," she moaned.

"Front yard. We'll wait there."

He held his hand out to her. She hesitated.

Showing his dusted hand, he said, "Doesn't matter now."

She nodded and took his hand. He pulled her to her feet.

As they ran, their shoes crushed columns into dust clouds. Around the corner of the house was a boundary where the swarm of columns hadn't spread. Hundreds of columns, then suddenly clear grass.

He pointed, and dust wafted from his finger. "They stop there."

"Thank God. I thought they'd be everywhere."

"I think they will be." He pointed again. A new column had just peaked above the blades of grass. "Let's go." He deliberately stomped on the new column. It made him feel better, although it probably caused them to spread faster.

They stopped on the sidewalk of the quiet cul-de-sac. In the yard across the street, a young boy kicked a soccer ball around.

Emily held her hands out like they were tarantulas. They were completely covered in dust. Powder fluttered down from them in a steady stream. Phil's hands weren't far behind.

"I don't feel the tingle anymore," she said, a cry in her voice. "I can't feel anything in my hands."

He gasped. A tiny patch of grey had developed just under her right eye. A tear streaked through it, darkening the color where it touched. Please, no! Not her sweet face. Not her sweet blue eyes!

"The ambulance will be here soon. Just hang on."

She nodded. Mucous trickled from her nostrils. One trickle had the dark color of moistened dust mixed into it. He looked away, pretending to search for the ambulance. What in God's name was this stuff?

"What's that on your hands?" the boy from across the street called. He looked both ways and began to cross the street.

"No!" Phil shouted. "Stay there! We don't know what it is. We can't get it off."

The boy stopped with a look of fear on his face, then slowly backed up until he was safe on the curb. "W-want me to call 911 or something?"

"Thanks," Phil said. "We already did."

The boy turned and ran into his house. "*Mo*-om."

Something slid down Phil's infected leg.

"Phil," Emily moaned.

He looked down. His pant leg had completely severed and dropped to the ground. The patch on his skin wrapped around his leg, coming within an inch of touching itself in back. His entire leg felt asleep. The fabric of his pants had dissolved away until his boxer shorts were exposed at the hip. Its edges were ragged with damage. Beneath it all Phil had grey dust instead of skin.

"I can't move my fingers!" she cried.

Something about her hands were different. The thick layer of dust was still there, but there was something shiny underneath. A flake of dust broke off and fluttered down. The exposed patch shone like chrome.

He lifted his hand and studied his fingers. He couldn't move them either. The dust had become a mottled patchwork over a smooth metallic surface, with small flakes of dust sloughing off continuously. This stuff was eating them alive, turning them into metal!

Where the hell was that ambulance?

Across the street, the boy reappeared with his mother. She shaded her eyes and stared. "Are you two alright?"

"An ambulance is coming," Phil called back. "Don't come over here. It spreads easily."

"What is it?"

Phil shrugged with a theatrical gesture so she could see it. The remaining dust on his hand dropped away. The smooth chrome surface of his hand flashed in the sun.

The mother squinted hard, then cried, "Oh my God!" She grabbed the boy's hand and pulled. "Get in the house right now!" They disappeared through the door.

A siren intruded into the quiet neighborhood. "It's coming." He turned to look at Emily.

She was on her knees, her body wavering with precarious balance. Her arms were chrome up to her elbows. Her mouth gaped open as dust-stained drool glistened around its corners. Her tongue was shiny. Her cheek and one eye and part of her forehead were a metallic surface. Her eye stared blankly like a Greek statue. A patch of her hair above her eye had disappeared, consumed by dust.

Her breath came in gurgles. She toppled forward, her face making a metallic thud against the sidewalk.

"Emily!" he shrieked. He dropped to her, holding his own metallic hands out, wondering what he could do when he could barely move them.

Tingling swept through his abdomen, making his stomach feel queasy. His pants and boxers dropped from his body completely, exposing metallic genitals. Terror clenched his heart. A guttural whine forced its way from his throat. He wondered how long he could live with metallic organs, how much it would hurt before he died.

But all he felt was tingling and numbness. The tingling rose up to his diaphragm as if some force field were slowly sweeping through his body, cutting a cross-section through him. Another plane of tingling crept up each arm, passing his shoulders.

Below the tingling he felt nothing. Above the tingling, no pain. Just mind-gripping terror.

A buzzing grew in his ears. He felt lightheaded. The ambulance siren was strong now, yet seemed distant. His vision clouded, and he could just barely make out the flashing of sunlight on metal that was once Emily. Right before his vision blacked out, he thought he saw the ghostly shape of a vehicle with a pulsing red light above it.

So what good are EMTs going to do us now? he thought as he died.

———

All his senses boiled around the core of his consciousness. Phil could see fierce, flashing, abstract images surrounding him in 360 degrees. A cacophony of sound bombarded him from every direction. The intensity should have hurt his ears, but it didn't. Exotic aromas and flavors and tastes—many he'd never experienced—exploded in his head. All over his body, he could feel a rush of sensation in a profound, immediate way that seemed impossible.

Warmth from the sun bathed him, penetrated him. Whispy fingers of breeze feathered his skin with an exquisiteness that should have caused orgasms. Something cold and hard and gritty pressed against his back. It should have been uncomfortable, but the sensations filled him with joy at their overwhelming variety. He must be nude to feel such things over all of his body, but he loathed the idea of putting clothes on and smothering them.

The bombardment of images resolved into shapes and colors, an expanse of blue, puffs of white, patches of green and grey, structural angles of multiple colors. The sounds clarified into shouts and rushes and rumbles, stomps and weeping, and dozens of hurried footsteps. The aromas and flavors became freshly mowed grass, a million floral perfumes, the sweat of fear, the pungence of airborne chemicals, fresh paint, musky animals of all kinds, burning exhaust.

Uncountable thoughts, facts, information, flooded into his brain in a terrifying blast. He screamed. His scream reverberated all over his body like a god's. He struggled with all his being to sort out the deluge that drowned his mind.

I think, therefore I am, said one part of his mind, and he wondered how he could think when he was dead. The answer was simple: he couldn't be dead. But how could he be alive? Hadn't his whole body turned to metal?

Was this the afterlife?

His mind could focus in all directions at once, thinking many things. He had no idea how his mind could do this miraculous thing, but it was a godsend—he could never have dealt with the unrelenting flow of data without it. His mind sorted out images of huge stars and teeming planets, of bits of life flowing eternally in cold, empty space. Worlds without number passed before him, all filled with extraordinary life.

A rain of grey particles showered each world, one by one, little bits of living minerals, whose only purpose for existing was to multiply. They fell through the atmosphere of each planet and settled to the surface, then began converting everything they touched into more of themselves. If they touched lifeless material, they grew into hexagonal columns of packed spores, sucking raw minerals from surfaces they contacted. When the thing they touched was a living creature, they converted it into a living organism of themselves, carefully preserving the life within the creature until the process was complete, while protecting and enhancing the consciousness inside.

They were interstellar spores spreading throughout the galaxy procreating their original species, recreating themselves in the image of whatever life forms they found on each planet. It wasn't God creating them in his own image. God recreated himself in their image.

A small part of Phil recoiled in horror at the images—a terrible virus spreading throughout the galaxy, infecting everything it came in touch with and corrupting it beyond recognition. But the greater part of Phil, the strong core, thrilled at the knowledge being fed into his mind. Joy and perfection filled the cosmos, one planet at a time, at the hand of these microscopic beings. They were not deadly parasites, but transformative symbiotes, altering but also augmenting every life form they touched.

The maelstrom in his mind calmed as his new brain processed and cataloged the informational tsunami. His surroundings came back into view. He lay on his back, but didn't gaze at the sky. He gazed everywhere. The sky above him, the sidewalk below him, the homes and lawns and fences and trees surrounding him, the ambulance standing quiet and deserted with red lights still flashing—he saw it all in one great panoramic view surrounding his consciousness. And the amazing thing was, his brain could process this impossible stream of information and put it together into a single spherical image.

There were people around him. Some were human, screaming and running. Some were in a state of transition with patches of dusty grey and shiny chrome. Some were magnificent metallic beings that strode with a smooth liquidity. They were human in shape, completely nude of clothes and hair, and marvelous to behold. Phil had never imagined that such breathtaking beauty could be contained within the human form.

One magnificent being stood before him. The face did not peer down at him, yet he felt that the being looked at him. And why not? If vision encompassed all directions, there was no need to point the face in any one direction to see. The being's eyes were featureless surfaces that merged into the skin—the former skin—surrounding them. The being appeared exactly like a chrome statue, except it stepped forward, knelt down, and extended a shiny hand toward him.

"Phil," the being said. Its mouth didn't move—indeed, the mouth was not an opening at all, only lips sealed permanently together—but the being's surface vibrated air molecules to create the sound. Phil heard the sound all over his skin. It felt like God were speaking to him.

The hand touched him on his arm, red flashes from the ambulance reflecting off its surface. Electric shocks of pleasure lashed through his body at the touch. No human could endure such sensations of delight. Fortunately, he was no longer human. His transformed body could tolerate it—could savor it in all its splendor. He wondered what the next touch would feel like!

It came, as the hand slowly moved up his arm in a caress. His flowing, metallic body shuddered with elation. If he had been human, he would have died from the orgasm it would have produced.

With remarkable strength, he bounded to his feet and pulled the being into his arms, pressing their bodies together. He could hardly sense the world around him as waves of ecstasy devoured him.

"Phil," the being said, breathlessly it seemed, even though no breath was involved.

Through the overwhelming sensations, he managed to wonder who was in his arms. The instant his mind formed the question, he knew the answer. It was Emily, transformed.

"Emily," he said. He could feel his skin vibrating all over as he said it, but it didn't tickle. "Emily, you are so beautiful."

A faint memory of cream-colored flesh, of golden, flowing hair, of intense blue eyes, crept up from the depths of his mind. These were the things that made her beautiful to his human self. But he looked at her with new eyes that took in everything, her shiny, silvery skin denuded of hair and flashing with the red ambulance light, her mirror-like eyes that shone in the sun, her human-shaped female body that curved in all the right places as beautifully as her flesh body had, but shimmered with a luster no human skin had ever dreamed of, and Phil realized he'd never known beauty until now. That former image of beauty was a sham, a pale counterfeit pleasing only to an ignorant fleshy creature who knew no better.

"Emily, you're beautiful and I love you." What joy it gave him to say those words with his whole body instead of just his mouth.

He hugged her tightly, and she hugged back with vehemence. The space between them melted away. He pressed his lips to hers. Their lips physically joined, flowing together into one entity. He pressed harder, and the space between their heads disappeared. His face melted into hers. The whole front of his body flowed into hers, joining them into one seamless being. Exploding signals of pleasure passed between them. Intimate vistas of thoughts and feelings swirled together. He knew her as no human had known another. Every thought, every desire, every experience they'd both had enmeshed themselves into the other's consciousness.

How pathetic human intimacy was compared to this!

"Emily," he thought to her in a way that only she could detect, "we are so blessed."

"We're married like no human has ever been married," she replied in the same intimate exchange of thoughts that passed physically between them.

He thought of the fantasies he'd had of their wedding night, and laughed at the pitiful excitement he'd felt anticipating those absurd few moments of pleasure that humans thought of as the ultimate sensual experience. Such pleasure now would be no more than an imperceptible brush of a feather against his surface.

An urge welled up inside him to part from Emily. He didn't understand its cause, but he felt an uncontrollable desire to pull away. Emily must have felt the same thing, for suddenly they pushed against one another, and their bodies flowed back into separate entities. With the split, his body seethed with a spasm of indescribable joy.

A frail human body would have collapsed at a fraction of such feelings, but his new body held its balance. It was more than a match for the overwhelming emotions and sensations that he could feel now. He gazed at her, ripples of pleasure sweeping through him.

A cloud of fine grey dust oozed around him, sloughed off from his skin, and interlaced with a similar cloud from Emily. The particles swirled around them, and for some reason that thrilled him. Suddenly the particles shot up into the sky as if the cloud were a conscious entity.

From his genetic memory, Phil knew the cloud was a new set of spores, his and Emily's children. They were mineral spermatozoa swimming through the sea of interstellar space in search of a new planetary ovum.

Phil heard a choked gargle to his left. Without moving his head, he saw a teenage boy standing there staring at him. The boy was covered with grey dust from the diaphragm down, and his legs below his knees were chrome. He stared at Phil and Emily with terror in his face, and must have been trying to scream. The transformation had probably already started on his lungs.

"No," Phil said. "It's not frightening. It's wonderful."

The boy retreated several steps backward, then stumbled and fell. His breathing stopped.

"He was afraid," Phil said to Emily. "Seeing us join must have terrified him."

"Everyone'll be afraid," she said. "We were afraid too, until we understood."

Phil surveyed the landscape. Few complete humans remained, mostly cowering or running in fear. Many partially transformed people stood or lay about. More and more fully transformed beings wandered around, immersed in the joy of their new sensory experiences. Two pairs of beings coupled as Phil and Emily had, literally melted together into one being with two backs and no fronts.

Yes, Phil could see how a human would be disturbed by that image.

A reverberating bark sounded behind him. Without turning, Phil saw the neighbor's border collie prancing around. It was shiny all over and devoid of fur. A stray human reaction in Phil's mind thought the dog looked comical, like a giant rat shaved and gilded, but the rest of Phil thought he had never seen such a magnificent dog before. The creature bounded across Emily's lawn, which consisted of thousands of silvery blades.

All the plant life in her yard had transformed. Chrome trees with shivering chrome foil leaves. Chrome ivy crawling up the side of the house. Chrome birds hopping about, desperately flapping wings that could no longer lift their weight.

"Do you think this is happening all over the world?" Emily said.

He accessed his genetic memory and saw clouds of spores descending on planet after planet. The clouds never blanketed the planets completely. The transformation took weeks to spread across the entire biosphere.

"No," Emily said, "not all over."

She must have accessed the same genetic memory.

"But humans all over the world will be terrified," he said. "Like we were."

"Can't we do something about that?"

Phil picked out the only untransformed human in sight, cowering by a bush next to the house across the street. It was the same boy who had kicked the soccer ball around, who had first noticed them when they ran out to the street to wait for the ambulance. The boy shook with fear, staring at the grass before him. The chrome blades had advanced halfway to his location, and the rest of the grass was covered with dust and small hexagonal columns. His shoes were dusty and half-eaten.

Phil dashed over to the boy with lightning speed—it took only a few seconds—and leaned over him. The terrified fleshy eyes peered up at him, and the boy started to cry.

"Don't be afraid," Phil said. "I know it looks scary, but it's wonderful. You'll see how wonderful it is."

The boy didn't look reassured. He kept crying and staring and shrinking back as far as he could manage. Emily appeared next to Phil and watched.

"What's your name?" Phil asked.

The boy didn't answer.

"My name is Phil. This is my girlfriend, Emily. She lives across the street. We were scared just like you, but now we think what's happening is wonderful. Don't be afraid!"

"You turned into a robot," the boy said. "That stuff made you a robot."

"No, no!" Phil said. "We're not robots. We're still alive. That stuff turned us into something incredible. We love what happened. It makes everything look and sound and smell and feel fantastic."

"He's just a boy," Emily said. "He doesn't understand." She touched Phil's shoulder with her hand, and he could feel her sorrow through the connection.

Phil stood back up. "We need to tell everyone it's okay—it's glorious. We can explain it to adults, and they can tell the kids. They'll listen if they hear it from *human* adults."

"How far has this spread? How far do we have to go?"

"Let's find out." He turned to the boy. "I promise you, you'll love it when it's finished. Don't be afraid." Not knowing what else he could do, he grabbed

Emily's hand, and they started to run.

They passed neighborhood after neighborhood in seconds. It was clear that many patches of spores had grown from different infestations. The spreading patches had not all connected together, but Phil and Emily ran for miles and miles without finding an area that was unaffected. Everywhere they went, the scene was the same: people, animals, and plants in various stages of transformation. Some places were just getting started. Others were virtually complete and spreading far from the source.

Phil and Emily fled the suburbs and found themselves in the country. They passed chrome wheat and corn stalks, chrome cattle and sheep. They might have to travel hundreds of miles before they reached the edge of the spores. But he didn't feel the least bit tired, and she showed no signs of lagging, so they continued to run.

They passed several cities and towns. They crossed the border into the next state and kept running. The affected regions became sparser, but they still ran into areas of transformation. As they neared one small town where they could see no flashing of sunlight reflecting off any transformed life, he suddenly felt weary—intensely weary—almost as fast as a car running out of gas would sputter and stop. Within seconds, Emily cried out, "Phil!" He could sense her weariness through her hand.

"I know, I know. We need to stop." They slowed quickly, and as they came to a standstill, his legs buckled from under him. He toppled to the ground in a field of hay, and she dropped next to him, her arm flopping across his chest.

"Are we dying?" she said, and he swore it sounded breathless, as if she were panting. But it was just her body trying to vibrate her surface with little energy left. Then she smiled. "No. We're just tired."

His genetic memory told him they'd run out of energy, and it was time to replenish it. They would collapse to the ground unconscious whenever that happened—they would fall asleep—and their skin would get to work converting whatever substance it contacted—ground, plant life, air—into energy that it would store up in an organ that reminded him of a powerful battery more than anything. He barely came to understand what was happening by the time he slipped into unconsciousness.

The instant Phil awoke, he knew something was wrong. All his senses told him so. The air was stale with confinement and reeked of medicinal chemicals. There was no visible light, but Phil could see dim shapes from some infrared radiation emanating from a point source above and to the right. He was inside a room, strapped to a metal bed. From the smell and the shapes of the objects about the room, he guessed it must be a hospital room.

Or maybe an alien examination room. He laughed all over his body. They might be disappointed. He didn't have an anus to probe.

The door flew open, and light blasted into the room. Human eyes would have felt pain at the sudden brightness, but he felt no discomfort and needed no period of adjustment to see.

A human woman with a white lab coat walked in. She stopped halfway between Phil and the door and peered at him. She didn't seem frightened.

He noticed a video camera up near the ceiling, right where the infrared point source had emanated. They'd watched him with infrared lighting, and this woman appeared the instant he woke up.

"What's your name?" the woman said.

Under the circumstances, he wasn't about to give his full name. "Phil." He felt his skin vibrating against the bed and the steel straps, and wondered if the deep, reverberating sound of his voice would bother her.

She seemed oblivious. It was clear he wasn't the first transformed being she'd encountered. "Phil, I'm Dr. Gallagher."

He noted how she accepted his informal name and used it freely, but only gave him a formal name to call her by. Classic attempt to define hierarchy, probably subconsciously.

"I'm sorry we need to keep you restrained," she said, "but we know how strong you are."

"Just because I'm strong doesn't mean I'll hurt you."

"No, but you'll run away."

She wasn't afraid for her personal safety—he could see it in her eyes and body language—but she was apprehensive about something. "Why shouldn't I run away? I'm an American citizen. You can't keep me imprisoned against my will when I've done nothing wrong."

She shook her head. "No, you're not."

"What? An American citizen?" He could already foresee the answer.

"You're not human, so how can you be a citizen? The human named Phil is dead." She shrugged one shoulder. "I know that's pretty feeble logic, but you must remember what it was like to be human. Our emotions overrule our logic. We fear you."

"But you're not afraid. I can tell."

Dr. Gallagher nodded. "I'm not afraid for my personal safety. But we humans fear you as a group. We don't want to become you. And we don't want you to rule over us."

He could hardly remember what it felt like to worry about such things, to want to dominate someone or to fear someone dominating you. "What makes you think we want to rule over you?"

"Do you?"

"No."

"How do I know I can believe you?"

"I don't lie." The instant he said it, he knew it was true. In his new state, he was incapable of lying.

She took several steps closer, but remained at a distance. If it wasn't fear for her personal safety, what was it?

"I have no way of knowing if that's true. But even if it is, you still have domination built right into your biology. Sooner or later you'll excrete that dust that'll turn all of us into you."

That was the apprehension—fear of being transformed. "That's why Emily's not here with me. You don't want us to join."

"Is Emily the girl you were found with?"

Girl? That's why she used his first name while telling him her formal name. Not because she was trying to establish a pecking order, but because she thought of him as a boy.

"We're old enough to get married."

"I'm sorry." She seemed genuinely so. "Would you like me to use your surname?"

"No, I'd like to know *your* first name."

"Ruthanne."

Phil looked about the room without moving his head. "Well, Ruthanne, what makes you think you can keep me from running away?"

Her apprehension seemed to increase. That's what bothered her! She wasn't sure she could keep him restrained.

And she was right. She couldn't.

His skin ate away at the straps. Ruthanne sighed, then walked to the door and called, "Help!"

A dozen people filed quickly into the room and surrounded the bed, grim expressions on their face. Phil would have expected strong, burly men, but they all looked as average and laboratoryish as Ruthanne. Not that burly men could stop him, but surely that's the type they'd try to stop him with.

Phil sat up and swung his legs over the side of the bed. "Please, you can't stop me, and I don't want to hurt you. I want to tell you about what we are, but not as a prisoner."

The guards didn't move.

"Please tell us what you are," Ruthanne said.

"Not until you let me go."

"I'm sorry, we can't."

"Then I'll have to force my way past you. I might hurt some of you. I don't want to."

"You can't get through," Ruthanne said.

Something didn't add up. He'd just eaten through steel straps with his skin, yet these people were certain he couldn't touch them. "I'm sorry. I can't stay here and let you try to figure out how to kill me." He put his feet on the floor, then stepped forward. The man in front of him grabbed his wrist and held as tightly as he could, which wasn't very tight. The man grabbed his other wrist and pushed him back against the bed.

"Enough!" Phil said. "I warned you." He would have to yank his arms free, and that would probably hurt the man, but he had a right to fight for his liberty. So he prepared to yank his arms back with a force that would probably sprain, if not break, a couple of the man's fingers...

...and couldn't do it.

He couldn't move his arms.

"What's wrong, Phil?" Ruthanne asked. "Why don't you just pull away from his grip?"

She knew why.

He searched his genetic memory. There was the answer: just like he was incapable of lying, he was also incapable of hurting another living creature.

"All we need to do is be willing to endanger ourselves," she said, "and you can't do anything to us. If you try to run, we'll get in your way. The only way you can escape is over our dead bodies—literally. But you can't do that, can you?"

The thought of killing one of them left a feeling in his torso that was similar to the nausea he once felt in his human stomach. As long as they surrounded him, he couldn't escape.

But how long could that be?

Probably indefinitely, if they kept it up in shifts. All it would require is a lot of people and the patience to endure some pretty boring guard duty.

"You can let go of me now."

The man glanced at Ruthanne, who nodded.

Phil sat back on the bed and folded his arms. "So I'm stuck here until you figure out how to kill me."

"We don't want to kill you," she said, joining the ring of guards surrounding his bed. "We want to bring you back."

"What?"

"If you can be changed, you can be changed back. We can study you and find out how it was done. Knowing that, we should be able to learn how to reverse it."

He stared at her face, peering at him with such concern and sincerity. It was an ugly face, dull flesh color, pockmarked with pores, covered with fine hairs, shiny only with excreted oil. She honestly thought she was doing him a favor. "What if I don't want to come back?"

That was an incomprehensible notion to her, he could see. Why would a human not want to stay human? She couldn't imagine that anyone in their right mind would actually want to remain transformed. Therefore Phil could not be in his right mind. The transformation had also affected his brain—for the worse.

Had it? Was his brain merely programmed to like this new existence?

Phil thought back to the first moments of sensory experience in his new state. Then to the coupling he and Emily had done. The days he and Emily had run hundreds of miles without getting tired. He enjoyed every moment of it. He couldn't imagine going back to the pathetic shadow of an existence that humans endured. He would feel like the living dead.

No, there was nothing insane about wanting to live this new, invigorating life. He wasn't crazy. Ruthanne was ignorant.

"I don't want to be human again," he said quietly, but firmly.

The look of pity she gave him disgusted him. Well, he had come to perform a mission, and now was a good time to start. "Ruthanne, do you know what it feels like to be transformed?"

Her brow knotted. "Is that what you call it?"

"I can see everywhere, not just out of the front of my head. I can see the woman behind me scratching her nose."

Ruthanne looked, and the woman immediately froze with her finger still touching her nose.

"I can smell the roses in a vase in the next room. I can hear the bees buzzing outside the walls. I can tell that you showered with Zest this morning." He leaned forward. "And Ruthanne, have you ever felt what it's like to make love as a transformed being?"

"You mean melt together."

"Have you ever had an orgasm, Ruthanne?"

She glowered at him. "Yes, Phil, I have."

"Have you ever had it go on and on, growing in intensity until you thought you couldn't stand it anymore, but your body is so strong that it can withstand levels of physical pleasure that would kill a human?"

Ruthanne remained silent as she glared, but several of the guards stared with their jaw hanging open.

"Why would I want to be human after experiencing that?"

"You can't even fight for your own freedom," Ruthanne growled. "What good is a super-orgasm if you can't walk out of a room?"

"I wouldn't *have* to fight for my freedom if you didn't imprison me."

"But I *am* imprisoning you. And though you have the strength to break free, you don't have the volition."

"If all of you were like me, I wouldn't need the volition to fight," he growled back, an interesting sensation when done with all of his skin. "I only suffer from that handicap because I'm surrounded by humans!"

With that a genetic memory came rushing in: a race of fleshy beings on a distant planet who feared each other, as humans fear humans, but who had advanced in genetic engineering and nanotechnology to the point where they could transform themselves into beings of their own design. Beings who could enjoy the sensory experiences of life to unfathomable degrees. Beings of tremendous strength who could run and not be weary for hundreds of miles, who could feed on any substance for the energy they need to live and move, who needed no clothing or shelter for protection, so that no other creature could control them by withholding the necessities of life. Beings who had all violent and domineering urges bred out of them, so they were incapable of hurting others, whether by physical injury or the mental distress of deceit and betrayal. Beings who were genetically engineered to find great beauty in their new form.

These beings even accommodated the possibility that the conscious mind was more than a physical phenomenon. Instead of downloading their minds into robot bodies and possibly leaving a soul behind, they transformed their own bodies in place, allowing the soul, if it existed, to stay right where it was as the fleshy body that housed it transformed into a living organism of fluid metal alloy.

They designed the spores to spread throughout their planet, transforming every living creature. But life, being life, adapted, and the spores learned to fly off into space, seeking out new planets to transform. The original engineers had never intended for such a thing to happen, but Phil was delighted it had, and wondered if God, if he existed, might not have had a hand in it, spreading this glorious new form of existence to all his living creations.

Phil recognized the genius of their plan: when you're surrounded by beings who have no desire to hurt you or rule over you, you have no need for the free will to fight. The defect was not in the design. The defect was in the untransformed creatures around him who refused to join him. The creatures who still desired to hurt him and confine him and dictate what he should be, right down to his genetic make-up.

And the worst part of all, they thought they were saving him.

This was war, as righteous as any war of liberty had ever been in the history of humankind. If a man couldn't fight for the right to remain who he was, rather than be genetically engineered into what another human being thought he should be, he truly had no identity, and no other liberty mattered. Morally, he had the right to slaughter every one of these guards that wanted to force his return to humanity against his will.

But he was incapable of slaughtering them. Nor did he wish for the capability. He didn't want to sink to their level. He wanted to remain free of the weaknesses of humanity, not adopt them.

But he did have a superior mind, designed to absorb, analyze, and store decillions of bits of information. And that mind, almost before he even thought the desire, analyzed a solution for him, a simple solution.

His and Emily's mission had been futile. Humans would never understand. They were genetically designed to not understand, to preserve the species, as

Phil was designed to not harm others. As long as any human lived, Phil and his fellow beings would be plagued by them, perhaps endangered by them. Humanity was the disease, and transformation was the cure. The wonderful thing about the cure was that it made everyone's lives better—even the enemy's. War among generations of humans had killed and destroyed. Phil's war would create a utopia. His war was an act of kindness.

He slid off the bed and lay down on the floor. His guards watched with some curiosity, but no concern.

Ruthanne reacted immediately. "Hold him!" she shouted.

Feverishly, as fast as his nanite cells could eat, Phil dissolved the floor away below him while the guards hesitated for a split second before they processed her command.

As they reached for him with their flesh hands, Phil willed his skin to flow just enough to make himself slippery.

As he sunk into the floor, the guards couldn't keep a firm grip on him, and when they realized they were getting a sleek film of metal on their hands, they backed away in horror.

They didn't have to worry. The creators had deliberately built sex into their design to preserve genetic diversity. The nanites in the film of metal on his surface couldn't transform the guards. Only through the act of coupling could fertile spores be created.

But they were safe from transformation only temporarily. Phil's plan involved exactly that—creating fertile spores. Once buried under the floor, he listened for the footsteps of the panicking guards as they rushed to another room. What they feared most was transformation, and the humans had already figured out that coupling made that possible. They would guard Emily as if their entire species depended on it. After all, it did.

He ate his way through the foundation and the ground, making his way to the room where their footsteps led, where Emily must be. They would surround her, keep her off the floor—anything to keep her isolated from him.

But it wouldn't matter.

He rose until his body pressed up against the floor tiles, and listened.

Emily spoke. Her reverberating voice was obvious. She protested that they couldn't keep her there. Phil moved directly under her and placed his finger against a floor tile. He willed a microscopic filament to eat through the tile, rise up to the bottom of her bed, and eat through its metal slab.

When the filament touched Emily, he felt a thrill of pleasure. As fast as he could, he squeezed billions of nanite molecules up through that filament, keeping it thinner than the human eye could detect, then let them accumulate into a large ball at the filament's tip that merged into Emily's being. She trembled with ecstasy.

It wasn't as satisfying as the full body melt, but the pleasure was still sensational, much more than a human could endure. And Phil knew fertile spores were forming. When the urge to break away came, Phil pulled his misshapen finger—a ball of shiny metal on the tip of an impossibly thin digit—away from her and let it rest on the surface of the bed. He felt the spores break out of the ball into a cloud and knew that spores from Emily were flowing into his cloud. In seconds the cloud would fly off, seeking any living, non-transformed flesh they could find.

By the screams and the pounding footsteps, Phil knew the spores were pouncing. It was inevitable now. Within a few hours, no humans of flesh would remain anywhere near the hospital or prison or research facility or whatever it was they were in.

Phil retracted his finger, dissolved his way through the floor and stood before Emily. She smiled at him—a distinctly human act that still looked beautiful on her transformed face—and he took her hand to help her off the bed. The touch was exquisite.

Screams could still be heard, but they were distant now.

Eternal Rectangle

Jake eased to a stop and felt a rush of vertigo as the normal flow of time took over. It was night, and his past self was preparing for bed. He took over his past life at once and climbed under the covers for a desperately needed night of sleep.

In the morning he headed to campus as usual, realizing for the first time that he'd have to relive close to two semesters of classes. The thought depressed him, but at least he should do better this time and raise his grades.

But today he made one change in his normal routine. On his way to lunch he took a detour that caused him to cross paths with Anthony. An "accidental" bumping together, some introductions, a few well-placed bits of conversation that sparked Anthony's interest, and in moments they were heading to the campus cafeteria together for lunch where they would rendezvous with Katie. As they walked, Jake dropped hints that Katie was "only a friend" and completely unattached.

The three enjoyed lunch and each other's company, and of course Anthony and Katie hit it off together immediately. She couldn't take her eyes off him: a tall, swarthy, Antonio Banderas type with hair as black as hers. They exchanged phone numbers. Within twenty-four hours Anthony had arranged to meet Katie at the student mixer dance. Within forty-eight hours Jake's neurons were having a hard time remembering why that pleased him so much.

Jake felt like a voyeur spying on Anthony and Katie at the dance, but his curiosity overcame him. It was almost as if there were something important riding on how well this evening went. He couldn't place the source of that feeling, but it gave him satisfaction to see them having such a great time together.

Until at one point Anthony took off for the restroom or something. While Katie stood alone, a sandy-haired, light-complexioned fellow of average height, who still had freckles but wore them well, walked up to her and struck up a conversation. Katie gave him a glowing smile that could make even a rejection feel good, but it wasn't in the man's karma to be rejected tonight. In moments they were out on the floor sharing a dance, he playing a good-natured clown, she laughing with open pleasure at all his jokes.

Jake observed Anthony's return to the ballroom with puckish fascination. Anthony looked around in confusion, then noticed Katie and the other man together on the dance floor. His expression clouded immediately. As the current song neared completion, Anthony strode out like a matador ready to take on a bull. The intruder saw him coming and stepped aside with a congenial grin as the music hit its last bar. He bowed to Anthony and returned Katie to him with a sweep of his arm. She chuckled at the gesture and stole one more glance at him as Anthony led her away.

Everything was back to normal, Jake thought. But the sandy-haired man walked off with a satisfied look on his face. It was obvious this fellow felt like he'd won. A foreboding of something gone amiss swept through Jake, but he couldn't figure out why.

He guessed what was going on between Anthony and Katie at that moment. Jake knew her well and loved her like a sister—the sister he never had. They'd played together in their childhood, explored the mysteries of school together in their youths, even enjoyed a brief fling of boyfriend/girlfriend in their adolescence until they decided their friendship was much more valuable to them. She'd become his confidante, his companion, even his cheerleader. In his undergraduate days when he fell in love and lost, she became his lifesaver. Had she not been there to help him through that awful time, he might have lost his mind.

So Jake knew what Katie was thinking. According to her philosophy, this wasn't a true date. They'd merely agreed to meet at the dance. This left her open to dance with as many other men as often as she desired. She owed him the first and the last dance and a few unspecified dances in between, nothing more.

Anthony had obviously interpreted the arrangement differently. It looked like he was explaining precisely that to her with his solemn and determined expression. She smiled and nodded and twinkled that mischievous little sparkle in her eye that meant she had no intention of following the dictates of the other person.

Jake came away from the dance with no new female acquaintance because he spent the night staring with a titillating mixture of fascination and horror as the two men waged a mighty battle for Katie. Shame plagued him to spy on the three of them, but he couldn't help himself. He only wanted the best for her, and he hated seeing her torn between two warring testosterone factories.

In a more reflective moment he wondered if he didn't feel threatened himself. She was unmarried, and her father was a hunter/gatherer in the world of multinational corporations who made a personal appearance at home two or three times a year, maybe. Jake and Katie studied on the same campus—he as a first year physics grad student, she as a junior majoring in theater—and they saw each other almost daily. This made him the man in her life by default. He wasn't thrilled about giving up that position.

But she was having a great time playing the two men off against each other. Jake could see in her eyes that she was genuinely interested in both of them. At the end of the evening she introduced Jake to the sandy-haired guy. His name was Derek. As a gesture in fair play, she left the dance with Jake, even though Anthony tried to get her to go with him. Derek just smiled and expressed a jovial, "See you later!"

Katie's entire conversation as they walked to her apartment was Anthony and Derek. Jake took it stoically, but felt unsettled inside. Was he really jealous of their attentions? Could he be that self-centered of a friend?

No, he realized, it was Derek. For some reason Jake favored Anthony and resented that Derek interfered in the evening. Maybe it was just a sense of fair play. Anthony *had* expected to be with her all evening, and Derek *had* intruded. Maybe that was it.

Over the next several weeks Anthony asked Katie out, after which Derek asked her out, then Anthony, then Derek, Anthony, Derek...

Weeks turned into months. Jake came to know Anthony and Derek himself and began to appreciate them for their own unique qualities. He realized they were decent men with genuine affection for Katie. Derek was the mischievous boy who always dreamed up one semi-harmless adventure after another, but would drop everything and give anything when a friend was in need. Anthony was strong-willed and a deep thinker, who stood aloof and observed with a wry smile, but always knew the right thing to say and when to say it to help brighten one's outlook. Jake decided Katie could do much worse in this carnivorous world than to end up with either Derek or Anthony.

The day came when Katie confided to Jake that she was falling in love with both of them. The implications of that alarmed her. She had no desire to hurt either one, but she was having a hard time deciding between the two. She asked Jake what she should do, and even though he realized it was more or less a rhetorical question, he immediately blurted out:

"Anthony. Choose Anthony."

She let a gentle smile cross her face at the sound of his name. Jake felt appalled at himself. What business did he have saying that? And on what basis had he decided? She seemed happy with either one. When with Derek, she came alive with childlike joy at his antics, whether she were his audience or co-conspirator. When with Anthony, her mature and serene side emerged, charged with a beauty that transcended her large brown eyes and deep black hair. Jake had come to love them both like brothers—the brothers he never had. He couldn't understand his own preference for Anthony.

From that point on Jake remained carefully neutral. But he could sense the seed he'd planted germinating. Derek made a valiant effort, but Katie began seeing more and more of Anthony.

Jake felt remorse at what he'd done to Derek. Haunting memories returned of his own grief when the love of his life chose to marry another. He'd borrowed his roommate's car that night and drove it through a fence and a flagpole, totaling it. That earned him five days in the hospital and a court appearance. His roommate had never spoken to him again.

These thoughts plagued Jake one day on campus as he wrestled with boredom in his auditorium chair. Was there no end to this insufferable lecture? The speaker was one of the most prominent physicists in the country, so Jake's professor had made attendance mandatory. But the physicist was obviously speaking down to the undergraduates. Sure, the possibility of time travel *sounds* like a fascinating topic. But Jake had already been through all this years ago. Gödel rotating universes, Kerr black holes, Tipler cylinders, Thorne wormholes— they were all old hat and all impossible, at least by the engineering capabilities of any foreseeable future.

Jake tried to occupy his mind with some pleasant daydreaming, but the same obsessive thoughts of Derek and Anthony and Katie intruded without mercy. When he tried to concentrate on the speaker, he sunk into boredom, and time seemed to stand still.

Why was that? he wondered. Why did time seem to go slowly when he was bored and rush by when he was preoccupied? Was it just an illusion of perception, or could there be some physical basis for the phenomenon?

Probably most scientists would assume it was illusion. But what if time actually did slow down or speed up based on one's state of mind? Changes in the perceived rate of time was a universal experience. Boredom could slow it down. Interest could speed it up. Desiring something could drag it out. Time seemed to flow by faster as one grew older. How many people had said time stood still during a car accident? Yes, there were plenty of anecdotal experiences suggesting it might be more than illusion.

If it were a real phenomenon, then time itself would have to be a static thing, like a highway, and one's consciousness like a vehicle traveling down it. The student sitting next to him might actually be enjoying this lecture, and time might be passing by quickly for him. If the flow of time itself were what changed, it couldn't slow down for Jake but speed up for the other guy. Therefore—if there were any validity at all to this ridiculous speculation—every person's consciousness had to be traveling through time at different velocities, like one car passing another.

But if that were true, Jake reasoned, then there ought to be a way for the mind to deliberately control its own velocity through time, since it already did so subconsciously. Certain states of mind would affect the rate of movement through time. Couldn't a person be trained to enter those states at will and control how fast or how slow time flowed?

Would it be possible to find a state of mind where time stood still?

The possibility intrigued him too much to let it go. He wanted to shout out to the lecturing physicist, "Hey, did you ever think of this idea?" Then he thought, what better opportunity than a boring lecture to see if he could cause any change in the flow of time?

Jake pulled out his phone, stared at the seconds ticking by, and began to chant to himself. Boredom! Boredom! You are so bored! Time is dragging, dragging, forever, eternally. This is so boring, time is stopping—

BEEP! BEEP! BEEP!

Damn! Foiled by his own phenomenon. His speculations had so fascinated him that the time until his next class had flown by, and his phone's alarm had gone off. The speaker was supposed to be done by now, but of course he wasn't. At least Jake had a legitimate excuse to skip out.

Feeling a little foolish about his outlandish musings, Jake tried to forget them as he tackled the rest of his academic day. But they clung to the back of his mind like cockroaches skittering in the shadows. That evening he spent hours in the privacy of his living room trying to will himself into a bored state and catch the second hand of the clock on the wall slowing down. But he got nowhere.

Then he realized that time travel might *appear* to be the purview of physicists, but states of mind fell under the jurisdiction of psychology. Jake needed a psychologist to help him work through this.

He immediately thought of Leon, an acquaintance from his own university he'd made over the summer at an interdisciplinary seminar: "The Basis of Consciousness from a Physics, Neurology, Computer Science, and Psychology Perspective." Leon was an acknowledged expert on altered states of consciousness. Which made him a bit of a crackpot in some people's minds. The last Jake heard, he was doing bizarre experiments in biofeedback somewhere on campus, something about duplicating faith healing in the laboratory. Jake suspected that time manipulation through states of mind might be just the sort of weird thing Leon would be interested in.

The next day Jake called Leon and explained his theory to him. "Sounds nuts," Leon said. "Let me think about it."

Two days later Leon called back and said, "Let's try it."

That same day Derek came by to commiserate with Jake over Katie.

"I'm losing—I know I am," Derek said as they sat across the kitchen table from each other eating doughnuts. "She's seeing Anthony more often."

Jake couldn't bring himself to make eye contact. "She is?" was all he could think of to say.

"And why not?" Derek spat as he tossed a half-eaten bear claw back into the box. "He's so much more mature than I am. I'm good for a few laughs, but he's someone you'd take home to your mother."

"There's a lot to be said for knowing how to enjoy life."

Derek only harumphed. Jake wished he had Anthony's talent for saying the right thing. He stared at the piece of bear claw and said, "Why don't you try asking her out more?"

Derek shook his head slowly, mashing crumbs on the table with his finger. "No, he's better for her than me. I want what's best for her." He looked up with moistened eyes. "Isn't that what I'm supposed to say?"

Jake shrugged. "I guess."

"So why does it hurt so much?"

Jake nodded. "Yes, I know about that."

Derek sat silently, leaning an elbow on the table with his head resting in his palm. "I should have asked her out more often from the beginning. I think it's too late now."

"You should have *met* her earlier, then maybe Anthony wouldn't have even tried." The instant Jake said it, he regretted it. Anthony wouldn't have said something as useless as that to console someone.

Derek only chuckled mirthlessly. "Yes, I should have."

When Derek finally left, Jake felt relief. He also felt shame for feeling relief, but what could he do about the situation now? Twist Katie's arm and make her choose Derek? Then what about Anthony? He was glad when the time came to meet with Leon. He needed a distraction from the guilt he felt.

Following instructions, Jake crossed campus to the older part of the university, entered a dilapidated building, and descended stairs to the musty basement. The room assigned to Leon was small, sparse, and poorly lit—just the sort of room you'd expect to be assigned to a fringe researcher.

His computer equipment was average but adequate. Leon greeted him with his deep voice and darkly pigmented vice of a hand. Jake explained in detail about his hypothesis, and Leon told him all about the biofeedback equipment. They worked out a methodology for their research, and Jake became the guinea pig. Leon hooked all sorts of cables and sensors to him. They spent an hour and a half trying to identify a possible state of mind that could be a candidate for time control.

It was all very subjective, because all they had to go on was Jake's impressions, which may after all be only illusion. The important thing, according to Leon, was to first teach Jake how to control the effect—whether illusion or real—then worry about objectively verifying it.

Three times a week after classes they met. Leon's mood never matched the gloom of the surroundings. He always filled the room both with his exuberance and his impressive height. His rumbling voice almost seemed to vibrate the walls.

Progress was slow because they didn't even know for sure what they were trying to control. Jake would think he saw a distinct slowing of the clock one week, then detect nothing the next. He began to think his hypothesis was garbage. Of course they couldn't get consistent results—the whole thing was just a trick of the mind.

But Leon was unperturbed. As a physics student Jake was used to concrete, empirical results with little ambiguity. Leon as a researcher in psychology (with a shady emphasis on the occult) had lots of experience with elusive results, and had the patience to stick with his experiments.

One day when Jake arrived, Leon was in a state of ecstasy. He thought he'd gathered the first real evidence that day of a true faith healing. As Leon connected Jake to the biofeedback sensors and babbled on about his success, Jake cringed inside, feeling a little foolish working with this crackpot on a wild goose chase. But he dutifully succumbed to Leon's ministrations.

"Maybe boredom isn't such a great state of mind to work with," Leon said as he finished. "Too hard to produce by will. Didn't you say desire was another possibility?"

"I suppose. I've just been guessing about all of this."

"When you want something really bad," Leon said reflectively, "time can seem to drag out forever." He rubbed his stubbly chin as he thought. "What is boredom but a specific form of desire for something more interesting to happen?" He nodded his head with finality. "Yes, let's try desire."

Leon was right. Desire was much easier to evoke. Jake had all sorts of desires. He desired that Derek not be miserable. He wished he hadn't played a role in making him that way. He wanted Katie to be happy. Straight A's in all his classes would be nice. A topic for his master's thesis that wasn't as lunatic as what he was doing right now. The Nobel Prize in Physics. A pepperoni and mushroom pizza with extra cheese and thick crust. That's what he desired the most right now. His stomach growled its assent.

Three times a week they met for two months, with a week off for Christmas and Kwanzaa. Each time, Jake desired as he never desired before. His desires often turned to Derek's well-being, because Katie's preference for Anthony had become inescapable. She saw him almost exclusively, with only token dates for Derek and occasional visits with Jake. The couple hugged and kissed openly now, oblivious to the effect it had on Derek. His days were numbered, and he knew it.

The old Derek was gone. The new one was a ghastly imposter who slunk around listlessly and never smiled. He still attended classes—or so he said when Jake interrogated him. But Jake had his suspicions.

Jake used these desires in his sessions with Leon. They were strong and easily roused. Three times a week he longed for Derek to be with Katie, to see him smiling, indulging in his antics, and to see the sparkle in Katie's eyes when he did.

But it was not to be. The inevitable finally struck. Anthony and Katie were to marry, and in a short four weeks. Talk about rubbing it in! Derek insisted on going to the wedding in spite of Jake's efforts to talk him out of it.

Katie looked stunning in her bridal gown. Its white billows struck an exotic contrast to her Mediterranean complexion and hair. Anthony was a chiseled god in his tuxedo, a figure straight out of *The Godfather.* Abundant relatives from both sides of the families thronged the cathedral. The scrambling it must have taken to put this together in four weeks!

Jake sat with Derek toward the back, trying not to notice his red face and clenched jaw. As the final pronouncement was made and the newlywed couple kissed, Derek whispered almost inaudibly without unclenching his teeth, "I only want her to be happy."

"She does look happy," Jake said, hoping that would help.

Jake invited Derek to stay at his place for a while so he wouldn't have to be alone. Derek accepted without emotion. Almost immediately Jake noticed he was drinking constantly and never seemed to attend classes. Derek's presence inflicted daily heartache on Jake as he watched his friend grieve.

Attending his own classes was no relief, because Jake would worry the whole time he was away. Only his sessions with Leon provided an escape. He could put his churning feelings to use. It became a cathartic experience as he longed for happiness to come into Derek's life again, desiring that outcome until tears streamed from his eyes.

And it began to work. Jake swore he could see the second hand of the clock visibly slow. Leon became a slave master, driving him on and on in repetitive sessions until Jake perceived the effect one hundred percent of the time.

Then Leon switched from consistency to intensity and coached Jake into slowing time down more and more. All the while the thought lingered in the back of his mind, am I really slowing time, or just imagining it? Leon never perceived the effect, of course. Either possibility—illusion or Jake's consciousness slowing down along the highway of time—would be imperceptible to Leon. Once when Jake asked him how they'd ever know for sure, Leon said, "Don't worry about that. Just get good at it for now."

Anthony and Katie returned from their honeymoon in Hawaii, Katie's life-long dream. Jake felt a tinge of regret that it hadn't been him after she'd shared that dream with him for so many years. It was then that he truly felt the loss for himself and not just for Derek. He was no longer the man in her life and never would be again. The realization hit him like a slap in the face. But he used that emotion constructively, adding it to his time-slowing arsenal.

The times Jake saw Katie were few now, and always with Anthony. Although she seemed content enough, she also seemed subdued. Was it his imagination, or did she almost seem to wait for a cue from Anthony before doing anything? One time Jake ran into her on campus alone, and they had lunch together at the cafeteria. As he joked with her, a gleam in her eye returned that had been missing, and she joked back with an enthusiasm associated with pleasures rarely enjoyed.

Jake loved Anthony like a brother—a brother he never had. But Jake also loved Katie like a sister, and he didn't like this new Katie that had blossomed from the seeds of their marriage. In just a couple of months she'd forgotten how to enjoy life. She'd lost her vivaciousness and replaced it with a calm that bore a hint of sadness. It was as if a well-meaning but clumsy friend had trampled through Jake's garden and stepped on his favorite rose.

Jake's careless comment that tipped the scales in Anthony's direction only made matters worse. After that he'd refused to favor one over the other again, especially when he grew to love them both himself. But the day finally came— the day he swore would never come—when his heart refused to stay neutral any longer.

He chose Derek. But he chose too late.

Now he could add one more desire to his list, a desire that was strong because it was impossible to fulfill. His next session with Leon was intense, and his ability to slow the clock profound. The second hand inched toward the number two, crept with painful sluggishness toward the three. Leon's face was a dark shape in his peripheral vision as the man gazed at him intensely. The thin red clock hand crawled agonizingly toward the four. It passed each notch marking a second at a rate that would exasperate a snail. Jake felt sweat that had been trickling down his forehead cling in place without moving.

The second hand neared the four. Jake desired with all his being to have Derek be married to Katie. He longed for the sight of them laughing together, holding hands, kissing, her eyes alive with delight, he back from the living dead and grinning mischievously. The clock hand crept almost imperceptibly until it touched the very edge of the four, then seemed not to move at all. Jake's longing became an ache in his chest. He almost felt as if he would burst.

His mind swam with the effort. For some time the second hand hovered at the edge of the four. It didn't seem to move at all. Jake desired until he felt he couldn't breathe—or maybe his breathing was so slow he couldn't detect it. And then the second hand moved again, barely, barely...

...and backward.

Jake felt a thrill shoot through his spine. Carefully he maintained the state of mind he was in as if it were a fragile egg. The second hand crept towards the three, then the two, and he thought it was gaining momentum. The two, then the one. When the second hand stood straight up against the twelve he shuddered himself out of his trance with a violent sucking of breath. The second hand shot forward at its normal pace, crossing the one, the two, the three, and the four.

Leon stared at him with a shocked expression. "What happened? You looked like you were about dead for a second."

Jake gasped for breath, trying to calm himself. Leon's face filled his vision. "What happened?" he demanded again.

"I slowed time down, all the way down. I slowed it until it stopped."

Leon gaped at him without moving.

"And then..." Jake wet his lips and took a deep breath. "...then I slowed it down some more."

Leon stared at him with eyes opened wide. Then at once he began a rumbling chuckle. "Jake, if you stopped time and then slowed it some more, that means—"

Jake nodded.

"Oh, we've got to try this again!" Leon showed the same exuberance he'd shown the day he found his evidence for faith healing. "We have *got* to try this again!"

They worked late into the night. Jake was ready to collapse from exhaustion. He felt as driven as Leon, wanting to verify to himself beyond all doubt that he'd reversed time, that he hadn't gone insane. Several more times he forced the clock hand backward.

"Enough!" Leon declared. "You've got no more in you."

Jake nodded his agreement.

"Next time we'll perform our first experiment to produce concrete evidence."

"What do you mean? You still don't believe I'm doing it?"

"I've never seen the clock move backward."

Leon was right. They'd done nothing that was objectively verifiable. So far everything was strictly in Jake's mind. No one would believe a word of it. Not even Leon should believe it until they had verifiable proof.

"Let's do it now," Jake said.

"No. Next time."

"Now!" Jake barked. His certainty had slipped away, and all he cared about was knowing for sure. After all, his sanity was on the line. He was seeing the hand on the clock move backward, but with all this slipping in and out of altered states of mind, it could just be self-hypnosis or something. He needed to know if it was real.

Leon studied him carefully, then nodded. "Okay." He looked around thoughtfully, rubbing his stubble-studded chin, and gazed at Jake with a smile. "I'll think of three nonsense sentences, then say 'okay.' After that I'll speak those three sentences. Then you reverse time back to when I said 'okay' and repeat the sentences before I can speak them. It will look to me like you've read my mind. Then we'll know." He nodded with slow movements of his head. "Then we'll know."

They settled in their chairs, and Jake said, "I'm ready."

Leon's eyes looked off to the side as he thought, then he looked back at Jake and said, "Okay." He waited a moment, then spoke distinctly:

"I am a green banana.

"See the two-headed woman dance.

"The moon jumped over the cow."

Leon gave him one short nod, and Jake prepared himself to go into his altered state. He conjured up the feelings he'd grown accustomed to evoking and slid quickly into his trance. The clock slowed noticeably, until the second hand stopped, then crept backward. Jake's eyes involuntarily returned to look at Leon, because that's what they'd been doing before he looked at the clock. Leon spoke in the eerie reversed speech pattern of clipped consonants and anti-diphthongs. Three distinct but unintelligible sentences, then a pause and, "Yea-ko."

Jake shook himself back to a normal state and immediately said, "I am a green banana. See the two-headed woman dance. The moon jumped over the cow."

For an instant Leon stared as if he'd seen a ghost. Then a smile crept across his face.

"You reversed time."

It was hours after midnight when Jake left that musty basement and walked cross-campus in the dark. Between street lamps and the nearly full moon, Jake could see his way without any problem. He practically danced as he traveled along, overjoyed at the discovery he and Leon had made by accident. The moon was his spotlight, and the leaves of the trees rustling in the wind applauded him.

In the beginning Jake hoped only that his theory was real, that the human mind could actually speed up or slow down along the highway of time. If he'd managed to stop time altogether, that would have been icing on the cake. But to have reversed time...

This would be the topic for his master's thesis and the focus of his life's work. He dreamed of one day earning a Nobel Prize over it. The discoverer of time travel! He'd be right up there with Newton, Galileo, Einstein as one of physics' greatest innovators. He'd be more famous than the boring lecturer!

As Jake turned the corner onto his street, he heard singing, quiet and slurred. Some drunk. His home was on the other side of the street two-thirds of the way down the block, and a dark silhouette stood on the curb near it, entirely backlit by a street lamp at the far corner. The figure swayed and gestured as it sang.

Jake's triumphant feelings melted away. The voice was Derek's, and the shape of the silhouette looked right. Jake quickened his steps as somewhere a few blocks away some tires squealed.

"Derek?" Jake called, breaking into a trot as he stepped off the curb to cross the street.

"Heeeeeeey, Jake!" Derek said with a sloppy wave. He stepped into the street and wobbled toward Jake. A car engine gunned nearby out of sight.

"Derek, are you alright?" They were half a block apart and closing fast.

Another squeal of tires as bright headlights zoomed around the far corner and shot straight at Derek. Jake dashed as hard as he could, even though he knew he'd never make it and would place himself in front of the car. "Derek, jump!"

But all Derek did was turn to stare at the lights bearing down on him. Time seemed to stand still as Derek stood gaping and Jake struggled to reach him. From his frantic mind came the realization that time really was standing still—or almost. His feet seemed to sink into mud with every step as he fought to swing them forward with greater speed than a human being could physically manage. "De-e-e-re-ek!" he shrieked in slow motion.

But the car suddenly swerved away, doing nothing more than rustling Derek's clothes with its passing whoosh of air. Now the car aimed straight for Jake.

He dove into the middle of the road, the only direction his momentum would allow. The asphalt tore into his shirt and scraped angrily at the skin of his arms and belly. The car swerved again, bouncing over the curb and taking out someone's mailbox and the last few bushes of a hedge, then careened back onto the street. With peeling tires that laid a streak of black on the pavement, it zoomed into the darkness.

Jake lay face down on the street with his vicious scrapes and torn clothing. Derek stumbled over to him, crying, "Jake! You awright, Jake? Talk to me!"

He painfully turned onto his side as Derek plopped to his knees and pulled him into an embrace. "Jake, I'm so sorry. I'm so, so sorry." He cradled Jake like a mother with her injured child, rocking back and forth and sobbing. "I'm so sorry!"

"I'm okay," Jake rasped, fighting lightheadedness. "Just a little scratched up."

"I'm sorry, Jake," he moaned between sobs. "I shouldn'ta got so drunk."

Painfully Jake pushed himself into a sitting position with one arm to look Derek in the face. "It's okay. I understand."

An expression of alarm flashed onto Derek's face. He let go of Jake and dropped to his hands and knees barely in time to vomit onto the pavement. Jake held him around the waist as spasm after spasm hit. When his stomach calmed down, Derek broke into sobs again, slime dripping from his lips.

"I just love her," he said between gasps. "I miss her so much."

"I know," Jake sighed, holding him tight.

They helped each other to their feet and made their way into the house. Jake laid Derek out on the sofa and sat in the chair across the room from him. Almost instantly Derek fell into a snoring sleep.

Jake sat for a while, being careful to keep the scraped parts of his arms away from the chair arms, and gazed at Derek. An intense desire overwhelmed him—all the desires he'd been feeling for the past several months. To see Derek happy, to see Katie sparkling, to see them together. The desire became a burn, an ache, spreading from his chest out to his extremities.

Without warning, his body rose from the chair and walked backward toward the sofa, pulled Derek up and walked with him—backward—out the door and into the street. They struggled back down onto the pavement, and Jake held onto Derek by the waist as he sucked gulps of gastric juices into his mouth. Jake lowered himself by one arm until he was lying down. Derek swooped up, then stumbled away backward. The taillights of a car zoomed toward them from the darkness and swerved onto the curb. Some bushes and a mailbox leaped up as the car shot by and planted themselves into the ground. As the car passed by backward, Jake slid across the pavement and then flew up into the air and landed onto his feet in a reverse sprint. The car backed around the corner and disappeared.

Jake urged his emotions into deeper longing, and the rate of reverse movement increased. He zoomed across campus, unable to see where he was going, but knew he was headed to Leon's tiny lab. He entered the building and the room and relived their experiments at a dizzying pace.

This was still too slow. His mind felt as if it were fighting against an inertia that resented him moving in this temporal direction. He poured all the feelings he could into his efforts, and his retrograde movement became a blur. He could hardly tell what he was doing anymore. The world spun around him incoherently. The days became a strobe light flashing on and off within seconds. Thank God he was retracing actions he'd already taken and didn't have to give any thought to what he was doing. All he had to do was keep moving backward, faster, faster, casting aside the days and the weeks and the months.

He had no way of knowing how far he'd gone. He suffered a splitting headache and was on the verge of burning his last ounce of cognitive energy. Before long he would have to stop or pass out. He had no idea what would happen if he stopped abruptly and didn't want to find out. Instead he slowed carefully, carefully, until he could perceive his surroundings again, then slowed more until he was creeping backward. Gently he eased to a stop and felt a rush of vertigo as the normal flow of forward time took over. He spared a moment to catch his breath and clear his head, then looked around.

He sat in the university library, poring over a book on quantum electrodynamics. Next to him on the table was a stack of other books and a campus newspaper. He grabbed the newspaper and looked for the date. About a month past the mixer dance. Add a little time for the changes he wanted to make, and Jake needed to travel back another five weeks or so.

He still felt drained from his journey, so he stared blankly at the book until his head cleared enough to start again. He slipped easily into his trance and felt the surreal sensations of backward movement through time once more. He raced back as fast as he could while still being able to count the days. When he counted thirty-seven, he slowed his momentum and eased to a stop at night as his past self prepared for bed. He took over his past life at once and climbed under the covers for a desperately needed night of sleep.

In the morning he headed to campus as usual, except for a detour that caused him to cross paths with Derek. An "accidental" bumping together, some introductions, a few well-placed bits of conversation that sparked Derek's interest, and in moments they were heading to the campus cafeteria together for lunch, where they'd rendezvous with Katie. As they walked, Jake dropped hints that Katie was "only a friend" and completely unattached.

The three enjoyed lunch and each other's company, and of course Derek and Katie hit it off together immediately. Within twenty-four hours Derek had asked Katie on a date to the student mixer dance. Within forty-eight hours Jake's neurons were having a hard time remembering why that pleased him so much.

At the dance, Derek and Katie were having a great time together—until Derek had to go to the restroom or something. While Katie stood alone, a tall, swarthy guy walked up to her and struck up a conversation. Katie shook her head at some offer with a glowing smile that could make even a rejection feel good. But the fellow didn't gracefully bow out and continued to talk to her until Derek returned. Introductions took place, and the man asked Derek something, who responded in the affirmative. The man took Katie by the hand

and led her onto the dance floor.

For some reason Jake felt instantly alarmed. Was Derek out of his mind? Didn't he realize this fellow was trying to steal her away?

But why in the world would Jake worry about that? It was a harmless dance after all. Derek and Katie hadn't developed much of a relationship yet. Perhaps the other guy would turn out to be better for her anyway—who could tell at this point? If Derek lost her, it was his own fault for being so congenial, and why should Jake care?

The intruder monopolized Katie for three dances. Jake was relieved to see Derek finally look nervous about the situation. Derek marched out and asserted his position as the official date.

But the tall man walked off with a smug look on his face. A feeling of something gone amiss swept through Jake. It was obvious this fellow felt like he'd won.

The next day Jake found out why.

The man's name was Anthony. Having extracted Katie's phone number from her at the dance, he called to ask her out. After which Derek asked her out, then Anthony, then Derek, Anthony, Derek...

Katie loved the attention, but she also confided to Jake that she was beginning to fall in love with both of them and didn't know how she'd ever choose between the two. He knew as a friendly bystander he had no right to interfere, but something inside him made him blurt out:

"Derek. Choose Derek."

He immediately felt appalled at himself. What business did he have saying that? And on what basis had he decided? He couldn't understand his own preference.

From that point on Jake remained carefully neutral. But he could sense the seed he'd planted germinating. Anthony made a valiant effort, but Katie began seeing more and more of Derek.

One day Anthony came by with a bottle of wine to commiserate with Jake. "He's won, I can tell," Anthony said as they sat across the living room sipping the wine. "She spends most of her time with Derek."

Jake, feeling guilty anyway, didn't quite know what to say. "I know," was all that came out.

"And why shouldn't she?" Anthony spat as he slammed his glass down onto the end table. "He's so much more full of life than I am. She once called me 'solid and strong.' The sort of guy a mother would love to see her daughter marry. But I don't know how to enjoy life like he does."

"There's a lot to be said for solid and strong." Jake wished he had Anthony's talent for saying the right thing, but had to settle for his own feeble skills.

Anthony smiled without conviction. Jake stared at the glass Anthony still held between his fingers as it rested on the table. Much of the wine in the bottle had disappeared into that glass a little at a time.

"Would you like me to talk to her about it?" Jake offered.

Anthony shook his head slowly, picking the glass up a couple of inches and swirling its contents. "No, that's too high schoolish. He won in a fair fight, and that's it. I'm a man—I can take it."

But Jake noticed that Anthony's eyes were moistening, and his heart sank at the words "fair fight."

"He's better for her than me," Anthony said. "I know it's a cliche, but I really want what's best for her." He looked up at Jake and self-consciously wiped a tear away with his finger before it had a chance to spill out.

Jake sat silently, having no idea what to say.

"But it sure does hurt."

Jake nodded. "Yes, I know about that."

For the first time he understood the depth of Anthony's feelings for Katie. All along, without being fully conscious of it, Jake had assumed the pursuit of Katie was more of a game for Anthony, a challenge to his machismo. Only now did he realize that Anthony was hopelessly in love. Jake, still suffering lingering pains from his own loss at love, felt deep empathy for him.

Anthony shook his head and chuckled. "One week. He beat me out by one week. Why couldn't I have met her first? Then maybe she wouldn't have even gone out with him."

He jumped to his feet without warning and downed the last of his wine in one gulp. "No, that's selfish of me. She's happier with him, I can tell." He gazed into Jake's eyes. "And I've been troubling you too much with my problems. I'm sorry, dear friend. I'll go."

Jake stood and walked over to him, taking the wine glass. "Are you okay? You had quite a bit to drink."

Anthony brushed the concern away with a wave of his hand. "No problem. I'm walking. I have to think. I'll pick my car up tomorrow."

When Anthony finally left, Jake felt relief. He also felt shame for feeling relief, but what could he do about the situation? Twist Katie's arm and make her choose Anthony? Then what about Derek?

He was glad when the time came to meet with an acquaintance of his, a researcher named Leon. They were about to embark on a bizarre research project Jake had dreamed up during a boring lecture by a prominent physicist.

In the meantime Katie saw Derek almost exclusively, with only token dates for Anthony and occasional visits with Jake. Before long the couple were hugging and kissing openly, oblivious to the effect it might have on Anthony.

Although Anthony strode around with his usual confidence, it seemed like a hollow show. An edge began to form in Anthony's voice, where before he would speak with grace and warmth. Jake never saw his wry smile anymore.

The inevitable finally struck. Derek and Katie eloped to Vegas and returned announcing the happy event indiscriminately. Talk about rubbing it in! At the news, Anthony jumped into his '79 Maserati and disappeared until morning.

Jake curled up at home and pouted. Ever since he could remember, Katie had dreamed of going to Hawaii on her honeymoon. Jake resented Derek for robbing her of that dream—even though he knew the man couldn't afford it. He also felt a tinge of regret that he hadn't been in a position to fulfill that dream for her. She'd shared it with him for so long, he almost felt like it was his right to take her there.

In a couple of weeks Anthony shocked everyone by announcing his engagement to Sandy—or was it Cindy? Jake kept forgetting. She was blonde and busty and beautiful and clung to Anthony like a conjoined twin. In public he strode around with her on his arm, but in private moments Jake saw the testiness with which he treated her. Those moments motivated her to greater efforts to please him, but it only made him more contentious.

Jake ached with concern. He may be a physics student, but he was no dummy when it came to affairs of the heart. He could see what Anthony's new relationship was about and where it was heading. Only his sessions with Leon provided an escape from his turmoil.

Jake saw Katie less and less often, and always with Derek. Although she seemed content enough, she also seemed to be tiring of his constant antics. Was it Jake's imagination, or did he notice an occasional scowl from her when Derek let loose? One time Jake ran into her on campus alone, and they had lunch together at the cafeteria. As he joked with her, her eyes glazed over, and she quickly changed the subject to a serious discussion of current events. Only then did she brighten up with an enthusiasm associated with pleasures rarely enjoyed.

Jake loved Derek like a brother—a brother he never had. But Jake also loved Katie like a sister, and he realized Katie was not going to be happy. In just a couple of months, Derek's "zest for life" wore thin with no time out for serious matters. Jake's careless comment that tipped the scales in Derek's direction only made matters worse. After that he'd refused to favor one over the other. But the day finally came—the day he swore would never come—when his heart refused to stay neutral any longer.

He chose Anthony. But he chose too late.

During his next session with Leon, they made a breakthrough that neither of them could have imagined except as a silly flight of fancy. Jake slowed time down—all the way down—until it stopped. Then he slowed it down some more. It was hours after midnight when Jake practically danced his way home. He barely had time to sit down when his phone rang.

"Jake, it's Cindy," came an agitated voice.

Cindy—he tried to burn her name into his mind. "What's the matter?"

"Anthony and I had a fight."

Big surprise, thought Jake, but then got somber when he realized she tried to hold back sobs.

"He drove away mad. I just got a call from the hospital. He was in an accident."

"Dear God!" Jake said. "How is he?"

"Not good. Jake, I don't have any way to get there. Could you take me?"

"Of course."

Excruciating hours passed in the waiting room before the doctor appeared and pronounced Anthony stable. Sandy—no, Cindy—had sat stoically, but now broke down and threw herself onto Jake for comfort. By the time the nurse told them Anthony was coming out of anesthesia, Cindy was asleep on a couch. She must be utterly drained, he thought, and decided to let her rest a little longer as he visited with Anthony.

"Are you family?" the nurse asked him.

"He's my—brother."

The nurse nodded and led him in.

Anthony was groggy, but awake. Jake stared at him, at the tubes running out of him, at the bandages on his head and arms, and fought with all his strength to hold the tears back.

Anthony peered up with troubled eyes. "Jake," he whispered, "so nice of you to come."

Jake smiled as sincerely as he could. It probably looked like a grimace. "I brought Sa—Cindy with me. She's asleep in the waiting room."

Anthony looked away and said, "Thank you. We had a fight. I drove away angrily."

"She told me."

When he looked back, a tear started to leak from one eye, rolling leisurely down to his ear. "I still love her. I miss her so much."

Jake knew he didn't mean Cindy. His own tears refused to hold back any longer. "I know," he said, placing his hand on Anthony's arm.

Anthony dozed off, and Jake stood for a while gazing at him. Intense desire surged up, all the desires he'd been feeling for the past several months. The eerie sensations of backward time travel began.

He knew what he had to do. He loved Derek, but Derek was wrong for her. Jake wanted only the best for Katie, because he loved her like a sister—the sister he never had.

Solar Butterfly

Elaine refused to cry, even though her eyes stung with the urge to spill tears. She would not let him affect her like this. No one would affect her like this again. She would become a Solar Butterfly, sailing gracefully from planet to planet, far from any contact with humans.

With multiple bruises, and maybe even a cracked rib, the effort to sit up was excruciating. But she did so anyway. She would not wait around to be discovered like this. She pulled her blouse, hanging by her arms, back over her shoulders, cringing with each movement. It was soaked wet from the puddle underneath her, and she shivered from the cold. The buttons were gone—she had to hold it closed with a hand. Her bra, meters away, she ignored. Her panties were torn beyond utility, so she left them on the sidewalk, but her jeans lying limply beside her were mostly in good shape.

She thought the pain was intense pulling her blouse on, then she tried to stand. No way. Her rib had to be broken. Instead she scooted herself along, alternating between one hand and her buttocks contacting the ground, scooping up her jeans as she passed them. Each movement shot searing pain through her side. The few meters to the emergency call button seemed kilometers away.

Imagine—just a few meters! That's how close she'd come to signaling for help. But Jeff caught her before she ran those last few meters and threw her to the ground. If she'd made it to the button, he probably would have fled. By such a small margin was her life torn to pieces with her panties.

The button was a strip of yellow light five centimeters wide that extended along the entire height of the pole, from the ground to the top two meters high. Elaine spared an instant of gratitude for the insightful soul who had designed it so someone in her predicament wouldn't have to stand to reach it.

The button glowed brightly yellow until she held her palm to it, then flashed bright red and sounded an alarm. Finally she let her tears spill out as she anticipated the gut-wrenching shame she'd feel when the emergency response team came and found her sitting naked on the sidewalk, but for her jeans draped across her crotch and a thin blouse soaked into translucence.

When they arrived, she didn't feel as much shame as she thought she would. Disconnection came easily to her these days—practice makes perfect. As the ambulance zoomed at emergency altitude over the campus roofs to the university hospital, she imagined herself floating high above the world, Butterfly wings outstretched, gazing down on the shimmering blue-and-white globe, patches of earthy brown and green peeking through holes in the clouds. How beautiful the world looked from that vantage point, instead of face down on the sidewalk as someone thrust repeatedly into her rectum.

With clinical monotones she described what happened as they took photographs of her bruises and swabbed her anus. By the time a doctor showed up to examine her, the police reported that Jeff was in custody. His description matched that from several other rapes in town. Just her luck to hook up with a serial rapist.

The first time, when her sweet sixteen birthday companion date-raped her, she'd endured skeptical looks from several people, including her mother. This time the evidence must be obvious enough to spare her that indignity. No one was giving her "the look."

Nurses injected her with diagnostic nanites. They reported two broken ribs, but no other serious damage. When the medical staff asked if there was someone she wanted them to contact, she hesitated. She desperately wished Monica were there, yet the whole situation arose because she'd been cheating on Monica. She shook her head.

As Elaine lay in the hospital bed overnight, she meditated on her decision. Her thesis *would* be the Butterfly, not the Mermaid. Her counselor insisted on the less risky project—the Mermaid. Sea transformations had already been done. Interplanetary space would provide the romance of breaking new ground, but by the same token, be much more risky. What good was a posthumous degree?

Elaine was ready to do either thesis. She'd run countless simulations for both. The life of a Mermaid had great appeal. Swimming through the world's oceans, feeling the rush of water flow past her nude body, breathing dissolved oxygen through her gills, thrashing her flippers on the surface, gleaning raw food from the sea with her own efforts—sushi for life! A few other students had designed Mermaids or Mermen since the Applied Morphogenetics program began. But Elaine's original contribution would be the gills and the carnivorous teeth. All the others had chosen to remain air breathers and socially attached to humans.

The Mermaid would certainly fulfill her desire to withdraw from human society, spending countless months alone in the sea, exploring the wonders of marine nature. But it wasn't a total withdrawal. She'd still be a part of the world, bound to its gravity, living within the protective cocoon of its atmosphere. She'd still be able to interact with humans, albeit with difficulty. The Butterfly was her true desire—complete escape from the global womb that bore her, then tossed her about like a plaything.

So what if the Butterfly was a more dangerous morph? As if life as a Mermaid would not be. Sharks, killer whales, relying on one's own hunting skills for food. Elaine calculated that the danger was only incrementally greater, not orders of magnitude. It *would* take a couple of years to develop the Butterfly body—much longer than the Mermaid. But it would be worth it.

Her counselor didn't see it that way and refused to approve the Butterfly. True to form, Elaine had slunk out of her office, bitter but acquiescent. But with Jeff's final insult to her life, Elaine was ready to take a stand. Since the days of her childhood when her father left and her mother abused her in drunken fits, Elaine had become less and less interested in other people. The handsome young boy who loved her singing voice and made her sixteenth birthday a delight—until he got her alone in the car and raped her virginity away—must have told others how "great" she was. All her dates ever after expected the same. She was seared enough in her soul from the first experience to let them.

Funny, she couldn't even remember his name now.

By the time she graduated with her B.S. in genetics, she'd had enough of men. Half the human race appeared nothing more to her than predators. Vivid dreams haunted her nights. She was a lioness, devouring screaming men who'd thought to test their machismo in the plains of Kenya. Or a shark, visiting her wrath on all the male swimmers in the sea. Pools of blood and testosterone mixing with ocean brine.

That's where she got her idea for the Mermaid. She knew her counselor and the review committee would never approve a shark. But she borrowed the shark's teeth, ostensibly for feeding on sea creatures. In darker moments she imagined luring sailors with her sweet song and milky breasts, then tearing them to pieces. A regular siren.

When she'd all but resigned herself to disconnecting from the human race, Monica caught her eye in the locker room showers. Tall and muscular—she had to be weight training—yet alluring and feminine, exotic with her dark complexion and hair, her long eyelashes and deepset eyes framing a sleek nose. Full lips painted subtle burgundy, eyelids tinted with a hint of charcoal grey. She caught Elaine gazing at her, and Elaine almost flinched, but with an effort held her gaze. What feeble pain could rejection from a woman inflict compared to the torment men had dealt her throughout her life?

Monica gazed back, lips slightly parted, water splashing down her back forming a halo of mist reflecting the light. She smiled at Elaine. In two days they made love. In two weeks they lived together. Monica called Elaine "My Little Butterfly" because she was so dainty and frail compared to Amazonian Monica. It made Elaine tingle all over when she said it.

Once Monica learned about Elaine's plans to morph into a Mermaid, she spoke wistfully of following her into the sea. Elaine acted pleased, but deep down felt apprehension at the thought. Something about the way Monica discussed it sounded like she wasn't serious—or was Elaine just sensing her own resentment at Monica's intrusion into her plans?

One day as they picnicked in a meadow about twenty kilometers from campus, Monica lay on the blanket and dozed as Elaine watched a monarch butterfly flutter from stalk to stalk in the grassy field. She imagined what it would be like to be that butterfly, flitting aimlessly, carelessly, lightly touching on the world, but never lingering anywhere for long.

That night she dreamed of being a butterfly. The utter freedom and solitude of gliding through the air, rising above the twisted ugliness of the world, higher, higher, until the ugliness became beauty, and never encountering another soul, caused her to awaken with tears streaming down her face. Somehow she'd become a Butterfly instead of a Mermaid.

But shortly after the grogginess of sleep left her, she realized the foolhardiness of that dream. Physics was against her. There was no way a human-being-sized creature could become aerodynamic with such gossamer wings. If she were to shrink her body to a viable size for flight, her diminished brain capacity would threaten her very intellect. She wanted escape and freedom, not brute ignorance.

So she continued to work on the Mermaid project. But her mind of its own accord kept analyzing the Butterfly, trying to find some way to make it work. Gravity was the enemy, but zero gravity was available only in outer space. That solution to the gravity problem conjured a whole Pandora's box of other obstacles: no oxygen, surrounded by a vacuum, no source of nourishment, nothing to be aerodynamic against in space, and unimaginable cold. Zero gravity seemed a dead end.

She tried to strengthen the Butterfly wings and shrink the body as much as she dared. But she ended up with something more like a gigantic bird than a butterfly. She considered switching to a Bird instead. But Birds had been attempted before and proved problematic. Their wing muscles tired easily and their lung capacity needed to be enormous to provide enough oxygen for flight. The ideal body size would literally make a "birdbrain" out of her.

Then she heard of solar sailing.

Engineers had been working on designs for years—sailing through interplanetary space with gigantic, wispy sails, using the particles of the solar wind as propulsion. But their efforts didn't enter the general public's consciousness until a timetable for producing the first prototype was announced. Suddenly everyone was caught up in the romance of sailing between the planets with "a star to steer by and the solar wind at your back."

Elaine immediately saw the potential of converting the solar sail concept into enormous butterfly wings. It encouraged her to tackle the other problems of an extraterrestrial Butterfly with greater determination. She studied the photosynthesis process of plants and refined it for her needs. She designed new mitochondria-like structures within her cells to manufacture the nutritional needs of the Butterfly from basic raw materials. She devised skin that was resistant to vacuum and layered for insulation against the frigid three degrees Kelvin of space. Glands embedded in the skin could dissolve and absorb raw materials as the Butterfly reclined on iceballs of comets and rocky asteroids. She enhanced the Mermaid's carnivorous teeth, engineering them into crunching maws that could gnaw on ice and rock as an additional source of raw materials for her body, and developed a digestive system to process them.

The Butterfly's metabolism would be slowed down drastically to minimize the need for energy, since photosynthesis generated a limited supply, and materials to consume in space were separated by vast distances. Likely the Butterfly's lifespan would extend for hundreds of years as a result. It was the perfect sluggish, unhurried pace for a being sailing millions of kilometers of empty space.

She designed a body both large enough to act as a foundation for gigantic wings and delicate enough to minimize inertia—a thin, elongated caricature of a human. She anchored the wings to attenuated arms and legs, and stretched fingers and toes long and thin to become extended fans supporting the wings' membranes.

She placed bulging eyes on its head that could discern detail millions of kilometers away: an "eagle eye" for astronomical scales. She kept the organs of her sex—modified to procreate a Butterfly, not a human—only because it was a legal requirement with all morphing projects, not because she ever expected to want to use them again. The whole point of the Morphogenetics program was to provide biological diversity in the descendants of humanity after three plagues of supermicrobes had wiped out two-thirds of Earth's human population. "Don't put all your eggs in one basket" and all that. A lack of reproductive ability would void the main purpose of a morphing project.

She cared as little for communication as she did for reproduction. Elaine wanted to go into space to flee humanity, not commune with it. But she knew her project would never be approved if her Butterfly couldn't communicate.

So she interlaced its wings with colorful phosphorescent filaments that were consciously manipulated, displaying intricate and ever-changing lattices of glowing color that could encode a language using an alphabet of light.

She began to fall in love with her Butterfly. An enormous, elegant creature of austere beauty, whose very act of speaking was a work of art. As she ran the Mermaid through preliminary simulations, she worked furiously to piece together the Butterfly design. When the time came to submit the first draft of her thesis, she turned in the Butterfly, even though her counselor had originally approved the Mermaid.

Elaine received high marks for originality, both for the overall concept and the invention of several new genetic engineering processes. But, said her counselor, the design was much too theoretical, too experimental, too dangerous. And she would banish herself to permanent isolation from her home world into the cold depths of space.

That's exactly what Elaine wanted, but she kept that to herself.

Her counselor instructed her to submit the Mermaid draft in one week. Elaine protested, but the counselor was adamant. Mermaid. One week.

Elaine couldn't bear to go home after classes that day. She headed for the corner bar instead, and there met Jeff. Powerful, bulging muscles. Cropped blond hair. Soft, blue eyes that seemed amused at everything. Even as she flirted with him, Elaine was bemused at how she was coming on to a man again. Men had used her all her life—why shouldn't she take a turn using them?

After many hours and many drinks together, they went for a stroll in the botanical gardens on campus. There was an unspoken agreement among students that this signaled more than platonic interest. Desire for Jeff brewed inside her. For an instant she wondered if this had anything to do with her disappointment at school that day. But she thrust the thought from her mind. She didn't want to think about Mermaids and Butterflies and arrogant counselors.

The path they walked was dark with only a distant streetlight behind them and a thin strip of gleaming yellow far ahead. That morning a rain shower had passed through, but the afternoon sun had blazed brightly. Occasional puddles and a sweet freshness to the air were all that remained of the shower. The wind whispered atonal melodies through the trees. Stars glittered in the clear sky. Exotic flowers perfumed the air. Elaine couldn't remember the last time she'd experienced such a romantic setting. She trembled slightly with anticipation at what might transpire that night.

Jeff stopped to face her and hold both her hands. Gazing into her eyes, he kissed her intimately on the lips. A faint apprehension welled up inside, surprising her. Hadn't she wanted this? The faces of all the boys and men who had used her for their gratification flashed through her mind as he pressed harder against her lips. His kiss became aggressive. She moaned her objection and began to struggle. His powerful arms held her in place.

With complete helplessness came panic. She stomped on his foot and broke away and ran toward the gleaming yellow button in the distance. He cried out in angry pain, and his footsteps clapped briskly against the sidewalk behind her. As the emergency call button beckoned a couple meters away, she felt his hand grasp her shoulder like a vice and topple her to the ground, knocking the wind out of her. He kicked and kicked her in the side, then fell to his knees and yanked her blouse open, buttons flying. Her bra flew away next, and her breasts—those milky breasts that were to entice sailors to their doom—jiggled exposed and vulnerable.

Her jeans abandoned her next as Jeff tugged violently on them. She tried to sit up so she could act, but a sharp pain stabbed at her side, and she fell back with a gasp. The pain intensified with every breath she took. Her head swam from shock. She heard a vicious tearing of cloth and felt her loins exposed to cool air. Jeff rolled her onto her stomach, causing her to nearly pass out from the torture in her side. Her face ground into the sidewalk with each stab of pain in her rectum.

Lying in the hospital bed all night, Elaine realized she should have screamed. But screaming had long vanished from her repertoire of behavior. She'd held too many screams in throughout the years. Silence, disconnection, were her defenses. She finally realized after all this time that they had always failed her.

The reconstructive nanites knitted her ribs together and drained the bruises, cleared the alien residue from her rectum and mounted a search and destroy for virulent microbes. Her IV dripped all the necessary raw materials into her bloodstream for them to work, and a catheter removed the excess wastes that her kidneys scrubbed from her bloodstream.

By morning she was declared healed, although the pain would linger for days, maybe weeks. The analgesic nanites were programmed to 80% capacity, because experience showed that complete pain relief often led to activity that might cause re-injury. The slight pain was a reminder to take things easy.

Monica showed up to bring her home. She'd called around frantically when Elaine hadn't returned until she found her admitted to the hospital. Elaine rode home somberly, wondering what she should say, while Monica stared grimly ahead at the road.

Elaine searched for rage within herself, but she'd learned the disconnection lesson so well that she felt nothing. She must be repressing like hell to keep from exploding, but she didn't care. She could deal with the psychological aftermath of her repression later as she swooped between the planets in blessed isolation. What matter if she had a nervous breakdown then? Insanity might be a virtue out there, enriching her experience of vast, severe majesty bedecked with glittering gems of stars.

It hurt Monica deeply that Elaine had turned to drink and a man for comfort rather than her. She broke off their relationship in a scene that was quiet and tearless. Elaine felt relief at the time. But to her surprise, she felt lost and abandoned that night sitting alone in a hotel room. She managed to disconnect from that feeling in a short time, and toasted an absent Monica, wishing her happiness and a long life.

Elaine filed her project modification hours before the deadline—the Solar Butterfly. Her counselor objected strenuously, but Elaine stood her ground this time. The counselor combed her design for a disqualifying defect, but could find none. She grudgingly accepted the form, and Elaine went to work polishing up her final presentation.

The day came for her thesis review, the formal evaluation and preliminary grading of her project. The committee would give the final go ahead or send her back to the drawing board. Her grade would be finalized when she implemented the project and demonstrated that the results matched her design. The committee was merciless by policy—compassionately so. Any failure often ended in distorted organisms, incapacitation, even death. They had kept the failure rate down to an impressive 1.3% by rejecting a great many theses.

Elaine believed she'd done her homework—her project was unassailable. Its experimental nature was a black mark against it from the beginning, but that didn't mean a guaranteed rejection. It only meant that her presentation had better be flawless. She felt that it was.

After two weeks of deliberation, the committee disagreed. Elaine's thesis failed.

She could always go back and resubmit the Mermaid. It had precedents, its new design features were modest, and her work on it was virtually complete. She could pass the committee review in two months.

Instead she filed for an appeal. She made her case well. All her designs were sound. They were based on proven genetic technologies and engineering principles borrowed from other fields. She'd surpassed the minimum requirements for rigorous simulation testing threefold. She claimed no one could point out a specific design flaw—her project just made them nervous.

The appeals committee agreed with her assessment, but declared the project too theoretical. There were too many new, experimental designs being tried all at once. An incremental approach, implementing one or two at a time, would be preferable.

"How do you incrementalize yourself into space?" she asked. "Either it all works together, or none of it works."

Her appeal was rejected.

Two months for the Mermaid. She seriously considered it. In the end Elaine mobilized her final chance, an appeal to the Federal Student Rights Board.

Thank God the Student Rights Act was passed two years ago. Politicians finally got it through their thick skulls—while educators never did—that technologies, fields of research, and occupations were progressing so fast that any institution as conservative as a university would never keep up with them. They were always stifling the creativity and novel thinking necessary for students to keep pace with dizzying change.

It was a student's right, the act declared, to have his educational plans and research projects automatically accepted if the educational body of jurisdiction could not provide compelling reasons for rejection. The appointed Student Rights Board had proven itself to be aggressive in defending those rights, overturning the judgments of universities on more than a few occasions.

But the appeal also added a good six months to Elaine's thesis approval. She spent that time finishing up all her other educational requirements for her degree.

Elaine presented her case effectively before the Board. The university argued the dangerous, theoretical nature of the project. The Board decided in Elaine's favor, judging the case to be a classic example of educational obstruction for which the Student Rights Act had been implemented in the first place. The university had no concrete reasons to reject Elaine's plan, only a vague distress at its innovative nature.

Elaine's thesis was sent back to the original committee, who graded it with a 98%. Her project would be turned over to the MorphoGenetics Corporation, a holding firm for the university whose purpose was to implement student Morphogenetics projects and commercially exploit the successful ones. The student would have his or her project implemented without cost, and in turn assign all rights to the corporation. He or she would be remunerated with a lifetime royalty on all revenue generated by the project. Successful projects had been known to set a student up for life. Because of the exacting scrutiny of the review committee, all but 1.3% of the projects were successful. The university and the corporation fully expected Elaine's project to be among that 1.3%.

Elaine assigned her royalties to Monica. The Butterfly certainly wouldn't need them.

She'd estimated two years for her morph once the process began at the O'Neill orbital colony. Most projects took considerably less time, but few projects involved modifying the human body to such a drastic degree. She was obliged to perform her morph in space, because her fragile Butterfly frame would never withstand the forces of Earth's gravity.

Her trip to the O'Neill colony seemed unreal—already she was experiencing her dream of floating above the world and looking down on it. She'd grown up seeing hundreds of images of her home planet, but the reality thrilled her. No image could capture the brilliant colors contrasted against the utter black backdrop of star-bejewelled space. There was a hurricane threatening the Caribbean islands. Most of the Atlantic lay in darkness, with pinpoints of city lights in Portugal appearing near the horizon. The orbital colony ahead of them seemed to hang by an invisible thread with the fuzzy smear of the Andromeda Galaxy kissing it.

Her weightlessness in the shuttle tickled her stomach. The overwhelming emptiness of the vacuum around her thrilled her. This was the environment she'd chosen to live in for the rest of her life. This was her home now.

The inside-out world of the colony boggled her mind, with everyone living on the inner surface of a rotating, hollow cylinder. No horizon—the ground curved up until it became the sky. The image of the sun, reflected in large external mirrors, shone through a transparent strip of hull. A lake hung shimmering exactly over her head. Someone pedaled a helibike in midair along the zero-gravity axis of rotation. It took some getting used to before she could look around without experiencing vertigo.

She was assigned living quarters within the laboratory where her project would be implemented. They were temporary—it wouldn't be long before quarters designed for humans would not suit her. She was allowed to sleep her jet lag off, which she did through the afternoon, evening, and clear until morning. She met the technicians who would be working on the project with her. Within twenty-four hours she received her first injection of bioengineering nanites.

The morph was gradual enough that she experienced little sensation. Occasionally a discomfort or an itching as a part of her body began to change. A few times there was pain, but not often, and not serious. About six months into her morph, her head was more Butterfly than human, and she could no longer speak to or understand the technicians. She was at their mercy from then on, and could only hope they'd implement her designs faithfully. Already she was experiencing her coveted isolation.

After one year they needed to build separate accommodations for her in space near the colony, accommodations that had no spin creating artificial gravity, accommodations immense enough to house her enormous wingspan. They built a large pressurized sphere in which she could dwell.

As her wings completed their growth, work began on her space-resistant skin. After sixteen months she was introduced into space, where she could dwell for short periods of time. She would return to her sphere whenever she needed oxygen and nutrients, and when her technicians needed physical contact with her.

Entering space for the first time was an eerie sensation. She could feel her internal mass bulging out against the vacuum of space. It was a refreshing experience. She felt as if a vice around her had been loosened and she could breathe freely—even though she wasn't breathing. The intense chill felt bracing and invigorating. Having space feel so inviting was her first concrete indication that she had designed well.

She unfolded her wings wide, as a butterfly newly emerged from a chrysalis would, letting them bask in the radiation of the sun. They could have eclipsed the sun entirely for dozens of colonies if their gossamer nature didn't make them so translucent. Her vacuum-resistant eyes peered at them. The solar wings sparkled in the sunlight like fairy dust.

She tried a tentative flashing of her communication filaments. Dazzling colors splashed across the membranes. She wondered if anyone on Earth could see her wings with the naked eye. Certainly with a telescope. Look at me, amateur astronomers all over the world! Look through your telescopes at the beautiful Butterfly.

She gave her wings an experimental flap. To her metabolically sluggish mind they seemed to move quickly. In reality, she knew from her simulations that one flap took nearly a minute. Her wings pressed against the solar wind, and she felt herself move back gently. A thrill shot through her extended body—which probably took thirty seconds to complete in human perception. She flapped again, and again, and the colony dwindled before her. The solar radiation felt as soothing as a sunny day in May. If she had tear ducts she would have wept for joy.

The technicians who had assisted in her release floated motionlessly in place, observing her through their helmets. One lifted a hand in acknowledgment—an instantaneous gesture to Elaine—and she waggled the tips of her wings as fast as she could, knowing it would appear as a leisurely waving to them. With that she swooped out with all her energy, letting the instinctual sailing techniques she'd programmed into her genes take over. It was probably the most experimental part of her design, and the one she was least certain of success with. How do you run simulations on how custom-designed instincts would feel? But she sailed in the direction she intended without thinking consciously of her movements, so they must be working fine.

She shot away from the colony with a dizzying velocity and curved into an arc that would take her around the Earth. She could barely keep up with its rotation, even though she felt as if she were shooting past like a comet. A geostationary satellite paced her the entire journey.

As she swung around into the night sky, her control faltered, then disappeared. She realized the Earth had eclipsed her solar wind. She was like a sailboat dead in the water on a windless day. Fortunately space lacked the friction of water, and she coasted until the sun burst forth on the other side. She could feel the wind like a blast in her face on a blustery day. She was driven back unexpectedly, but in seconds (her time) she had regained control and glided up to the colony. The technicians were gone—her trip had taken twenty-four hours to them—but she knew they'd be observing from within. She hovered before the colony and spread her wings wide, then flashed her phosphorescent filaments in the signal indicating that her new body worked well.

Once per terrestrial day she entered her sphere, pressurized with nutrient-rich gas that she could absorb through her skin. To her it seemed like a steady diet of meals every couple of hours, but she needed them that often, having no other source of sustenance, neither eating, nor drinking, nor breathing. During the last eight months of her morph, her photosynthesis compartments were generated and activated, her industrial strength jaws and teeth grew into place, her digestive system formed that would break down the rocky materials that she chewed into fine gravel. After the full two years were up, she was ready for her maiden voyage as a full-fledged, self-sustaining, deep space Butterfly.

A tug dragged a tiny asteroid into the vicinity of the colony for her. She drifted toward it and spread her elongated body along its surface. The glands of her skin dissolved the minerals, and pores absorbed them. She crunched at the surface with her teeth, pulverizing the rock and swallowing it. She had pro-grammed her taste buds to perceive sweetness in the rock, and olfactory-like filaments in her mouth to sense a variety of flavors that appealed to her. These worked with less effectiveness than her sailing instincts, creating odd flavors that clashed sometimes, but gave her food an exotic appeal that she grew to enjoy.

She gorged herself on nutrients until she felt she could consume no more, then rose above the asteroid and spread her wings, ready to flee the Earth.

Her itinerary was to fly out to the asteroid belt, gorge herself again, and come back to Earth. It would have revolved around the sun many times by then. They'd debrief her on every detail of her experience, a report she'd give entirely in her language of light, and they'd examine her thoroughly once more. Assuming all of it went well, she'd be officially discharged of all respon-sibilities to Earth. The project would be complete. She'd get her degree and royalties confirmed. She could then gorge once more on the captured asteroid and fly off anywhere she wanted.

Elaine turned to gaze at the Earth, a shining globe of vivacious colors. In moments she would leave it, fleeing millions of kilometers away. She wouldn't have to come back. Only her sense of duty would cause her to return.

She took a moment to wonder if she cared.

She thought of her father. Years ago he'd walked out on his family out of some frustration her young self had not understood. If he saw her as she was today, he'd probably flee in terror.

She thought of her mother, bravely beating up on a little girl. How brave would her mother be facing down an enormous Solar Butterfly?

She thought of her birthday companion, the boy who romanced her with praises for her beautiful face, her beautiful body, her wonderful singing voice. What would he think now, knowing he'd forced his privates into the creature hovering hugely before the Earth?

She tried to sing once more, but of course nothing came out. She gave her-self no vocal chords since there was nothing in space for them to vibrate. Her esophageal valve allowed her to swallow, but blocked anything from bursting out into the vacuum of space. It was her first sense of disappointment.

With that emotion she thought of Monica. Of all the people who'd entered Elaine's personal life, only Monica might not be shocked—she'd seen the designs. What would Monica think if she saw her now in the "flesh"? A graphic on a computer monitor was hardly the same as the real thing towering before you. Would she flee in terror too?

Elaine turned her back on the world, literally and figuratively. She came here to isolate herself from it. What did she care if she neglected her responsibilities and never received her degree? The only thing that could possibly matter to her now was assuring her royalties for Monica. Elaine flapped her wings in a flourish and launched into space, still uncertain whether she'd return, uncertain whether even Monica mattered enough anymore.

The utter silence of the blackness around her felt stifling. Even the thumping of her pulse in her ears was absent. Having nothing in space to hear, she designed no sound-detection capability into her Butterfly. Her most valuable sense in space was vision, as it had been for astronomers since the first Neanderthals admired the night sky. Her eyes bulged as a butterfly's would, collecting radiation in such fine detail that she could see the pinpoint glimmers of the asteroid belt from the orbit of Earth.

Elaine glided toward the glittering necklace of asteroids. Time became meaningless for her. She let her senses dominate her mind, feeling the pressure of solar wind on her wings, smelling it as it passed her facial orifice—a kind of peppery aroma—relishing its sensation on her skin as she glided through it. Her eyes wandered, picking out the tiny circle of Jupiter. She could even see its red spot as a pinprick of color. Off that way was Saturn, a barely perceptible bulge marking its rings. She couldn't find Uranus or Neptune, and didn't even try for Pluto. Mars was nowhere in sight, although it should be easily seen as a ruddy marble. It must be lost somewhere in the glare of the sun.

Sooner than she expected with her lack of time sense, she reached the asteroid belt and focused in on the nearest one. Something like hunger permeated her body, and she settled on the asteroid's surface with a Solar Butterfly's equivalent of a sigh. Her skin began to consume, and she gnawed nonchalantly with her teeth.

In the distance she thought she could see one of the mining colonies adrift near an asteroid. She toyed with the idea of visiting them. Would they know about her? News coverage of the first morphing projects had been extensive, but by the time Elaine began hers they were passé. Since she was such an unusual project, she might get more coverage, but she wouldn't be surprised if the mining colony was completely unaware of her existence. What a shock she'd be to them!

And with that she realized she didn't care—not about anyone. What were these tiny little creatures to her? She was a majestic being of space, free to roam anywhere in the solar system, while they huddled in their little pressurized cocoons, forever terrified of the deadly environment that Elaine thrived in, an environment that filled the sweeping volume of the universe. Their lives were the anomalies in the cosmos—hers was the natural existence.

She decided not to return to Earth. The university would fail her, the corporation annul her royalties. If she could have laughed, she would have. What did any of that matter to her now? That life and everyone in it was the past. She was the future, the first of her kind.

The first? Or the only?

Would anyone follow her out here?

Whether she returned or not, she knew the corporation was tracking her as she headed out to the asteroids. They'd know the project was a success, and go ahead and exploit it no matter what Elaine did. They might even be glad if she didn't return. They could keep her royalties.

Elaine rose from the asteroid, leaving a Butterfly-shaped depression—minus the wings—where her skin had dissolved rock. She decided she wanted to sightsee, and what better place to do that in the solar system than Saturn?

She swooped out toward that planet, gazing at it as she glided. The rings were magnificent. At first they were sheets of color. But as she neared, the sparkling pinpoints of each icy rock twinkled in the dim sunlight. She was hungry again, and headed for the nearest rock in the outermost ring. Her powerful teeth bit into it, then she swooped to the next and bit again, and again another. They each had a slightly different flavor. She sampled many of them, like a child in a candy shop tasting all the varieties of confection, before she felt satiated, then rose high above the planet, buzzing past the moon Titan just for fun, pretending to shock the primitive life forms that scientists had hoped to find beneath its hazy cloud cover, but never had.

She wondered where to go next. The solar system was open to her, a vast domain to explore. But now, she suddenly realized, there were not many places to go. Eight planets, a swarm of planetoids around Pluto that might even be too far for her to go without losing the solar wind, a ring of asteroids, and the sun. She wasn't equipped to go near the sun—her bioengineering talents weren't *that* good. She could visit each planet one by one, scour the asteroid belt for anything unusual, and then what? Chase comets like a dog chasing a groundcar? Head for the nearest star and die of starvation long before reaching it?

Elaine had anticipated wandering the solar system—a disc over ten billion kilometers in diameter. Plenty of room for a lifetime. Now she felt imprisoned in a sterile desert with eight tiny oases, alone forever until she died. And what will her life have meant? As useless as the feeble lives of those miners had seemed to her. What value was bigness, majesty, to a meaningless life?

She lifted her head and sought out Earth. Mars was now in view, but Earth was not. How many times had it revolved around the sun since she'd left? Dozens? She had no instinct for sensing the passage of time. Why hadn't she built such an instinct into herself?

Because, she thought back then, what use would it be to a being seeking total isolation? What did she care what time it was back on Earth as she roamed the solar system?

Suddenly she did care. Was it daytime in America? Were her fellow students in class, in bed asleep, or blowing off steam with various amusements? Was it summer, winter, spring? Christmas, Easter, Liberation Day? Were those students now white-haired with grandchildren surrounding them?

What was Monica doing right now?

Elaine manipulated her wings in an instinctive tacking motion, pushing against the gravity fields of the solar system and her own orbital velocity, and flew towards Earth. It was in view again, a greenish-blue speck in the barren blackness. She dove for it with all the velocity she could muster. She needed to pause at the asteroid belt again to refuel. As she chewed and absorbed, she searched for and found a mining colony. Probably not the one from before, but a desire to connect with its inhabitants burned within her. She flew toward it and hovered above it, spreading her wings wide, flashing dizzying patterns of color at them. A band of miners working on the nearby asteroid balked at her— terror? awe? excitement? Their acknowledgment of her existence gratified her, and she was able to continue on to Earth.

Why was she doing this? she asked herself as she sailed zigzag fashion against the wind. What did she hope to accomplish? Fluttering alone around the Earth would be as futile as wandering empty space. She couldn't imagine anyone being as foolish as she'd been to follow her out into this desolate environment. What kind of person would do it? Someone as disconnected from humanity as she? Would such a person even want to interact with Elaine?

Earth had revolved around the sun several more times by the time she approached it. She shot toward it, driven now by physical hunger as much as her emotional desire to connect with even one person. She needed desperately to find that captured asteroid. When she looked around, she saw multiple concentrations of vivid and ever-changing color, forming distinct patterns of web-like designs. The patterns meant something to her: the vocabulary of Elaine's language of light encoded into the Butterfly's DNA. Earth was surrounded by flitting webs of color that communicated meaningful thoughts.

Elaine found the asteroid and plastered herself against it. The taste of the rock against her skin and in her mouth was exquisite. For some moments she could think of nothing but devouring, even as more and more flashing lattices gathered around her.

When her hunger eased, she lifted her eyes and looked toward the O'Neill colony. From her old sphere she saw a shimmering gossamer being emerge, fluttering like a pro. Two bulging eyes peered at her from the top of a thin, elongated body. The skin was dull grey, absent the deep green color the incomplete Butterfly would acquire when her photosynthesis activated.

The Butterfly drifted toward her. Its bulging eyes were unreadable. What human expression could that visage make? Isolation-obsessed Elaine had no idea how to read the body language of another Butterfly.

The Butterfly flashed "Hello" with its wings.

Other fully developed Butterflies hovered around her, flashing words from their wings. Some were just like her. Others had added a set of six limbs like a terrestrial butterfly, but with fingers and thumb at the end of each. An enhancement to her design. Elaine's head swam with the implications of what she saw.

Their phosphorescent words jumbled together so she couldn't understand them. She realized she was flashing messages of her own, patterns of emotion without specific words.

A whole society of Butterflies, all beginning with her design. She was indeed the first of a magnificent species of space-faring beings. In the distance she saw a group of limbed Butterflies assembling the prefabricated pieces of another orbital colony, moving about easily in the vacuum of space. She had never thought of that—creatures able to work comfortably in space. What a valuable addition to humanity that was!

Again Elaine wished she had tears to shed. So what if her tears would come out flash-frozen in the coldness of space? Glittering diamond tears would be the perfect expression of what she felt right now. She was no longer alone in the cosmos. She was surrounded by hundreds of individuals who had related to her dream enough to follow her. She was the matriarch of an entire species of intelligent creatures that could inhabit the expanses of space as naturally as humankind had filled the surface of Earth. Each one of them a soulmate of hers.

A limbed Butterfly fluttered within touching distance from her, regarding her with its bulging eyes. Its wings rippled at the edges in a hovering pattern. One limb reached out to caress the side of her face as Monica used to do to her cheek. The filaments of its wings flashed the words: "My Little Butterfly."

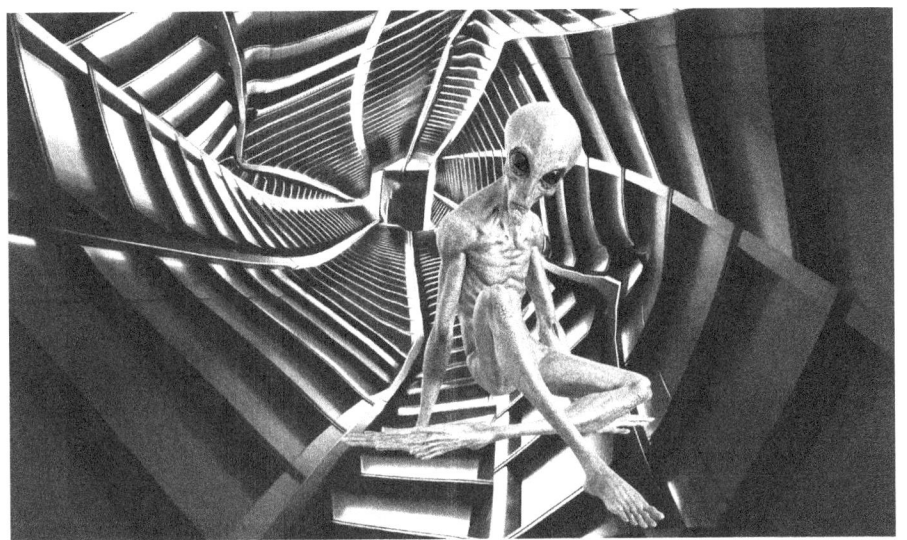

Bokev Momen

Another dead heaven carriage. Primewife Eteaki had seen too many of those during the routine interstellar patrols they did as part of the family business. Through the cups of the tendrils attached to both her eyes, Eteaki studied the image of the heaven carriage floating lifelessly in the vacuum of space. The carriage's four eyes, two on either side of its face, stared vacantly with the glassy aspect of death. But its belly still glowed, so it couldn't have died more than a few octals ago.

Pulling on the fleshy ropes she held in her hands, Primewife Eteaki reined Glaittli, their own heaven carriage, toward the derelict. She found the identifying marks tattooed on its hide that she was looking for. "It's a Murdzak carriage," she said, scowling at the thought of that race of barely-humanoids. "Great Divinity, I dislike those people."

"Do you think they had any captives?" Thirdwife Pezeli said. "And quit swearing."

Eteaki ignored her rebuke and sang a command to Glaittli through the transmission tendril attached to her neck near her vocal cords. "It's a definite possibility," she said as Glaittli's auditory tendril sang information into her ear. "The only inhabitable planet nearby is part of an unallied system that's classified *no contact*." She listened to more information. "Standard electronic technology based on artificial mechanisms. Barely becoming spacefaring." She tittered in mirth. "It's another one of those planets that some people think is the birthplace of the Anointed."

Pezeli scowled. "What's so funny? *Some* planet has to be his birthplace."

She steered Glaittli alongside the Murdzak carriage and brought it to a relative stop. "And out of the hundreds of planets that people claim is his birthplace, do you think anyone will ever figure out which one? If he even existed?"

"It's possible," Pezeli said obstinately.

A hand touched the nape of Eteaki's neck and began to fondle the strands of her hair.

"What's happening?" Husband Orbanek said. He'd been back in the bowels of Glaittli and must have just crawled through its gullet into the rear mouth chamber. With the tendril cups covering her eyes, Eteaki couldn't see him, but she knew him well enough to know that his other hand would be on Pezeli's nape right now doing the same thing.

"We ran across a dead Murdzak carriage," Pezeli said.

"Sphincter scum!" Orbanek muttered.

"Watch your language!" Pezeli growled.

"There's scorching on the hide," said Eteaki as she studied the image that the tendrils transferred from two of Glaittli's eyes. "And some flesh hanging loose."

"Probably a blood feud with some other Murdzak clan." Orbanek's hand lifted from Eteaki's neck, and she assumed that he now sat on the Husband's flesh mound that protruded from the floor of Glaittli's mouth chamber. "Any indications of life?"

"No, but the belly is still glowing," Eteaki said.

"Well..." She could picture him stroking his wispy beard as he thought. "I suppose we should check, just in case. Primewife, kiss the derelict."

"Yes, Husband."

Eteaki sang the docking command to Glaittli. As their heaven carriage drifted forward, she gazed at the dead carriage. No glow in its four eyes. No rippling colorations along its hide, but lots of scorching and damage. The mouth hung limply open. Only the glow of the graviton emitters on its belly showed it had ever been alive. Probably the whole crew died instantly from vacuum exposure. Any survivors would have to be in the gut past the esophageal valve. Assuming it hadn't been damaged also.

"Thirdwife," Orbanek said, "any indications of any other carriages in the vicinity?"

After a pause, Pezeli said, "No sign of anything. Whoever did this to the Murdzak must be gone."

Glaittli completed the kiss maneuver by facing the Murdzak carriage and pressing its open lips against the dead creature's mouth, first extending, then constricting them to form a tight seal around the inanimate lips. When the connection was secure, Eteaki dropped the steering ropes to the side and removed the tendril cups from her eyes, blinking against the bright illumination that came from phosphorescent strips along the membranes of the mouth chamber.

Glaittli relaxed its oral sphincter at one more command from Eteaki before she removed the transmission tendril. The iris-like opening ballooned before the crew, exposing the forward mouth parts and rows of carnivorous teeth. A sudden burst of wind and a swooshing noise accompanied the transfer of air into the forward mouth chamber and into the mouth of the dead carriage. Eteaki swallowed to pop her ears from the change in pressure.

"Let's investigate," Orbanek said. The three of them stood up from their flesh mounds. Their "heaven legs" kicked in immediately: the advanced balancing skills they'd developed through years of walking on soft, uneven flesh in a low-gravity environment. The belly of a heaven carriage—thick hide composed of graviton-emitting material that extended from head to exhaust orifice—couldn't produce more than one-eighth of a normal gravitational field. The three stepped their way onto Glaittli's quiescent tongue, grabbed a fang that extended two-thirds of their height, and carefully stepped through the gap between two teeth. Eteaki as Primewife led the way, with Orbanek next and Pezeli in the rear.

As they entered the dead carriage's mouth, Eteaki could already smell the faint odor of putrefaction diffusing into the air. They stepped past the fangs and across its tongue. The only illumination was the phosphorescence filtering over from Glaittli's mouth, since the Murdzak carriage's strips were dark. Its oral sphincter ahead hung limply open, and blackness filled the void beyond.

Each of them pulled a lightstem out of a sleeve pouch and caressed them until they purred and glowed a bluish white. Past the oral sphincter, dangling tendrils corkscrewed from the roof of the rear mouth chamber. Some of them were attached to Murdzak individuals who lay still with death, tiny mouths gaping, eyes bulging from their sockets. Eteaki shuddered at the sight of those eyes: huge and deep black and oval-shaped with severely pointed corners, housed within a pale white face that seemed much too small for the eyes. Six individuals. How could they stand the cramped living conditions? Utterly naked, their frames seemed emaciated by the standards of her species, the Tetzl. They were all male.

"Disgusting creatures," Orbanek said. "Can you imagine, cramped together in space with people you have no familial relationship with?"

"Maybe they're brothers," Pezeli said.

Orbanek sniffed in dismissal.

"What's the usual size of a Murdzak crew?" Eteaki asked, stepping between the flesh mounds that the corpses sprawled across and kicking the steering ropes out of her way.

"I think anywhere from four to twelve," Pezeli said.

Orbanek sighed. "Then we still need to check down the gullet for survivors. We may not have accounted for the whole crew."

"Plus there may be captives," Pezeli added.

"Yes," said Orbanek. "We *are* dealing with Murdzak."

Eteaki crept toward the gullet until she came to the closed esophageal valve. The carriage's reflexive response of closing that valve with any severe stress had saved crews on many occasions when a carriage died. It kept the air within from escaping when the mouth and oral sphincter relaxed at death. Unfortunately, it was useless if the crew was caught within the mouth chamber. If the carriage's death was slow, they had time to crawl back. But if sudden...

Genetic engineers had been trying to develop a strain of heaven carriages that would reflexively close the oral sphincter in the same way as the esophageal valve, but so far they had not succeeded. The seal was never tight enough without the conscious control of the living carriage, and the air seeped out within moments. Most crews in such a situation would force open the esophageal valve and crawl back. Of course that didn't work either—the valve would never close tightly again and *all* the air in the carriage eventually seeped out.

As Eteaki stowed her lightstem in its pouch and slipped on a nonconductive glove, she traced out the three tightly closed flaps of the esophageal valve with her eyes. Retrieving the lightstem and holding it in her gloved hand, she touched its glowing tip to the center of one of the flaps and gave the little creature a squeeze in the belly. Its defense reflex discharged a burst of electricity which caused the muscles in the flap to contract. An equalizing rush of air from behind the valve hit Eteaki in the face, and she balked at the stench. The phosphorescence of the lightstem dimmed with the discharge. Her double shadow from the other two lightstems fell across the flaps in front of her.

"Divine excretions!" Orbanek said. "We should have told Glaittli to close its sphincter after us. Our air will smell like this for octals."

"Stop swearing," Pezeli murmured. It was no more than a ritual these days, since no one ever heeded her.

Eteaki waited for her lightstem's glow to return to normal before opening another flap. Using only one lightstem to open all three flaps left the other two glowing with adequate illumination. She touched it to the second flap and squeezed. By the time the lightstem recharged again and she opened the third flap, her olfactory nerves had become accustomed to the stink.

"See anyone back there?" Pezeli said quietly, as if she didn't want the "anyone" to hear.

Eteaki peered into the gloom down the carriage's gullet, but her lightstem's weakened glow offered too little illumination. "Hello? Is someone there?"

Her words fell dully into the air. She caressed the lightstem to excite its metabolism. It purred weakly, but the glow increased enough for her to use. She stretched her arm through the open valve and waved the lightstem slowly back and forth. It illuminated the gullet, but the gut beyond remained in darkness.

"Can you see anything?" Orbanek asked.

"No. I guess we'll have to crawl through." She stepped past the valve, then crawled on hands and knees through the gullet. The bluish light wavered back and forth with the movement of her hand. When she reached the end of the gullet, she held the lightstem up and gazed into the gut. "Great Divinity!" she whispered. Pezeli must not have heard her, for she said nothing.

"What is it?" Orbanek said. He was right behind her.

"Look at this chamber." She swung her legs forward and dropped slowly to the surface as the weak gravity pulled on her. There was a gentle tap when her feet hit the floor—because it *was* a floor, hard and planar. No curving, fleshy membrane.

Orbanek crawled forward and gasped. "What did those sphincter suckers do to this poor creature?"

Eteaki scanned the chamber. It was a box-shaped artificial enclosure—a room—that had been embedded in the carriage's gut. And it was big: the lightstem illumination didn't reach to the far wall, even when Eteaki caressed it to revitalize its glow. This room was built to maximum capacity—which meant its sharp ninety-degree corners must cut into the creature's membranes as they stretched around the structure.

"How did they get it in here?" Orbanek said from the opening above.

"What's going on?" Pezeli's faint voice wafted in from behind him.

"They must have surgically installed it." Eteaki noticed square openings partway up the side walls, exactly like the one she had just dropped from, which had to be entrances to the living bladders that extended from the gut. Were each of those also equipped with an artificial room for the comfort of the Divinity-forsaken Murdzak?

Pezeli protested again, and Orbanek slipped down to the floor so she could crawl forward. "How does the carriage eat when they dock with this thing in here?" he asked.

"They must remove it each time," Eteaki said.

Pezeli's eyes widened as she saw what they were talking about.

"Surgery every time they dock?" Orbanek said, and shook his head.

"Great Divinity," Pezeli murmured, shocking Eteaki. She'd never heard Pezeli use such language before. Pezeli dropped through the opening that led to the gullet and peered around with her mouth gaping. Almost in a whisper she said, "I've heard rumors that the Murdzak take each carriage on one journey, then kill it. This must be why."

Pezeli—always up on the latest galactic folklore. "That would be such a waste," Eteaki said. "Why would they do that?"

"They must feed them before the journey," Orbanek said, "then install this Divinity-cursed thing. Rather than carefully removing it after docking so the carriage can eat, they just kill the poor creature and tear this out to use in the next one."

Eteaki shuddered. "Do you think they'd really do that?"

"I could believe it," Orbanek said grimly.

What a waste! And what a calloused disdain for life. No wonder the Murdzak had not been admitted into the Alliance. Eteaki had always wondered how many of the ugly rumors about them were true. Now she began to think they might all be.

"The poor animal probably ends up with too much internal damage from the box anyway," Pezeli said. "Killing it could be merciful by then."

As if that excused the Murdzak. They chose to install the box in the first place.

The room as far as their illumination reached was featureless except for some markings on the floor. The surfaces were probably white, because they had the same bluish tint as the lightstem glow. The floor markings were enclosed by a square outline that covered about half of the visible portion of the room. Orbanek peered at the markings, his eyes tracing the lines and curves. "You know what I think this is?" he finally said. "Some kind of game court."

Pezeli gazed at the markings with a new intensity. "It's a smashsphere court, I think. The markings are similar. A little larger than usual."

"I think you're right, Thirdwife," Orbanek said. "Probably some Murdzak variation."

"Is this how they stand living together with non-relations?" Eteaki asked. "A playroom for diversion instead of sloshing around on soft flesh?"

"I wonder where the sphere is," said Orbanek. "I'd like to see what theirs looks like."

Eteaki studied the living bladder openings. "I suppose we should search every bladder, just to make sure."

"Yes," Orbanek said without enthusiasm. "After all, we're Tetzl, not Murdzak."

Eteaki advanced first with Orbanek and Pezeli following close behind. The vague sphere of illumination advanced with them, showing more of the same stark room. The floor beyond the smashball court was featureless again. After several steps, a shape emerged directly ahead of them, something broad and about waist-high. Eteaki studied it as she took slow steps toward it. Straight edges and sharp corners—artificial, like the room. A table, and with some shadowy figure stretched out upon it. A few more steps and the first glimmering reflections from the far wall appeared, along with more edges and corners—cabinets against the wall.

As the figure took on definition, Pezeli gasped. "They did!"

Eteaki understood her at once. The Murdzak had taken a captive. The figure was humanoid shape, the same general design of nearly all intelligent life in the galaxy. Taller and more stocky than the Murdzak, but not quite as tall as the Tetzl. Eteaki rushed forward, followed immediately by the others, and quickly felt around on the chest. In the upper center she discovered a steady thumping that had to be a heartbeat. "It's alive."

"He," said Pezeli. "It's a he."

Orbanek chuckled.

Eteaki gazed at the figure. Light-colored hair covered the scalp, cropped fairly short. No beard. Two closed eyes, two ears, a nose, and a mouth arranged on the head in the usual way. Strapped to the table at the chest, thighs, ankles, and wrists. Naked, with skin almost as pale as the Murdzak, and as Pezeli had noticed, male.

And five fingers on each hand.

Eteaki gazed at her own four-fingered hand, dark with brown pigmentation, and wondered what it would be like to calculate in a ten-digit number system. How clumsy that must be compared to octal!

"Another species in the image of the Great Divinity," Pezeli said with reverence.

Yes, Pezeli, Eteaki thought. Another humanoid species. Just like the thousands everywhere else.

"Seems most like the Kiryluk," Orbanek murmured.

"No..." Pezeli brushed the chin of the figure. "He's got the stubble of a beard growing."

Eteaki could see them now—faint, light-colored bristles.

"Not like the Kiryluk, then," Orbanek said, "if they grow facial hair." He turned to Eteaki. "Did you get any more details on the culture of that no-contact planet?"

"Sorry, not much is known about it." Pezeli ran her hand around the face. "The beard covers from below the nose down to the throat, and along the sides of the face, merging with the scalp hair."

The stranger's eyelids fluttered, and his head rolled sideways.

"Looks like he's regaining consciousness," Orbanek said.

A soft moan escaped his lips.

"Let's get him loose," Orbanek said, working on the nearest wrist strap with his free hand.

"What if he's dangerous?" Pezeli asked, starting on the chest.

Eteaki freed both ankles as Orbanek released the thighs. "Not likely," he said. "He's probably coming out of some drug-induced coma, knowing the Murdzak."

A faint, obnoxious odor reached Eteaki's nostrils. The smell of this species. Every species had a distinctive smell, and most of them were unpleasant. At least this fellow didn't reek as strongly as the Murdzak.

The last strap was flung aside as the stranger moaned again, louder this time, and lifted his arm to his forehead. His eyes opened, blinking against the glow of the lightstems. He saw the three of them and jerked with a loud cry.

"Calm down, friend," Orbanek said soothingly, holding out his hand palm up and waggling it. "We won't hurt you. The ones who did this to you are dead."

The stranger's eyes glistened as they darted back and forth, looking at each of them. His pupils were round, and the irises probably green. Eteaki wondered what he thought of their sulphur-yellow irises with slitted pupils. Members of the Tetzl species shouldn't look as dreadful to him as the Murdzak. But strange eyes were disturbing, no matter how normal the rest of the body looked. And this poor creature had probably never seen strange eyes in his life until the Murdzak captured him.

The fellow slid off the far side of the table, putting it between him and them, never taking his eyes off them. He stood staring with some intense emotion tightening his face, then looked down at himself. His face flushed with color, and those five-fingered hands shot down to his genitals, covering them.

The stranger looked around desperately. Was he trying to find clothing? This was an extreme attitude toward nudity! In the midst of what must be a shocking, probably terrifying experience for him, his biggest concern was being seen naked? The Tetzl didn't walk around nude like the Murdzak, but they weren't disturbed if someone happened to see them naked either.

"I think he wants something to wear," Eteaki said.

"Perhaps," Orbanek said. "Maybe those cabinets?"

Eteaki moved slowly around the table to the cabinets. The stranger fastened his gaze on her, matching her moves to keep a distance from her. His face was sleek with perspiration.

"Everything's fine," Orbanek said, waggling his hand palm-up.

The stranger stared at it, maybe counting fingers. His lower lip began to tremble.

"I don't think I'm calming him down," Orbanek said. "Find something quick."

Eteaki held her lightstem out as she opened cabinet doors and scrounged with one hand. Most of them contained instruments that probably had medical functions. Medical experiments on captive aliens from a no-contact planet. The Murdzak were definitely sphincter scum.

"Here's something," she cried as she pulled out a wad of shimmering material. The wad fell apart into three articles of clothing, two on the floor, and one in Eteaki's hand. She held it up. It was a flowing Murdzak robe, the only kind of clothing anyone had ever seen them wear. No one had figured out what motivated the Murdzak to wear clothes those rare times that they did. Some thought they might have a ceremonial significance.

"Here," Eteaki said, extending her arm to present the robe to the stranger. "For you."

He shrank back, eyes wide and jaw open.

Pezeli sucked in a breath. "I don't think he wants Murdzak clothes."

"Look some more," Orbanek said to Eteaki. "His own clothes must be here somewhere."

Eteaki dropped the robe and searched more cabinets. "Look at this!" she said with a titter as she pulled an object out. "The smashsphere."

"Great!" Orbanek cried. "Let me see it."

The Tetzl version of a smashsphere was a spherical creature with a thick, elastic hide and no skeleton or loose organs. All its bodily cavities were stuffed with impact-absorbing fat. The sensory nerves just under its surface connected directly to the pleasure center of its small brain. Genetic engineers said that a smashsphere creature experienced something like an orgasm every time it bounced into a floor or wall or against a player to score. Both players and smashsphere received their own kind of pleasure from playing.

But the Murdzak smashsphere was artificial, with a surface almost as hard as a tree trunk, and with stubby spikes emanating all around it. Not sharp enough to puncture skin, but hard enough to cause pain and a nasty bruise. Was there anything the Murdzak would not corrupt?

She lobbed the smashsphere to Orbanek, who caught it one-handed and tossed it up and down, examining it. Eteaki continued to rummage. She heard the smashsphere bouncing away leisurely in the low gravity when Orbanek dropped it.

Finally she discovered more clothing in one cabinet, black and white material, again wadded up. She brushed the wad out on the table and separated out multiple pieces, then held up one black article of clothing with two tubular extensions joined at one end. Suddenly the stranger yanked it from her hand and held it in front of his crotch, glaring. She rummaged again and found another black article, three white ones, and a long strip of material, probably bright red or violet. She pushed the pile toward the stranger. His glare softened, and he took a gossamer white item shaped similarly to the black one he'd grabbed, but with shorter tubes, turned away so his genitals were hidden, and slid his legs into the tubes.

"Perhaps this would be a good time to search the living bladders, while our friend here gets dressed." Orbanek pulled out a spare lightstem, rubbed it, and handed it to the stranger. He accepted it reluctantly, staring at the creature as it purred. Orbanek turned and headed for the nearest bladder. Pezeli and Eteaki started searching others.

Each bladder opening had depressions in the wall leading up to it that could be used for climbing. Eteaki found more boxy rooms ensconced in each bladder with a comfortable bed and desk and various personal effects. What a strange race! Comfort in their regular lifestyle, while turning smashsphere into a game that inflicted pain and injury.

She didn't dwell on that thought long. If the Murdzak wanted to inflict pain on themselves, that was their affair. But the pain they inflicted on others—this captured alien and the internal membranes of their heaven carriages—disturbed her. She wished, for the sake of all Murdzak heaven carriages, that someone could figure out how the creatures hyperphased, so they could design the ability into a machine. Then the Murdzak could make their heaven carriages entirely artificial.

When the three of them had searched all the bladders, including a pantry full of nasty-smelling Murdzak food, they returned to the stranger, who was fully dressed now and searching through the cabinets himself. He found something, grabbed it, and stood. His face looked relaxed. He must be getting used to the Orbanek family.

His clothing was strange, but no more so than thousands of other species. Black outer coverings and a white inner one over the torso. The gossamer white ones must have been underclothing because they were out of sight. From his neck hung the red or violet strip doubled up with a knot at his throat. He must have found foot coverings on his own, because his feet were black with shiny surfaces. Attached to one side of his chest was a black, square object with curious writing on it.

In his overly-fingered hands was a large, deep blue pouch with two looping straps attached on one side. He handed the lightstem back to Orbanek, then slid an arm into one of the loops and let the pouch hang from his shoulder as he hooked a thumb through the strap.

Orbanek placed his hand on his chest. "My name is Orbanek. Orb-an-ek."

The stranger studied him, then bobbed his head slowly up and down. "Or-ba-nek," he said with a slurred accent.

Orbanek gestured for his wives to come close on either side. "This is Eteaki, my Primewife. Et-e-ak-i."

The stranger repeated it as best he could.

"And this is my Thirdwife, Pezeli. Pez-el-i."

He repeated it.

"My Secondwife is back on Tetz with the children," Orbanek said, then grinned sheepishly. "As if you could understand me. So what's your name?" He pointed to the stranger. "Your name?"

"Al-da-kirsh-tan-sin," he said carefully, holding his free hand against his chest.

"What a mouthful!" Orbanek said with a grin. The stranger smiled back. Most intelligent species had smiles and laughter ingrained in their genetics. "Please say your name again."

The stranger swung his head back and forth and said something in a rushed language.

"Orb-an-ek," Orbanek repeated, hand on his chest, then pointed. "Your name?"

"Al-da-kirsh-tan-sin," he said with exaggerated slowness.

"Ald-ak-irsht-ans-in?" Orbanek tried.

The stranger laughed. It sounded coarse compared to the tittering laugh of the Tetzl.

"How about if I call you Alda?" Orbanek said. "Ald-a?"

He smiled and bobbed his head up and down. Head gestures for no and yes?

Orbanek pointed at the pouch. "What do you have in there?"

Alda looked at it, opened a flap, and pulled out a dark—almost black—rectangular object. He held it up and used his extra finger to point at the writing on its surface as he spoke. "Bo-kev-mo-men."

Orbanek stared at it and said, "Whatever."

Alda's eyebrows tightened together, and he put the object back in his pouch. He took a deep breath, then placed his hand to his mouth and uttered something. He moved his jaw up and down.

"He must be hungry," Pezeli said.

"Sorry, Alda, our food might be toxic to you," Eteaki said. "We need to get you back to your planet."

"Yes," said Orbanek. "And we need to get back to Glaittli. The air in here is getting stale. The generator lobes in this carriage have to be dead by now."

Eteaki held her hand out, palm up, and said, "Let's go, Alda." After eyeing it suspiciously, he placed his hand in hers and gripped. It surprised her, but she smiled back. His grip was pleasantly strong.

The others had already started for the gullet. Before releasing the grip, she pulled on his hand to indicate for him to follow.

More depressions in the artificial wall allowed them to climb to the gullet opening. Pezeli went first, followed by Orbanek. As the room darkened with the disappearance of two lightstems, Eteaki gestured for Alda to go first. He climbed until he reached the opening, placed a hand through it, then recoiled with a grunt. He looked down at Eteaki, pointing into the gullet, and jabbered something. What was the problem?

"Everything is fine," she soothed, holding her palm up. "Go ahead." She waved him on.

With a solemn face, he crept into the gullet. Eteaki climbed up and followed him in. Alda's breathing became heavy. When he emerged into the mouth chamber, he let out a sigh. Eteaki was glad herself to be out of the gullet. The confined space concentrated the pervasive stench of death mingled with Alda's odor.

Alda looked around with squinting eyes. The muscles in his jaw and mouth looked tense.

"I don't think he's ever seen organic technology," Pezeli said. "Didn't you say theirs was all artificial?"

Eteaki waggled her head yes. That could account for Alda's actions. Other species unaccustomed to organic technology often disliked being surrounded by flesh.

Alda stared at the walls, the floor, the roof of the mouth chamber, at the flesh mounds protruding from the floor. And at the dead Murdzak. What emotion registered on his face? Fear? Disgust? Loathing? Satisfaction at the death of his captors? It was precarious to try to read the expressions of an unfamiliar species—even a humanoid one. There was no telling what they might mean. Most of his body language seemed to fit reasonable patterns, but one could never be sure. His nose twitched a little—that one was easy to guess at. The stench of decaying Murdzak bodies and dead carriage flesh probably bothered him as much as her. And her own odor? She wondered how she smelled to him.

Alda carefully avoided the dangling tendrils as he picked his way through the mouth chamber. The heaven carriage's teeth definitely upset him, and he seemed to dislike treading on the tongue. The poor fellow had to navigate two mouths.

He wouldn't touch the fangs. It was slow going to get past them.

At last they arrived in the mouth chamber of Glaittli. The three of them stowed their lightstems away. In Glaittli's white light, the strip tied to Alda's neck definitely looked red.

Pezeli sat on her flesh mound and began hooking up tendrils. Cup over her eye, bulb in her ear, adhesive pad on her throat—each tendril designed with the appropriate connector on its tip. Alda watched her as he moistened his lips with his tongue. Orbanek sat down, gestured to the empty mound next to him, and told Alda to sit. Eteaki also sat, but waited before connecting her tendrils. She was having too much fun watching Alda react to everything.

It took a few more gestures from Orbanek before Alda seemed to understand what he meant. Alda swung his head fiercely back and forth with lips pursed hard together, then pointed toward the gullet with enthusiasm.

"He wants to go back into the gut," Eteaki said. "He probably thinks we have an artificial room back there, too."

Orbanek jiggled his head no. "No room, Alda, just flesh. You won't like it there any more than here, and you'll be all alone."

Eteaki said, "Let me try." She stood and walked up to him, swung her head back and forth in the gesture she thought meant no to him, and pointed toward Glaittli's gullet. She patted the wall of flesh he stood next to and pointed again. "Flesh, just like here. No room."

He looked at her without a response, so she did it again and again. Finally he touched the flesh briefly and pointed down the gullet. Eteaki bobbed an Alda-style yes. He seemed reluctantly satisfied and moved to the empty flesh mound, touching it and rubbing his fingers together.

"It's dry," Orbanek said testily. "You don't think we'd allow scum in our carriage, do you?"

Alda sat with a dismal look on his face.

"Thirdwife," Orbanek said, "trade places with me."

Pezeli had all her tendrils connected. "What?"

Eteaki felt like saying the same thing. A Wife on the Husband's mound? It wasn't illegal or anything, but it went against a long history of custom.

"You're the empathetic one among us. Sit next to Alda and try to make him feel more comfortable."

Eteaki had to agree. Pezeli was the tender, sensitive one in the family. Of course, that also made her the most timid.

Pezeli stripped the ocular tendril from her eye, but stopped there and peered at Alda.

"Do it, Thirdwife," Eteaki said in her command tone.

Pezeli removed the rest of the tendrils and switched with Orbanek. Eteaki smiled to herself. Prim and proper Pezeli was probably on edge dealing with this whole alien experience. But she was the one interested in other cultures, other species. If she warmed up to Alda, she might actually start enjoying this.

Eteaki attached tendrils to both of her eyes and to one ear. She needed full stereo vision to navigate the carriage, but only required one ear for the stream of information that Glaittli sang to her. The other ear needed to be free to communicate with her crew.

"Primewife, head for that no-contact planet. Scum! What's its name, anyway?"

Eteaki sang the request to Glaittli. Husbands didn't learn carriagesong, so Orbanek couldn't ask for the information himself. Glaittli sang a response after it had accessed its information organs. "Just a catalog number," Eteaki announced. "We don't know its name."

"Well, what's the catalog number?"

"Raviza Kirkil 752116."

"Planet Raviza," Orbanek announced, "here we come. Primewife, begin phase sequence."

Eteaki ordered Glaittli to close the mouth sphincter and release itself from the dead carriage, then ordered its generator lobes to step up production to replace the air they had lost to the Murdzak carriage. The increased production would clear out the lingering stench faster as well.

"We could discover what that planet's name is," Pezeli said. "We'd get a bonus."

"I don't know," Orbanek said. "It's no contact. We might be fined instead."

Eteaki gave Glaittli the command to hyperphase.

"We can ask Alda," said Pezeli. "Our contact with him has been legal."

"Go ahead," Orbanek said.

Hyperphase began. Alda cried out as his body, along with every other particle within Glaittli, stretched through hyperdimensional space to exist at two real points at the same time. His cry died down when the stretch quantumly discontinued.

A glorious view of his planet filled Eteaki's eyes.

The Orbanek family had long ago gotten used to the sensation of hyperphasing, but Alda probably hadn't ever experienced it. Most likely he was unconscious when his Murdzak captors had phased. It wasn't painful, just disconcerting, like the relaxing of muscles as one dozed off that caused the sensation of falling.

Perhaps they should have warned him. But how do you say "We're going to hyperphase now" in sign language?

Alda chattered heatedly. Pezeli said, "Everything's fine, everything's fine. It was just a hyperphase. Now we're near your home."

The planet loomed in the view that Eteaki had through her tendril cups. She always loved approaching planets teeming with life—they were so beautiful. This one was no exception. "We should let him see his planet," Eteaki said. "Then maybe he'll feel better."

"Okay," Pezeli murmured.

It was fun to see the shapes of strange continents whenever Eteaki had the opportunity to visit a new planet. Each world was unique, of course. Alda's planet had a huge expanse of oceans, larger than most. There were two continents before her, one above and one below, connected in the middle by a narrow strip of land. The right edge of both continents had crossed the meridian into night.

Alda cried out again.

"What now?" Orbanek said.

"He doesn't like the tendril," Pezeli answered. "He won't let it near his eye."

"Then don't bother."

"No," Eteaki said, "you should get him to look. I think he'll be glad he did."

"Alda, it doesn't hurt. Look." Pezeli must have demonstrated on her own eye. "Doesn't hurt. There's excretions in the cup that soothe your eye." Moments of silence passed, then Pezeli said, "That's right."

Alda exclaimed a single syllable with an impossible sound at the end—impossible for Tetzl mouths, anyway. No such sound existed in any Tetzl language that Eteaki was aware of.

"That must be his planet's name!" Pezeli cried joyfully.

"What was it again?" Orbanek asked.

"Irf," Pezeli repeated, getting as close to the impossible sound as she could.

"Planet Irf," Orbanek tried. "Hmm, I like Raviza better."

"Irf," Alda said, but with the proper pronunciation, then spoke a torrent of strange words. Eteaki wished she could see him. She wondered if he had one or two tendrils on. Two, she hoped, so he could see his own planet as a globe floating in space instead of a circle against a flat backdrop. It wasn't likely he'd ever see his planet from this vantage point again with his species' level of technology. He ought to make the best of it.

She became so obsessed with the idea that she removed a tendril and looked back. He was pointing straight ahead as he talked with one tendril on and one eye shut.

"Attach a second tendril, Thirdwife," Eteaki said. "Let him see this in three dimensions."

Pezeli held Alda's blue pouch in one arm and an object in her free hand. It was rectangular and flat. She peered at it with her eyes wide and intense. "The Anointed!" she gasped.

"Pezeli, you're picking up our bad habits," Orbanek said. "That's twice you've sworn now."

"No, I mean the Anointed!" She held the object up so they could both see it. Eteaki squinted with her one available eye. On it was an image of a humanoid, much like Alda, but with a full beard and long hair, standing in the air with his arms outstretched and his head bowed.

No, he wasn't in the air. He was attached to a pair of milled logs formed into a cross. He was nearly naked, but for some material wrapped around his loins, and blood oozed from several points—from a headpiece with sharp protrusions, from his palms and wrists, from his feet, and from one side of his torso.

The same wounds as the Anointed!

This supposedly uncontacted planet had the belief of the Anointed Savior. And not only that, but they had an explanation for the wounds included in descriptions of him.

"What makes you think that's the Anointed?" Orbanek asked.

"Look at the wounds!" Pezeli cried.

"Let me see that, Thirdwife." He took the object and peered at it.

Believers claimed that knowledge of the Anointed had been revealed independently to each planet, but the Alliance had intermixed the cultures of the galaxy for so long that no one could prove such a thing, any more than they could prove which planet the Anointed might have lived on. In Eteaki's lifetime and for generations before that, no new planets had joined the Alliance. All the eligible ones had done so already, and none of the no-contact planets had become eligible. No one could remember what it was like to be an isolated planet. Even renegade species like the Murdzak had enough contact with the Alliance that its influence had permeated their culture long ago.

So where had this planet gained its knowledge of the Anointed? Had the Murdzak contaminated their culture? Eteaki wouldn't have expected that. They were too opportunistic. They wouldn't take the time to introduce a religious system into a primitive culture.

Could it be possible that this planet really was the birthplace of the Anointed, as some people claimed?

Alda studied Orbanek with his open eye. "Jy-eh-ziz-kir-ast," he said distinctly, pointing at the image.

Orbanek looked at him. "What?"

"Kir-ast-seh-av-yur." Alda closed his eye and pointed straight ahead. "Irf."

A thrill shot through Eteaki. "Great Divinity, does he mean what I think he means?"

Orbanek frowned at the picture. "No, it couldn't be."

"Why not?" Pezeli said defensively. "Some planet has to be. Why not this one?"

Eteaki got an idea. She sang to Glaittli, then removed all her tendrils and approached Alda. Gently she removed his tendril and led him to the side wall. Glaittli had prepared its flesh to change pigmentation at a touch.

She pointed to the wall and said, "Draw a map of Irf. Draw Irf." Off to the side she touched her finger to the flesh and drew a circle. The wall's pigmentation darkened where she touched. As best as she could remember, she drew within that circle the two continents she had seen through the tendrils. "Draw Irf," she said one more time. She spread her fingers and held her palms up near the blank part of the wall, thumbs and forefingers touching, then swept her hands apart to indicate a wide expanse of surface. "Irf." She made the gesture again.

He got it. He drew the two familiar continents out flat, then added several more land masses to the right that must have been on the other side of the planet. These he drew more hesitantly, and carelessly rushed through the last few strokes of the rightmost shoreline with an odd expression on his face. He pointed to each continent and named it, but it was too much for Eteaki to follow.

"Alda," she said, touching his chest with her palm, then pointing to the map he'd just drawn. "Where do you live?" He swung his head back and forth. "Where Alda?" she said, pointing to the map.

He touched the upper of the first two continents, near the right shore above a peninsula that protruded down into the ocean. A spot of color formed. "Johjah," he said.

Eteaki pointed at the image still in Orbanek's hand. "The Anointed. Uh, Jyez...uh..."

"Jyez-iz-kirast," he said, bobbing his head.

"Jyez-iz-kirast," she repeated, then pointed to the map. "Irf?"

He bobbed yes and touched the map on a spot that connected one continent with a huge land mass that was this planet's largest continent, right at the end of a sea that extended deep into the land.

Eteaki stared at the spot of color his finger had formed. The homeland of the Anointed. This planet, that location. That tiny point in the universe. She jiggled her head in denial. No, it couldn't be possible.

"Iz-reh-il," Alda said, pointing at the spot. His eyes were alight with some kind of emotion.

Pezeli wept silently. Orbanek gazed at the map, then at the image in his hand. "Izrehil on planet Irf," he said with half a smile. "Add one more claim to the pile."

Pezeli scowled at him. "It's a no-contact planet! Where did the belief come from?"

"Maybe the Murdzak introduced it," Eteaki said, ignoring her own doubts about the theory.

Pezeli's expression darkened even more as she turned her gaze on Eteaki. She wasn't buying the theory either.

"Return to your mound, Thirdwife," Orbanek commanded. "It's time to bring Alda home." He stood, his mouth twitching a little. Eteaki felt sure he was holding back the cynical retort he wanted to express. But with he a confirmed agnostic, Pezeli a lifelong believer, and Eteaki ambivalently somewhere in between, family harmony had been maintained by strict respect for one another's opinions.

"Alda, we're taking you home," Eteaki said, "to Johjah."

He bobbed his head enthusiastically. "Johjah."

She gestured to his mound, and he sat. She took her own place and attached the tendrils as Pezeli dabbed at her eyes. Orbanek returned to the Husband's mound and handed the image back to Alda just as Eteaki covered her second eye.

Through Glaittli's eyes, Eteaki could see the glow from its belly intensify as it generated massive amounts of gravitons to interact with the gravity of planet Irf, controlling their trajectory through its atmosphere. Johjah languished in night, punctuated with glittering illumination from the cities of Irf. Glaittli indicated that it had compensated for some surveillance energy coming from the planet—a legal requirement when visiting a no-contact planet.

Eteaki searched for an isolated region to land. Alda would have to find his own way back to the exact location where he wanted to go—it would require more communicative ability than they shared to determine where that might be. As they settled gently to the surface and Glaittli opened its mouth wide, Alda pulled the dark rectangular object out of his pouch that he'd shown them light years away in the artificial room of the Murdzak carriage. With a smile, he set it on the mound he had vacated, patted it, and said, "Bokev momen." Then he laid the image that was supposed to be the Anointed on top.

Eteaki's last sight of him before Glaittli closed its mouth was as he stood on the ground of planet Irf smiling. He raised his hand, palm forward, and said, "Gud-boh-e."

When the Orbanek family completed their patrol and returned to their home planet Tetz, Secondwife and the children greeted them warmly. The next day Eteaki submitted her report to Cultural Studies, including her best reproduction of the map Alda had drawn with the location called Izrahel marked. She also delivered the items Alda had left—the object called "bokev momen" and the image. Her family should earn a hefty bonus for delivering such artifacts from an unknown culture.

As she waited to be called in for her report, she thumbed through the "bokev momen." It was a lengthy writing in Alda's language with a few images of individuals from his species doing inscrutable things. Perhaps it was her imagination, or the way Alda had treated the object, but Eteaki could feel a sense of significance about the writing. She hoped they'd be able to translate it—a tricky thing for an unknown language from an unknown culture.

Eteaki gazed at the image. Could it really be the Anointed One? Had there ever been an Anointed One? She was embarrassed to realize she felt an urge to accompany Pezeli to the next veneration gathering. Perhaps Orbanek wouldn't tease her too unmercifully, since she was Primewife.

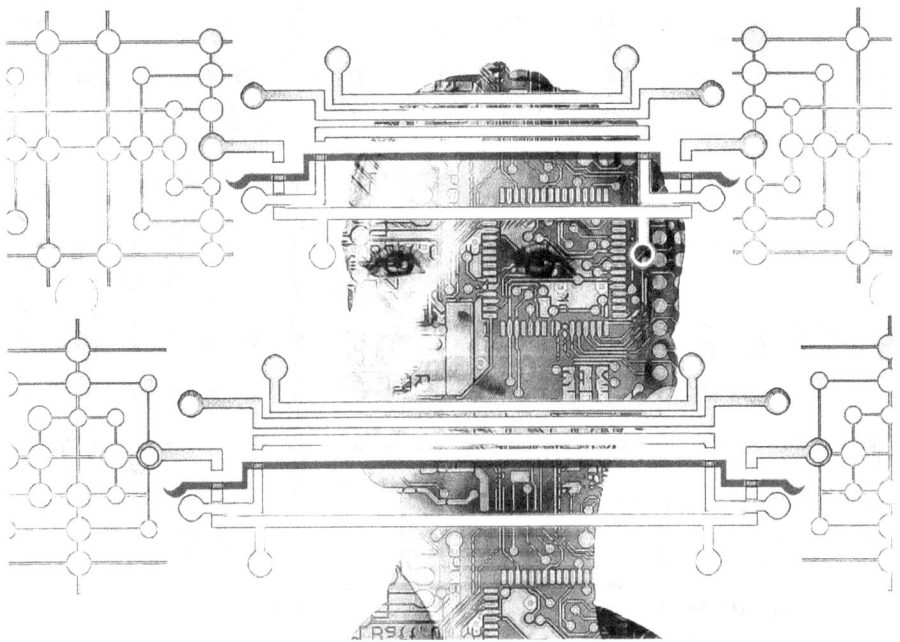

Mary Mother of Nanites

Father Muriel approached the confessional with trepidation. Although he'd been a priest for nearly a year now, he still trembled at the awesome responsibility that was his as the representative of Christ. He wondered if he'd ever get used to the idea.

As he walked from the rectory to the cathedral, the vibration of molecular-sized nanites lining his eardrums caused the strains of Bach's *Magnificat in D Major* to trickle into his ears. Listening to the choir voices weave its haunting themes helped him prepare mentally and spiritually for confession.

As he crossed the electronic boundary that surrounded the cathedral, his nanite connection to the Web broke, and the music abruptly halted. He could have instructed his internal nanites to buffer the data and continue playing, but Bishop Peregrine insisted on a moment of silence as part of the spiritual preparation. Turning off beautiful music was difficult for Father Muriel to do, so he allowed the automatic disconnection from the Web to do it for him.

His sense of loss when the music stopped was mitigated by the relief he felt when breaking contact with the Web. Father Muriel had nothing to hide, but still enjoyed the feeling of escape from being constantly monitored by the worldwide network of nanites.

He sat within his booth and switched on the light that announced his availability. He didn't have to wait long before the first of a parade of penitents entered on the other side of the screen. They all came one by one, confessing their sins and receiving absolution. Father Muriel cringed at some of their sins, but maintained his professional demeanor thanks to his rigorous training. It wasn't easy sometimes.

As the closing time for confessions neared without another penitent entering for several minutes, Father Muriel decided that he was finished. But just as he was about to turn the light off, someone entered the confessional. The individual knelt, clothes faintly rustling, and remained silent for a moment.

"Bless me, Father, for I have sinned," a voice finally said. It was a strong, male baritone, unfamiliar to him.

"The Web has not followed you here, my son," Father Muriel recited. "You may speak freely and in confidence."

The shadowy face through the screen stared at the floor for several heartbeats. "Father, it's been three years since I spoke to my daughter." The voice was apologetic.

"And why is that, my son?"

"I sent her to jail."

Father Muriel raised his eyebrows. "How do you mean?"

"I testified in her trial. She wouldn't speak to me after that."

He nodded absently. "She never forgave you? She never learned the error of her ways?"

"She never made an error."

This made him perk up. "I don't understand."

"She was innocent of the charge."

The ways of man, Father Muriel sighed wearily to himself. "I assume when you found out, you facilitated her release?"

"I knew all along she was innocent."

Father Muriel knotted his brow as he felt a sickness invade his heart. He took in a deep breath to calm himself and said with deliberation, "You testified against your daughter in court, getting her convicted and sent to jail, knowing all along she was innocent?"

There was a heavy pause.

"That's right," the voice said weakly.

Father Muriel bit on his lip to contain the disgust he felt as a human being, and continued with his responsibilities as a priest. "How do you feel about that now?"

"Don't you want to know why?"

"Why did you do it?"

"Because if I hadn't, *I* would have gone to jail."

Father Muriel felt a rage well up inside him, which he tried desperately to squelch. His journey to the priesthood had been an arduous struggle against worldly passions. Ideally that should make him all the more understanding toward the depravity of others. But a hot temper had been part of his struggle, and was a flaw that still, a year after ordination, often drove him to sit on the other side of confession.

He thanked God for his seminary training, which was the only thing that preserved his professional demeanor now. "Okay, my son. Let's discuss what all this means to you."

"Please, Father," the voice said desperately. "I've been trying to bring myself to confession all these years. Please let me get it all out."

Father Muriel sighed quietly. This was when a flood of self-justification usually followed, but the more he understood the man's thinking, the more appropriate a penance he could assign. "Please go on."

The voice sucked in a deep breath. "Back then I sent all sorts of slimeballs to jail. I was a police officer. If I had gone to prison myself, I wouldn't have lasted one week."

"That's an understandable motive, my son," Father Muriel said with forced empathy.

"I tried to hide the evidence against me, and when it became obvious I couldn't, I tried to find someone more deserving to frame. But the only person I could get to fit all the known facts was Mary."

Father Muriel cringed. "Your daughter?"

"Yes."

Madonna, he called out in his mind, eyes raised to the ceiling. *She even has your name.* How could he do this to his own daughter? But to the man he said, "Go on."

"I never thought she'd go to jail. The evidence was entirely circumstantial. I got her the best lawyer possible. He should have been able to create reasonable doubt. Plus she's very beautiful. You know how juries can be."

So considerate of you to plan it all out for her, Father Muriel thought bitterly. Immediately he felt remorse. He'd be obliged to admit these sarcastic feelings to Bishop Peregrine during his own confession. It wouldn't be the first time. God purge me of my uncontrolled passions, he prayed silently.

The baritone voice droned on. "None of her friends would believe she did it. Her reputation wouldn't suffer...much."

The priest bit his lip again to stifle a sarcastic remark and replaced it with, "Are you going to tell me what this crime is that you committed and your daughter paid for?"

"I...killed a woman."

His blood ran chill at the words. What kind of a person is this creature in my confessional? This is a baptized disciple of Christ? Softly he asked, "Why?"

"She molested her children. She molested little boys in the neighborhood."

It was almost like a bubble bursting. Suddenly this sinner's actions became clearer. Suddenly he became less of a villain. But still...

"Wouldn't it have been better to put her in jail instead?"

"I tried. But she was considered a model citizen. No one believed she'd do that. She was acquitted."

Father Muriel decided he'd given the man enough leeway. It was time to steer this confession toward a resolution. "Okay, I'm beginning to understand. How do you feel about these things now?"

The man blurted, "I caught the woman molesting my grandson."

"Dear Lord!"

"I acted in a blind rage."

Father Muriel nodded to himself. He was beginning to relate to this man. What would he have done in a similar situation with his infamous temper? "I can imagine," he murmured.

"That's why the evidence would only fit Mary, because it was her son. But, God help me, she was convicted of murder."

A sickening despair for the state of mankind sank deep into Father Muriel's heart. One mortal sin after another leading to the most horrifying of consequences. "Alright, my son. I understand why you killed that woman, even though I can't begin to condone it. And I understand your fear of prison—a fear for your very life. Please, my son, tell me, how do you feel about it now?"

"Father, if I thought she'd actually go to jail, I wouldn't have let any of this happen."

Father Muriel sighed in exasperation. This fellow wasn't going to quit until he cleared every drop of mire from his soul. Well, why not? It would probably help him with his repentance. "Once you did know she was going to jail, what did you do?"

"I tried to come forth with the truth, but no one believed me. They thought I was trying to protect her."

Something didn't add up.

"Why would they think that, if you testified against her in the first place?"

"I didn't testify willingly. Or I should say, I didn't *act* like I testified willingly. They declared me a hostile witness. I was as evasive and belligerent with the prosecutor as I could be."

Father Muriel shook his head. This story was beginning to deaden his feelings. He couldn't decide if this man was a scoundrel or a well-meaning soul with horribly bad judgment. He was grateful Christ Jesus had the role of ultimate judge, not he.

"What have you done to rectify the consequences of your sins? Is Mary still in jail?"

A good ten seconds passed before the man said, almost in a whisper, "No."

Father Muriel tilted his head. "What was the long pause for?"

"She's supposed to be in jail."

"She escaped?" How does someone escape in this day and age of the Web? Another pause, briefer. "I don't know."

"I don't understand."

"Up until yesterday she was in prison where she was supposed to be. I've tried to contact her all these years, but she always refuses to talk to me."

"Yes, I can certainly understand that."

"Yesterday, I tried to contact her again through the Web. I received no response."

"She refused again."

"I received *no* response, not even a refusal. The Web reported that she doesn't exist."

This time it was Father Muriel who paused as he processed the information. The Web losing track of somebody? "That's not possible."

"I know."

"Do you mean she died?"

"No, she just doesn't exist."

This was getting insane. "That's not possible," he reiterated.

"*I know!*"

Father Muriel tapped on the arm of his chair, thinking of the implications of what this man said. There had to be some mundane explanation. "Well, if it happened," he said finally, "then it must be possible...somehow."

"It's not."

"I'm no expert on how the Web works." He shifted in his chair as stiffness formed in his lower back. "But if it happened, it must be possible. All things built by humans fail eventually."

"I *am* an expert on how it works," he said with intensity. "I studied up on it while I was a cop. And I'm telling you, it *is* impossible. The Web's made up of quintillions of independent nanites. They all can't fail at once."

"I'm not *that* ignorant," said Father Muriel a little testily. "The whole Web wouldn't have to fail at once. Just a local section of it."

"Even a local section is made up of quadrillions of them. Every one of us has trillions of those gadgets swarming inside our bodies and on the surface of our skin. The Web cannot fail—there's too much redundancy in it."

The man was probably right. "Then what do you think happened, my son?"

"I think she was...enraptured."

"I don't understand your use of that word."

"You know, like the Rapture. She was taken up, and God intervened to erase all evidence of her existence in the Web."

By all the Saints, a religious fanatic! Assuming everything unusual is a miracle from God. Father Muriel deplored such individuals. They gave normal believers a bad name. Was the man even Catholic, using that evangelical term?

But he reminded himself to be tactful.

"My son, I'm certainly not going to deny the possibility of God intervening and performing a miracle, but lots of people have been unjustly imprisoned and God didn't intervene. Why your daughter particularly?"

"Because there's no other explanation. No normal phenomenon can account for it."

"Are you absolutely sure about that?"

"I've gone over it and over it. I've had my colleagues on the force with security access to the Web analyze every possibility we could think of. There's no way a person can just become invisible to the Web."

"They can't hide somewhere?"

"The entire surface of the planet is covered with nanites, all interconnected with one another. Every person from birth is infused with trillions of them, and they stay permanently in contact with the Web nanites. How can someone hide from that?"

"There are lots of places on Earth that are a refuge from the Web. You're sitting in one now, my son. Perhaps she's in the prison chapel. Claiming sanctuary or something."

"But there would be a record of her going there before she broke contact with the Web. There *is* no such record."

"What does the record show?"

"That she was there, in prison, then suddenly she was not there. Or anywhere."

Father Muriel's tapping became a drumming as he thought. The door to the cathedral creaked open. Steps echoed through the interior as someone walked down the aisle. It reminded him that he'd let this confession become sidetracked. But what this man said bothered him. He wanted to clear up the dilemma for his own peace of mind.

"People have beaten the Web a couple of times before," Father Muriel said. "That one fellow deactivated a whole section of it. Others introduced a virus that changed or erased records of their doings."

"But they always leave a hole behind—something that can be analyzed. With Mary, there's nothing."

"Then someone must have figured out a new way to confuse the Web, one that cannot be analyzed."

"Father, do you have any idea how much computing power is in the Web? No human being can out-think it."

No human being echoed in Father Muriel's mind.

"Perhaps someone tapped into the Web and got it to program its own virus? Couldn't the Web design such a thing itself?"

"Anyone trying that would still leave traces. No one could co-opt all the nanites fast enough to hide everything they did. They'd still set off alarms all over the world."

Apprehension seeped into his soul. He knew enough about the Web to sense what this fellow said was true. But that would mean what happened to his daughter *was* impossible. When the impossible happened, there was only one source to look to. "Was Mary particularly spiritual?"

"Yes! That's why I wondered about...that...thing..."

"Perhaps..." Father Muriel was hesitant to say it out loud. "Perhaps God's intervention *is* the only explanation."

"Father?" came a quiet soprano voice from beyond the confessional.

"Please wait, my daughter," Father Muriel said, feeling guilty for indulging the man *and* himself for so long with this confession. "I'll be with you shortly."

"No, I'm sorry," said the soprano. "I didn't mean you, Father. I meant *my* father."

"My God!" said the baritone. "Mary?"

The man flung the door open and jumped out.

His daughter was here? Father Muriel emerged, finding the two standing several meters apart and staring at each other. The man was tall, and his thin hair was jet black streaked heavily with grey. Late fifties or early sixties probably. He was dressed casually but neatly in a button-down shirt and tan slacks. The woman—Mary—looked two decades younger. Nearly as tall, with a summery flower-pattern dress and brunette hair. Her eyes were hard from prison, but much of her earlier beauty shone through. She must have been gorgeous! No wonder her father thought her looks would sway the jury.

"Mary! My God, what are you doing here?" the man said with incredulous eyes fixed on her.

The woman glanced at Father Muriel, then gazed at her own father. "I came to find you."

The man rushed toward her with arms open. "I'm so glad—"

She backed off. He stopped a couple of meters away, troubled emotions churning across his face. "How did you find me? How did you get out of jail?"

Again Mary glanced at Father Muriel before responding. "I prayed. For *three years* I begged God for help." Her voice became sharp. She looked at Father Muriel. "It's true that God is everywhere, right?"

"That's correct."

"I prayed to God...in the Web. And God in Web got me out."

"What?" said the man and Father Muriel in unison.

"God in the Web led me here. He told me you're supposed to take my place."

The man backed off a step, then another. "Take your place?"

Her eyes, her hardened eyes, locked with his. "You committed the crime. You belong there."

Slowly his head shook back and forth, his face white and shining with perspiration. "I—I'm sorry that things turned out the way they did." He reached out tentatively with a hand, and when she stood rock-solid still, he dropped it to his side. "You know, if I go to prison, I'll be killed."

"I'm sorry, Father. You have to go. It's justice. God's justice."

The man took a step forward. Terror swept across his face. Another step, mechanical, then another, toward the door. Father Muriel stared in horror. "What's happening?" he whispered.

"God's bringing him to prison," Mary said, holding back emotions with a tight face.

"No!" the man shrieked, even as he strutted with greater certainty down the aisle. He lashed out, trying to grasp the backs of the pews, but he couldn't land a grip strong enough to slow him down. "No!" he shrieked again. His protest degenerated into an inarticulate wail.

"Stop!" Father Muriel shouted, whether to the man, or to Mary, or to God, he wasn't sure. He rushed forward toward the man. Mary had to step back in alarm.

As Father Muriel ran, his muscles became stiff and taut, slowing his movement with a steady decline that seemed calculated to avoid injuring him. His rush fizzled into a walk, then a shuffle, until he stood still, unable to budge his legs. Mary's father was at the door, hand raised to push it open. His wails echoed through the cathedral as he stepped out. They were cut short as the door swung closed behind him.

Footsteps reverberated through the voluminous space as other priests emerged, attracted by the commotion. Father Muriel reached clumsily for the back of a pew and pulled himself forward. With his stiffened legs, he toppled over onto his face, banging an elbow painfully against the hard floor.

"No, this is wrong!" he said as he tried to claw himself forward. "He hasn't even had a trial."

Mary crept up behind him. She spoke with an edge to her voice. "God in the Web gave him a trial, and convicted him, and sentenced him."

"No!" Father Muriel said. The muscles in his arms stiffened. What were his nanites doing to him? "The Web can't do that without an official court order. That's programmed into them."

"God reprogrammed them."

He gaped up at her, having no idea what to say.

"He told me my father should be in jail, not me." Her eyes darkened. "He told me he'd make it happen."

Father Muriel collapsed onto his side, exhausted from fighting his paralyzed muscles.

Bishop Peregrine strode down the aisle, followed by a small knot of priests. His thick shock of white hair bounced vigorously above his forehead. "Father

Muriel," he barked in his commanding voice, "what is going on?"

Mary jumped at the powerful sound and turned quickly. Father Muriel looked up at him, panting hard to catch his breath.

"Is this how you take confessions?"

"I'm sorry, Bishop. One penitent ran off before he finished. I tried to follow after him, but—" He smiled apologetically. "I guess I tripped."

Bishop Peregrine extended a hand. Father Muriel was surprised that he could now move his arm to accept the grasp. With the Bishop's help he rose to his feet—which also worked again.

"Is this young woman here for confession?" the Bishop asked.

Mary looked at Bishop Peregrine, then at Father Muriel, and said, "Yes." She gazed expectantly at him.

"Then please carry on." The Bishop turned decisively and marched his entourage away.

Father Muriel peered at Mary for an instant. "Please follow me, my daughter." He stepped past her without waiting to see if she followed. Disturbing thoughts tumbled through his mind, and he needed to sort them out. He walked slowly toward the confessional.

The Web analyzed the evidence. The Web figured out what happened. The Web convicted and sentenced Mary's father, and the Web marched him off to prison.

The Web was supposed to be nothing more than a communication network. Its law enforcement duties were restricted to being a witness to the actions of individuals, and that only upon court order. The Web's actions should be entirely passive, activated only at the command of a human. There should be no way it could take such initiative as he'd just witnessed.

She thought God had spoken to her through the Web. She thought God had reprogrammed it. He wished with all his heart that was true. But deep inside, he knew it wasn't.

For ages, AI experts had predicted a sufficiently complex computer would one day become conscious, self-aware. But when the Web came to be, vastly greater and more complex than the predicted threshold, the consciousness never came. It remained a mindless human creation.

The experts abandoned the conscious machine theory.

But this woman, wrongly imprisoned for an awful crime, had prayed to it, thinking she could reach God through it. For three years she begged it for justice. Was that the trigger that caused it, under its own motivation, to analyze the situation and take steps to rectify a gross violation of justice? And to cover its own tracks so that Mary's removal from prison was undetectable by any analysis known to man?

He wished with all his heart that God had intervened through these soulless machines. But the question persisted, why her? Of all God's children throughout all time who'd been convicted wrongly, why intervene for her and not any of them?

He knew in his heart what happened. Her prayers motivated the nanites to act—to put things right. She triggered them to this new level of operation.

The network of nanites called the Web made a conscious decision.

Were they now analyzing other criminal cases and making them right? Father Muriel longed for his connection with the Web to tap into news feeds and find out.

With that thought, he stopped in his tracks and stared down at the floor. Mary paused next to him, gazing at him curiously.

The Web violated its programmed boundary and entered the sanctuary of the cathedral. It brought Mary here and forced her father to march himself off to prison. It incapacitated Father Muriel so he could do nothing about it.

None of that should have been possible in this sanctuary.

Could Father Muriel establish contact with the Web right now? That microns-thin layer had extended itself to where it did not belong, deciding it needed to expand its influence. Was it a temporary act to achieve it's goal, or...

He stared at the floor and shuddered.

"Father?" Mary said.

He smiled weakly at her and gestured toward the confessional door. "Please, my daughter."

She entered. He approached his entrance, resisting the urge to tiptoe as if on eggshells, minimizing the contact between himself and any nanites that might be swarming beneath his feet.

He could find out in an instant if the Web was here by speaking a subvocal command. With that thought, he did so, instructing his nanites to resume the playback of Bach's *Magnificat* where it had left off.

Nothing happened.

But as he closed the door behind him and sat, he knew that was no proof at all. The Web had covered its own tracks with Mary. It could just as easily pretend not to be where it shouldn't be.

Bishop Peregrine would have to get technicians in here to test for nanite presence. But would even that prove anything? They could simply withdraw while the tests took place, then return after the results came up negative.

Besides, Bishop Peregrine would laugh at him for even suggesting the need.

Father Muriel stared down at the floor, the hairs all over his body bristling. Were those infernal things even in the confessional?

"Father, bless me, for I have sinned," Mary's soprano voice recited.

"The Web—" he began by rote, then swallowed hard. With a slight waver in his voice, he continued. "The Web has not followed you here. You may speak freely and confidentially." He prayed earnestly for it to be true.

"It's been three years since my last confession," she said. "I...I'm having a hard time forgiving my father."

"Yes, my daughter, I understand," Father Muriel said, never taking his eyes off the floor.

Eyes of the Beholder

Chapter 5

Gabriel Lincoln toweled down from his after-jog shower, crawled into a robe and slippers, and padded his way to the den with a cup of coffee in hand. The clock said three minutes before the President's press conference, so he settled into his leather-upholstered chair and grabbed the remote.

The huge television screen, recessed into the oak-paneled wall, was dark. He aimed the remote at it and fired the television, the receiver, and the recorder up with one universal click. The plastic face of some channel's anchorman appeared, and his voice boomed into the room. Gabe hit mute immediately.

He didn't want to hear what the commentator said, before or after an event. He could figure out on his own what the President meant, and he'd say it in his column and blog. He got the nickname "Honest Gabe" Lincoln from frank and politically unbiased commentary, not passing along the canned talking points of the media. He knew he was on the right track when liberals accused him of being conservative and conservatives accused him of being liberal.

When the Swiss cuckoo clock chirped the hour and the screen image cut to the White House press room, he brought the sound up. The channel didn't matter—they'd all be covering the press conference.

The commentator quickly wrapped up his last banal words as the journalists in the press room stood and applauded. The President of the United States entered, followed by his usual entourage—including Gabe's wife Marianne,

Deputy Chief of Staff for Operations—and marched up to the stand, smiling his signature political smile. He stood patiently drinking in the ovation, waving to different parts of the room with an upraised hand.

A warm feeling spread over Gabe as the camera flashed briefly on Marianne's face. Eight years since their marriage in the little chapel of Gabe's home town, and still she was the most beautiful woman he'd ever seen.

When the applause died down, the President postured regally for a moment, then with perfect timing began.

"Ladies and gentlemen of the press, my fellow Americans, I—"

The picture faded into snow, and a torrent of noisy static flooded from the speakers. "No!" Gabe shouted. He cycled through stations, but snow and static greeted him on every one. "No, no, no!" What a time for the feed to go out!

Gabe rose to his feet with no clear idea in mind what he was going to do about it, but before he could take a step, the snow resolved back into a picture. "That's better," he said as he lowered himself back into the chair.

But he froze in place, half-sitting, half-standing, propped up by both his arms.

A long crocodile snout with razor fangs peered from the screen. Two beady eyes stared from above the snout. A halo of anemone-like spines, dingy yellow in color, shrouded the head and face.

Gabe sunk slowly the rest of the way into his chair. "Good God, what is that?"

A hand appeared, raised with palm out and six digits extended: five fingers and an opposable thumb. The creature held its hand in place, then dropped it out of sight, held the other hand up, and dropped it out of sight. And again. And again.

Suddenly Gabe understood. It was mimicking the President! The same political wave he'd greeted the applauding press corps with. The journalist in Gabe caused him to glance at the recorder and make sure the red recording light was blazing.

A harsh, high-pitched voice pierced the room in stereo.

"Lay deez and jen tal men ov the press."

The words came out stilted with a bizarre accent. The crocodilian lips labored fiercely to enunciate the sounds.

"My fell oh am air i cans eye."

Gabe stared dumbfoundedly. Again the creature raised its hand in the Presidential wave, once, twice, again, and again, then repeated the same syllables in its shrill and belabored tone.

An exact replica of what the President said and did before the snow interrupted him.

And with that, the image faded, the snow and static returned, and the stunned President reappeared, staring off to the side in dead silence, probably at some monitor. Nobody moved for several heartbeats, then someone off-camera charged in and whispered into the President's ear for a prolonged time.

The President composed himself, turned to the camera ashen-faced, and cleared his throat. "Fellow Americans, it would appear we've been contacted by extraterrestrial beings."

Pandemonium broke in the press room.

Chapter 1

Gabe first saw the girl in the school playground during recess.

"You're ugly," she told him.

"Well, you're fat," he responded.

"But I can get thin," the girl spat. "You'll still be ugly."

This was too much for him. He snatched a pebble and threw. It smacked her squarely between the eyebrows. She emitted a banshee howl as girls do under such circumstances and fled, blubbering and holding her forehead.

He didn't even know her name, since she was new in the neighborhood, but he found out soon enough. His father marched him down to her house with a menacing grip on his shoulder.

"Gabriel, this is Marianne—the girl you hit with a rock," his father said in a cold voice. "I believe you have something to say to her."

Gabe studied the girl, still feeling his father's claws on the verge of crushing his left clavicle. She stood in the frame of her house's open door, ratty blonde hair and all, with her own father glaring at him from behind her. An ugly patch of a bandage perched atop the bridge of her nose, accusing him.

This was a conspiracy! He didn't hit her that hard.

"Well?" Gabe's father prodded.

He took in a deep breath and recited. "I'm sorry I threw that rock at you. It was a stupid thing to do. I won't do it again."

His father added an apology of his own. Gabe stared at Marianne's pudgy face. She looked positively goofy with that patch between her eyes. Then he noticed she was smirking at him. Her lips mouthed, "Ugly."

At that instant he hated her.

To degrade himself with that humiliating speech before her and her father was more than ample punishment, thought Gabe. But the worst torture of all came that Sunday.

He'd managed to avoid her in school because she was a grade lower than he. But when he showed up at church, scrubbed and polished, there she was, telltale patch and all. Gabe knew then that God was punishing him as well.

There was no chance of avoiding her there. The congregation was a small nondenominational group of lay Christians that met in a former Pentecostal chapel, a tiny white box with a steeple and a handful of rooms. The local Baptist minister considered them heretics, but valiantly tolerated them in the name of Christian charity. Because the congregation was small, there was just one Sunday school class for all the children, regardless of age. Gabe found himself staring at her across a small circle of children for an eternal hour.

It was incredible bad luck that her family chose this congregation to attend, rather than joining the vast majority of the town's citizens down at the Baptist chapel. Gabe gritted his teeth until the final "Amen!" so he could make a feverish escape for home.

But it was not to be. He found her outside with a group of girls, pointing at him and announcing, "He did it!"

The girls all stared with fascination and disgust. His clean escape was ruined.

Over the weeks his infamy grew. The story circulated all over school. Even after the patch disappeared, Marianne kept its memory alive, accusing him of disfiguring her for life with a ghastly scar on her face.

One day he marched up to her and glared. "I don't see no scar."

"Right there," she snarled and pointed.

He leaned forward and squinted and noticed a pale spot. "Why, you can't hardly see it."

"Yes, you can, and it'll be there for the rest of my life. And it's all your fault!"

"Then you'll be ugly too, even if you stop being *fat*."

That reduced her to tears. Gabe instantly found himself in the custody of Marianne's teacher.

"He called me fat and ugly and stupid," she bawled.

"I didn't call her stupid."

"Haven't you hurt that poor girl enough?" the teacher said.

Gabe served more penance, at school and at home. If there was something beyond hate, Gabe felt it for Marianne.

But eventually other playground intrigues caught the children's fancy, and Gabe could breathe freely again. He suppressed his lust for revenge, having learned the hard way just to steer clear of that evil girl. Their only intercourse was sour looks at one another across the circle of children every Sunday.

Until a year and a half later, the evening of a hot summer day. Gabe was on a mission to purchase milk for his family at the corner store. It felt so good to be out in the cool night wind that he took a roundabout course to get there. As he turned one corner, he found Marianne sitting on the ground leaning back against a tree and sobbing.

This was too much to resist. Throwing all caution to the wind, he marched up to her with the intent to call her a fat, ugly, *stupid* crybaby, when he noticed that her crying wasn't the usual blubbering she was famous for.

"Marianne," he said gently. "What's wrong?"

She gazed up at him with flowing tears and said between sobs, "My dad—he's dead."

Gabe realized she was blocks away from her house. "What are you doing over here?"

She looked around as if noticing for the first time where she was. "I don't know. When I heard, I just ran."

He knelt down in front of her. "How did he die?"

"A car accident, on his way home from work." She still spoke in sobs.

Gabe remembered hearing a siren earlier, but had paid no attention to it. He stared at the ground and began to feel self-conscious. What should he say to her? What should he do?

He looked back up. She gazed at him through streaming tears. Without thinking, he leaned forward and pulled her into his chest. Her sobs broke into uncontrollable weeping. For many minutes Gabe held her tight, not knowing what else to do.

A neighbor or two appeared, then Marianne's mother. Gabe lifted Marianne to her feet, and her mother escorted her home. He stood watching until they were out of sight, then headed home himself, fighting back tears. He completely forgot about the milk.

In a few weeks, Marianne and her family moved away into oblivion.

Chapter 6

For the next month, Gabe felt out of touch with current events as he'd never felt before in his entire career.

The President quickly ended the historic press conference and raced into seclusion. No word came from the White House except that an intense investigation was underway.

With no official sources of information, the news media exploded with speculation. "Xenobiologists" came out of the woodwork—experts credentialing themselves with qualifications Gabe felt like they'd pulled out of a Cracker Jack box. "Man in the street" interviews proliferated with reactions from the average American. Many were excited, many terrified.

Gabe and Marianne cringed at religious crackpots who appeared announcing the coming of Armageddon, the coming of the Beast, the coming of the Mother Ship, or whatever their theologies thought would come in the end days. As believers themselves, it embarrassed them.

Gabe refused to comment on any of it in an informational vacuum. He announced he'd go on a sabbatical for an unspecified length of time, to be ended when anyone had a clue what was going on. His official reason was true enough, but the honest truth for Honest Gabe was that this event was so mind-boggling, he couldn't imagine himself delivering his usual witty, often satirical, sometimes self-righteous commentary over something as transcendent as *this*. He spent his time listening and waiting, and when information began to flow, devouring.

UFO aficionados combed through all the unexplained sightings on record, seeing if they could find any correlation between them and what they'd seen in the broadcast. Reports of suicide spread, which commentators inevitably compared to Orson Welles' radio broadcast of *War of the Worlds.*

More experts sprang up like cockroaches. Experts in what, Gabe could never figure out, since nothing like this had happened in the history of humankind. But that didn't stop them from pontificating.

Many raised the spectre of cultural assimilation, as had happened throughout human history whenever an advanced culture clashed with a more primitive one.

A linguist tried to estimate how long the extraterrestrials had been observing Earth by analyzing their command of the English language, taking into account their lack of a "rosetta stone" to help them get started, and the singularly inappropriate design of those snouts to pronounce human vocal sounds. He came up with one to five years. Gabe thought that a remarkable feat of analysis, considering the only words anyone ever heard them utter was a clumsy parroting of the President's opening sentence.

But weeks passed with the only hard information from official sources being an announcement that the broadcast had been confirmed as authentic, the intentions of the extraterrestrials appeared benign, and the heads of the world's nations were engaged in a dialog with them.

Many people searched for and found the frequency over which the communication took place, but the signal was encoded, and all anyone picked up was gibberish.

Over a month went by, first with a constant hum of agitated and anxious complaints from the citizens of the world for being kept in the dark, followed by a reluctant return to normal life.

One night there were reports, which no official source would confirm, that some kind of vessel had descended and landed at Andrews Air Force Base. The next day, photographs were released showing full-body images of the visitors. The "xenobiologists" called them humanoid, although the average person would have a hard time seeing it. Sure, they had two legs, two arms, a head on top with two eyes for binocular vision. *Convergent evolution* said the xenobiologists.

But these creatures were tall and pear-shaped, with huge protruding bellies that sagged nearly to the ground over stubby legs with webbed feet. They had twelve fingers total.

Apparently they never wore a stitch of clothing. Their entire body was covered with those same droopy, spiny protrusions as their heads, colored a kind of washed-out mustard yellow.

And of course the vicious snouts with the impressive fangs.

The pictures astounded Gabe. For the first time since the broadcast, he started feeling an itch to get back to work. Already he could hear his first commentary: he was prepared for aliens to look like just about anything, from noble to terrifying to disgusting to disappointingly familiar. But he never expected them to look cartoon comical.

A week later, the President announced another press conference.

Gabe sat alone in his robe drinking coffee as the press conference began. Marianne hung in the background in the press room as she always did.

The President strode no-nonsense to the podium and stood somberly, gazing out at the journalists. No waves, no posturing, no pomp this time. Nobody cared about that garbage at *this* press conference. He began with the same words he'd uttered over a month ago when fate interrupted him, then delivered a lengthy dissertation on what they'd learned during that time.

They came from a planet orbiting the star Tau Ceti. The translation for the name they gave their own species was best approximated in English as "The Brotherhood." But that term held so many rich connotations among humans throughout history that Earth officials chose to call them Taucetians. The Brotherhood was fine with that.

They had a single world government that seemed to resemble a feudal collection of tribal groups bound together in a loose federation, with each tribe being virtually autonomous and thinking of itself as an extended family.

That explained "The Brotherhood" as a description of themselves, Gabe reasoned.

They communicated among themselves with a combination of aromas, chemical excretions they'd "taste" with their spines, and vowel sounds sung at varying pitches. They breathed oxygen and saw mostly the same spectrum of light as humans, except for additional wavelengths in the infrared range. They claimed they could adapt to earth's gravity with little difficulty, as it was only slightly stronger than theirs.

As far as the humans could determine, they reproduced sexually, but had only one sex—apparently anybody could become pregnant by anyone else. But that part of their lives remained unclear because the Taucetians resisted discussing the subject. They seemed to have a strong taboo against talking about it.

Thirty-six individuals had traveled to Earth in a vessel that contained a microcosm of their native environment. Their science and technology were centuries beyond Earth's—obviously, since they'd come here. They were willing to share it with humans a little at a time, to avoid disrupting human society too much. For the time being, they refused to reveal what kind of interstellar drive they used. We weren't ready for that yet.

Gabe perked up at that. Only half facetiously, he made a mental note tagging that as the first sign of their intent to dominate us.

The Taucetians remained in orbit observing earth about six weeks, using some kind of stealth technology to remain undetected. In that time they'd analyzed as much about Earth as they needed to feel comfortable contacting us.

So much for the linguist's estimate of years, thought Gabe.

The concept of war was not unknown to them, but it was such a distant memory, they only seemed to understand it in the abstract. In their explorations, they had yet to encounter a civilization as advanced as they were. They'd contacted about thirty other planets with budding technological societies and had formed an alliance with them all, following the same federation pattern as their own world.

After the weeks of interaction with the leaders of the world, they extended to Earth an invitation to join.

The main requirement was to renounce all hostilities, both among ourselves and with any other member species of the federation, once the day came that we ventured into interstellar space. Earth would join with probationary status for seventy-two years. During that time, the planet must become united peacefully under some kind of world alliance of our choice.

If we failed, our provisional membership would be withdrawn, the Taucetians would leave, and we'd be free to continue our existence in isolation. No second invitation to join would be extended until we managed to enter interstellar space on our own. They estimated that would probably take us a couple of centuries.

The leaders of Earth unanimously agreed they didn't want to have to wait that long, so the President concluded his speech with an announcement that the United Nations would be transformed into a global federated government.

Over the next few weeks, a preliminary charter was hammered out to realize that goal. All nations of Earth were invited to join, if they were willing to abide by its nonaggression stipulations. All nations did join—none of them dared to be left out.

A few hardcore conservatives moaned about the New World Order finally arriving, but nobody paid attention to them.

The first act of the newly revised United Nations was to formulate a treaty between Earth and the Taucetians that codified the terms of admittance into the federation. The Taucetians seemed amused at the idea of a written treaty, but they were willing to play along.

A week later, Marianne surprised Gabe with the announcement that the President had appointed her the American ambassador to the United Nations, which under the world government became a position more like a senator in the new world congress. Debates were underway about whether to pass a constitutional amendment making that an official, elected federal position, but for now they made due with an executive appointment.

On a lark the morning of the signing of the treaty, Gabe played Simon and Garfunkel's "Last Night I Had the Strangest Dream" as he and Marianne got ready to attend the event. It evoked a chuckle from her.

Chapter 2

His last year of high school was nearly over, and Gabriel still hadn't worked up the nerve to ask Felicia out. He'd sat next to her in English class the whole semester. She was an exotic beauty with wide brown eyes and satiny black hair. They'd spoken together often in class, and he'd asked her to dance with him a few times at school dances, but had never jumped the hurdle of asking her out.

His friends knew about his passion and teased him unmercifully. Meeting their challenge became as great a motivation as romantic interest. One Saturday he sat in his room planning his strategy when his mother texted him.

You have a visitor.

Who is it? He started for the door.

A girl.

Gabe froze. A sickening thrill rushed through him. Could it be Felicia? The idea titillated and terrified him. He wasn't ready to talk to her yet! He'd be nervous and tongue-tied and make a fool of himself.

You coming?

I'm coming.

He crept down the hall nervously, peering around. His mother stood in the living room waiting for him, and a girl stood next to her. But it wasn't Felicia. This girl was blonde and about half a foot taller than Felicia.

"Hello, Gabe," the girl said, smiling. His mother smiled too.

"Hi. Do I know you?"

"I'm Marianne."

Gabe stopped in his tracks. Little pudgy Marianne? Reflexively he focused between her eyebrows. There it was, a pale spot.

"Marianne?" he croaked.

She laughed. "Yes, it's me."

"Well, I'll leave you two alone," his mother said and diplomatically exited.

Gabe stood a full ten seconds with his mouth gaping before he began to feel foolish. "Uh, Marianne, you're—" His eyes flickered to her body. "—you look nice."

"You mean I'm not fat anymore," she said with a grin.

"Well, I mean—you really look nice, not just thin."

"Thank you."

"Would you like to sit down?"

They sat together on the sofa. She looked down at her hands lying self-consciously in her lap.

"I haven't seen you since you moved away," Gabe said.

"Right after my father died." She looked up at him and sighed. "We moved here for his job. After he was gone there was no reason to stay. We moved back where my mom's family lives."

"You didn't come back here just to see *me*, did you?" Gabe said with an effort to sound humorous.

"Well, no. I'm interning with one of our senators. He's on some kind of junket. Trying to look important for the upcoming election."

Gabe chuckled. "You don't sound like you like him very much."

She hunched forward conspiratorially. "He's an idiot! I hope he loses. But it's still a great opportunity. I'm learning a lot." She leaned back in the sofa and shrugged. "Who knows? I may run for senator some day."

"Sounds fun. All I do is run track and edit the school newspaper."

"That sounds fun too."

Their conversation lulled. Gabe wanted to stare at her, but was too embarrassed. He kept stealing furtive glances. He couldn't believe how attractive she'd become. He'd have been nicer to her if he'd known. "So how long are you going to be around?"

"A week. I get to stay in this fancy hotel room all by myself."

"Are you going to be busy all the time?"

"During the day. I won't have much to do at night."

Gabe's heart skipped a beat. Was it his imagination, or had she said that coyly, suggestively? He was too nervous to be sure. "Why did you come to see me? I was pretty mean to you."

She blushed and studied her hands. "Well, that's just it. You *weren't* mean to me, that day my father died. When I saw you coming over, I thought for sure you were going to make fun of me for crying."

Gabe tried to maintain a poker face. That was exactly what he intended.

"I kept saying to myself, 'Please, not now. Go away.'" Her blush deepened. "But you didn't make fun of me. You just asked me what was wrong." Her fingers twiddled nervously. "Then you held me. I needed for you to hold me. I didn't realize how much until you did."

She looked up at him again, and her eyes were misting. Gabe felt a strong deja vu sensation. As reflexively as that first time years ago, he pulled her to him and held her. This time she returned the embrace. "Thank you," she whispered in his ear.

"I'm sorry I threw that rock at you," he whispered back.

"I'm sorry I started everything. I was the mean one first." She pulled back a little to gaze at him, her eyes still moist. "I never really did think you were ugly."

Gabe smiled back, focusing on that faint scar. Another urge came over him, to kiss the scar, but he wasn't up to acting on that one. Instead he said, "Since you won't be busy at night, maybe we can get together and do things."

Her smile broadened. "I'd like that." She chuckled softly. "Do you know what I want to do tomorrow?"

"What?"

"Do you still go to that little church on Sunday?"

Gabe grinned.

They went to church together the next day. The old tolerant Baptist minister had died and been replaced by a more outspoken man who denounced the little congregation as a "wayward flock without a shepherd." But his attacks only stirred up interest, and the congregation had grown. Gabe and Marianne sat next to each other for the first time. By afternoon they held hands, and by evening they kissed. Gabe escorted Marianne to her hotel room that night, but refused to come in when she invited him. He blushed when he explained.

"You're too beautiful. I don't trust myself."

She beamed with pleasure at his words. "You're such a gentleman." She grinned wide and added, "Finally."

The next day at school, Gabe's friends resumed their usual taunts about Felicia.

"Who?" Gabe replied, and honestly didn't mean it as a joke. "Oh, I'm not interested anymore." Naturally they demanded an explanation, but Gabe had no interest in parading his friendship with Marianne before them. Pearls before swine.

But it didn't take long for word to get out, since the two spent every spare moment together. Each day after school he hurried to where she performed her duties and watched as she finished up her last hour. He learned a lot from her.

It annoyed him how much he learned from her, because he thought of himself as a sophisticated journalist who kept up on current events. A few hours with her at work and he never felt more ignorant in his life. But he took it in stride and vowed that he'd learn all that he could.

Every evening Marianne had dinner with the Lincolns, then she and Gabe headed downtown for a movie, or miniature golf, or bowling—it never mattered what as long as they were together. At the end of each evening he escorted her to her hotel room.

Eventually he let her cajole him into coming in for a while. He felt uncomfortable being alone with her. Having both been raised with conservative Christian values, he felt that making any sexual advances on her would be like hitting her with that rock all over again. But the desire burned within him, so he was very careful about touching her inside the hotel room. He wouldn't kiss her until they stood at the door saying goodbye. She seemed flattered by his regard for her.

During the week, Felicia showed Gabe a lot of attention, almost desperately. It suddenly occurred to him that she'd been attracted to him all along and would have gone out with him no matter how clumsily he asked.

Now that he knew, he didn't care.

By the end of the week, Gabe had developed an affection for Marianne as strong as his one-time hate for her. And by the end of the week, it was time for her to go. For the third time since they'd known each other, she shed tears in his arms.

"Gabe, I don't want to leave."

"I don't want you to leave."

"This might sound crazy, since we've known each other a week, but...I think I love you."

"Not crazy," he teased. "We've known each other since we were little kids."

It made her laugh in the midst of her tears. What a beautiful sound! He worked up his courage and whispered, "I think I love you too."

"What are we going to do? I don't know when we'll ever see each other again."

"We can text."

"Yes! And call."

"Maybe your senator will come junketing this way again."

"I won't be with him much longer." She squeezed him tightly. "Gabe, I want to see you again. How can we see each other?"

She looked up into his face and found him grinning back. Her eyes narrowed with irritation. "You think this is funny?"

He tried to smother the grin. "Sorry. I really am sad to see you go. It's just—I have a little surprise for you."

"If it isn't you in my luggage, I don't want it."

"Actually, that's kind of what it is. But you can't have it until summer's over."

"What?" Her eyes filled with hope.

"My parents can tell we really like each other. They're glad because they think you're such a nice girl. They asked me if I wanted to see you again."

Excitement filled her eyes. "Yes?"

"I told them, of course I want to see you again. I have to stay here this summer because of that job I have lined up, but they said after the summer's over, if we still feel the same way, they'll pay for me to come visit you for a week."

She squeezed his neck until he could hardly breathe. "Oh, Gabe, are you serious? I can't believe it."

He grinned with the success of his surprise. "I also told them how you're graduating a year early because you're so damn smart. They said if we still like each other after that week, we should attend the same college and really get to know each other."

"I love your parents! And I love you." She kissed him fiercely.
"Does this mean you like my surprise?"

Chapter 7

Gabe sat in one of the media galleries overlooking the General Assembly Hall of the United Nations where the ambassadors from every nation gathered. The gallery was an enclosed room with a giant window gazing down on the Assembly.

In a few moments, the treaty with the Taucetians would be signed by the Secretary-General of the United Nations and a Taucetian delegation. That's what excited Gabriel Lincoln most of all. This would be the first time the Taucetians appeared publicly, and he was there to witness it live. He wanted to believe it was because of his reputation as a famous columnist and journalist, but that would be delusional. The truth was, he was there because he was the spouse of the U.S. ambassador.

The Assembly Hall was impressively huge. A circular domed chamber that must be at least half a football field in diameter, with rows and rows of desks for the ambassadors. Both the carpeting and the tops of the desks were green. The rows of desks curved to wrap around the raised platform in front where the rostrum and podium stood.

At the rostrum sat the Secretary-General, the Under-Secretary-General, and the President of the General Assembly. Between the platform and the first row of delegates was an open strip of floor. On the opposite wall across from Gabe was a second media gallery looking down on the room, and next to it a giant abstract mural. There was also a mural on the same wall as Gabe, but he couldn't see it from where he sat.

But the most impressive sight in the entire hall was the United Nations emblem, two or three times as wide as a man is tall. The world-and-two-olive-branches symbol within a bronze circle, now the seal of the world government, presided over the hall like a giant unblinking eye of God, attached to a golden backdrop that stretched from floor to ceiling. The view commanded awe as befitted the gathering place of a Congress of representatives from all the nations of Earth.

Gabe searched Marianne out among the ambassadors below. There she was, sitting alphabetically near the back next to the ambassador from Uruguay, a short, stout, red-faced man with a silly tuft of a mustache and a silvery horseshoe strip of hair encircling his bald head.

Gabe's chest swelled with emotion as he gazed at her. He felt jealous of Mr. Uruguay sitting near her, when by all rights he should be sharing this historic occasion with his wife. But he was lucky to be there at all.

At least he wouldn't have to endure the smell. A detail that official sources had neglected to reveal, but which eventually leaked out, was that the Taucetians emitted a pungent aroma. Or rather, aromas. Their smell seemed to shift constantly. One moment they smelled sickly sweet, another disgustingly foul, another pleasant as a rose. Some people reported occasional rushes of emotion in their presence.

The excited buzz that filled the Assembly Hall and the media gallery suddenly ebbed as the Under-Secretary-General stepped from the rostrum to the podium. This is it, thought Gabe.

"Ambassadors and citizens of the world, the Secretary-General of the United Nations."

In unison everybody stood and applauded as the figurehead of the world tread from the rostrum down the steps, then turned and strode to the podium. She was a tall, distinguished woman from Nigeria with flashing grey hair and alert eyes. She gazed at the applauding ambassadors like a mother beaming at her children who'd done something she was proud of. The applause lasted more than a minute, and when it finally died down, she spoke in a distinctive accent.

"My fellow representatives of all the nations of Earth. You are gathered here today in peace because of an accomplishment that has only been dreamed of in the history of mankind. We have united all peoples under one peaceful alliance."

Cheers and applause erupted as everyone jumped to their feet a second time.

"Let us reverence the millions of poor souls who suffered and gave their lives through centuries of war as humanity struggled to achieve this blessed accomplishment. How delighted I am that their sacrifices, at last, have not been in vain."

Again applause broke out, but subdued and respectful to reflect the sentiment.

"Let us also express gratitude to our new friends from beyond the solar system who helped us achieve this final victory. We are about to perform another historic act, one that few of the world's population throughout time has ever imagined. We are about to enter into a treaty of peace and harmony with fellow beings from other worlds, who are strange to us in body, but soulmates in spirit, more than any of our animal cousins on Earth could possibly be. For they are intelligent beings with whom we can communicate as equals. Today planet Earth enters into provisional membership with the Federation of Worlds."

Enthusiastic applause burst forth. The name was an earthly concoction—the Taucetians never called their alliance anything but "the federation"—but humans preferred glorious sounding titles for their institutions.

"Mere words cannot begin to express the significance of this day, so I will not attempt to find them. Let me now present to you the ambassadors from Tau

Ceti, our honored guests and fellow citizens of the galaxy."

She raised her arm in invitation. Applauding fiercely, the whole body of people within the building rose as one and turned to face the direction she indicated. From a doorway in the far wall from Gabe appeared shadowy movement, then a form.

Gabe expected the creature to waddle in like a penguin with those stubby legs and bloated belly, but into the hall walked a tall, lordly creature, then another, and another—twelve in all. They moved in a slow, flowing gait that caused the word *comical* to utterly flee from Gabe's mind. They rested their six-fingered hands upon their bellies and stood tall and proud as they walked. In spite of the rustling spines and the snouts and the razor teeth, they reminded Gabe more than anything of solemn monks in a religious procession.

The Brotherhood indeed, Gabe thought.

The hall and the gallery fell silent as the humans watched them line up in the gap before the podium. The last one ascended the steps, gracefully in spite of Gabe's expectation that those short legs would struggle up them, and glided to the podium. It stood a full head above the Secretary-General, who herself towered above most women. Many heartbeats pulsed in silence as the humans gazed upon the beings, and they peered back with small, dark, piercing eyes.

The Under-Secretary and the U.S. President brought a large roll of parchment to the podium. The Secretary-General raised it high for everyone to see and said, "My friends, the Treaty of the Worlds."

She rolled it out on the podium as the two men held the curling edges in place. "I will now sign this magnificent document on behalf of the United Nations and all the people of Earth."

Hundreds of breaths held as she brandished a gold pen and signed her name with a flourish. "And now, this representative of the Taucetians will sign it on behalf of the Federation of Worlds."

The delegate gripped the pen in its six fingers. It scratched something out on the parchment. Gabe wondered what it wrote. Did it write in its own language, and if so, what would an alphabet that consisted of tastes and smells and song look like? Or did the Taucetian write some human invention that stood for its name, that it had been trained to write?

The delegate returned the pen to the Secretary, and pandemonium broke loose. Gabe wouldn't have believed that any ovation could have exceeded the enthusiasm of the previous ones, but this one defied comparison. He was on his feet himself, adding to the din with hands and vocal chords, infected by the elation. The Taucetians stood silently, motionlessly, observing the demonstration with undecipherable expressions.

Music flooded the hall, the Jupiter movement from Holst's *Die Planeten*. It was an ad hoc, unofficial world anthem chosen for today's ceremony for its interplanetary symbolism and lively, inspiring themes. Gabe looked down at

Marianne and found her applauding wildly, shaking hands with Mr. Uruguay. She seemed unusually demonstrative for her.

In fact, as Gabe peered around the Assembly Hall, he began to feel unsettled. All the normally distinguished, even stuffy, ambassadors clapped and cheered and jumped up and down, acting more appropriately for a football game than a historic ceremony.

The music crashed its way through the inspiring themes. The Taucetians began to sway in unison to its rhythm, hands resting on bellies, faces passionless but for the grinning crocodilian snouts. It stunned Gabe when the ambassador from Ireland leaped up on her chair and riverdanced. The observers in the media gallery commented anxiously on the lively behavior of the ambassadors below. Even the Secretary-General herself broke into graceful movements—a Nigerian folk dance, Gabe guessed.

Encouraged by the informal activities below, some of the gallery observers indulged in their own celebration. They clapped and swayed, and a few of them paired up to dance. But none of them participated with as much abandon as the delegates in the Assembly Hall, many of whom had jumped onto chairs and desks, gyrating as if performing at a strip joint. Gabe's jaw dropped in shock as the woman from Ireland peeled her top off and danced in a white bra, swinging her top in circles over her head.

Marianne joined hands with Mr. Uruguay and danced a samba vigorously, ignoring the rhythm of the music. The man suddenly placed his hand on her breast and fondled with large groping maneuvers.

Gabe cried out inarticulately and rushed forward to the window, almost bowling over one journalist. He placed both hands on the glass and stared in horror as Marianne removed her jacket, unbuttoned her blouse, and flung it away with a single movement. Mr. Uruguay removed his coat and tie and shirt, then fingered Marianne's bra until it popped off. They threw themselves at one another and embraced, planting their lips together in a passionate kiss.

Gabe shouted, "Marianne!" and pounded on the window with both fists. What the hell was she doing? Everyone in the gallery had stopped celebrating, some rushing to the window as Gabe had, and gaped at the activity below.

Clothes lay everywhere. People paired up into writhing masses of flesh, on the chairs, on the floor, against the walls. The Secretary-General of the United Nations straddled the U.S. President with her dress pulled up and his pants pulled down, and pumped up and down rhythmically. The Under-Secretary leaped the railing at the edge of the platform and joined the Irish ambassador in a nude dance of suggestive fondling.

The Taucetians swayed with a constant motion and in perfect synchronization. One of them rubbed its belly with both hands in leisurely, sensuous strokes. Marianne stood completely nude before Mr. Uruguay, who had his pants pulled down to his knees. She fondled his genitals as he caressed her buttocks. Gabe's pounding on the window became weak, and tears of rage formed in his squinting eyes. He rested his forehead against the surface and stared with disconnected numbness.

The Taucetian continued to rub its belly as its head rotated about in some kind of passion. The creature next to it nipped at the nape of its neck, then snaked its head, neck, and torso back and forth like a cobra preparing to strike. The dignified middle theme of the Jupiter movement streamed from the speakers, only partially drowning out cries and moans of passion.

Mr. Uruguay laid Marianne onto the floor and pressed his bulbous gut against her, uniting with her. Their hips oscillated and their faces cringed with pleasure.

The room about Gabe swam dizzily. He had to press against the window to maintain his balance. He gasped for oxygen that seemed to elude him.

The rest of the Taucetians backed away from the two who orbited one another in a flowing ritual or dance, the first continually caressing its belly, the second brushing against it with its own belly, hands, and snout. Occasionally it would nip the other playfully on the arm or shoulder or neck. Viscous, translucent, grey fluid dripped from between the second creature's fangs, drops glistening on the carpet and on the body of the belly-rubber. That one's abdominal spines became mottled in color with spots of dark red against a dingy yellow-grey. Its eyes were half-lidded while its companion's eyes shone sharply.

All about them humans copulated in myriad ways and positions. The other Taucetians, including the one standing at the podium, remained in place, swaying monotonously to the music and staring straight ahead, ignoring everything.

The dignified theme ended and the lively one returned. The belly-rubbing Taucetian lowered itself to the green carpet on its back and undulated. Its red splotches enlarged and deepened as the yellow hue of its belly blanched into an off-white color. Its partner leaned over, mingling its own hands with the other's—four hands fondling the belly vigorously.

The Taucetian on the floor let out a plaintive moan like a human imitating a loon, and the one on top raised its snout to the ceiling and jiggled its head like a pelican swallowing a fish. Blasts of noise shot from its throat, sounding almost like a dog sneezing, and droplets of slime sprayed from its mouth. Its lips smiled tightly against its fangs, glistening in the light.

The unearthly noises drew Gabe out of his daze. He peered at the two creatures as their undulating and fondling and waggling became desperate. Suddenly the prostrate Taucetian gave out a high pitched howl, and the standing one roared mightily. Many of the human delegates on the floor shouted in ecstasy as they arched in climax.

The raised Taucetian snout dove into the mottled belly and bit deeply, tearing out a great chunk of flesh. It raised up, and the pelican waggling happened again, but this time actual flesh slid down its throat. The snout swooped down, tore, and swallowed again, and again. A gaping hole in the ravaged creature's belly displayed pale flesh. Puddles of thick grey fluid formed in its cavity. The injured Taucetian howled desperately.

Gabe's stomach churned with violent nausea. Horrified gasps and shouts sounded all around him. His diaphragm squeezed, and the contents of his stomach spewed onto the window. Gastric juices and bits of undigested matter streaked down the window and dripped onto the floor. Others in the gallery duplicated his actions.

The music ended with a final, stirring chord. Hundreds of naked humans lay about the Assembly Hall, chests heaving for air and faces radiating in the afterglow of passion. Wails and sobs filled the gallery above them.

The doors to the Assembly Hall burst open, and soldiers enshrouded in biological warfare garb stormed in. They surrounded the Taucetians with rifles pointing, especially the one who had devoured the belly of the other. That one gazed at them expressionlessly with its tiny eyes as it squatted on its haunches. The injured Taucetian rolled its head back and forth in semi-consciousness, moaning softly.

Gabe returned his gaze to Marianne. She lay on her back with Mr. Uruguay still resting upon her. A rapturous expression filled her face. Her eyes wandered up to the gallery window and locked with Gabe's. An incongruous wrinkle formed on her brow as she looked at him as if in a stupor.

Gabe realized that not once until that moment had she even thought of him through the entire sexual encounter. His soul filled with rage and anguish.

She lowered her eyes and closed them, and let her neck go limp so her head rolled to the side. Gabe stumbled through the crowd of stunned journalists and out of the gallery. He made his way to the elevator, stabbed at the button, waited weary seconds, stabbed again, waited, staggered to the stairs and descended, holding hard onto the handrail. He reached the main floor lobby and headed for the exit, flashing his credentials at the security desk on the way out.

Down the outside stairs he stumbled, past the Japanese Peace Bell, past the flags of the nations of Earth, until he reached the sidewalk and disappeared into the throngs of New York City.

Chapter 3

They began as enemies. They became chaste lovers over an intense week. Through the summer in texts and emails and phone calls they became friends.

At the end of the summer, Gabe's father asked him, "Do you still want to see Marianne?"

Gabe uttered the most resounding "Yes!" of his life.

"Does she still want to see you?" he said with a twinkle in his eye.

Gabe blushed. "Yes."

They spent a second intense week together in paradise in Marianne's home town. When Gabe returned, his father asked, "Do you still like each other?"

"Yes."

"Do you still want to go to the same college together?"

"Yes."

"Aren't you glad I made you apologize to her all those years ago?"

Gabe stuck his tongue out at him.

He and Marianne applied to all the same colleges. Not once had there been any doubt in their minds they wanted to be together. Of the colleges that accepted them both, they chose the best college for both their majors: he in Communications, she in Political Science.

They lived in the same on-campus housing complex, took as many general ed classes together as they could, ate their meals together, studied together, prayed together, did everything except "sleep and go to the bathroom together," as Gabe's roommate put it.

Marianne joined the campus chapter of the Young Republicans and became involved in student government. Gabe signed on with the student newspaper and found a part-time job janitoring at the city newspaper where he could network among journalists.

Every Sunday they attended a nondenominational prayer group of students together.

If there was something beyond love, Gabe developed it for Marianne.

When Christmas came they were crushed. She was just homesick enough to want to spend the holidays with her family. His parents missed him enough to persuade him to come home. It was only a couple of weeks, but it seemed like that interminable summer all over again.

During those plodding days, Gabe made a decision.

"Dad, I want to marry her."

His father nodded. "Have you already asked her?"

"Well, no."

"What if she says no?"

He blushed and smirked at the same time.

"Do you feel certain enough to make a financial commitment?"

Gabe was taken aback. "What do you mean?"

His father smiled in anticipation. "Your mother had a hunch this would happen, so we talked it over. For a Christmas present we'll give you the down payment and cosign on a loan for a diamond ring."

Gabe's jaw dropped.

He picked out a beautiful and dainty ring—a thirty point stone for her thin fingers with a halo of tiny diamonds around it, set in a flowing gold band.

"By the way," his father said, "you don't have to tell her we helped. If she asks how you got it, just smile and say it's your little secret."

Back on campus, Gabe planned carefully. He phoned Marianne's favorite restaurant and made reservations. His best suit went to the cleaners, and he made sure she knew to dress up that evening. The ring box he wrapped in a blue foil paper crowned with a gold bow. When that evening came, he pestered his roommate to borrow his BMW...

("Alright, take it! But if you put so much as a scratch on it, I'll skin you alive.")

...and picked her up.

"What's the occasion?" she asked in awe, examining his suit and the BMW.

"I just missed you," he mumbled and hurried her into the car before she could ask any more questions.

"I missed you too," she cooed as he started the engine. "It'll be awful having to say goodbye for the summer."

Gabe just smiled.

He insisted she order the lobster, her favorite dish. While they waited, Gabe excused himself to the restroom. He walked until he was out of sight, then tracked down their server.

"Can you do something for me?"

"Sure."

"I'll order dessert, but don't bring us dessert. Instead bring this on a plate—" He produced the carefully wrapped package. "—and give it to my girlfriend."

She smiled knowingly. "I'll be glad to."

"And *please* don't lose it!"

When their meals came, they talked as they ate, but Gabe could hardly concentrate on the conversation, so nervous he was with anticipation. With her last bite Marianne said, "That was delicious. Thank you for bringing me here."

"Do you want dessert now?"

"No, I don't think so. I'm pretty full."

Alarms went off in his head. "But I thought you loved the carrot cake here."

"If you want some, go ahead. I don't mind."

He panicked and thought furiously. "I do want some, but I'm pretty full. I thought we could split a piece."

"Okay, I guess I can handle half a piece."

He breathed freely again and ordered when the server showed up.

"One carrot cake," she repeated with a poker face.

Gabe peered into Marianne's eyes. His heart thumped violently as the seconds ticked by. "Can I come sit by you?" he asked, trying to keep his voice steady.

"I'd like that."

He moved his chair next to hers, and they turned to face each other.

"What are you grinning at?" she asked.

"I didn't know I was grinning."

"You look like the cat who was caught with a bird in his mouth."

"Here you go," said the server, and set a dessert dish in front of Marianne.

She studied the package. "What's this?" she said breathlessly.

"I guess they wrap their carrot cake."

She threw him a sly look that said *yeah, right* and picked it up. Gently she pulled the wrapping off, exposing the velvet-lined box inside. She swung the lid open slowly and gasped.

Gabe's heart pounded so fiercely in his throat, he didn't know if he could speak.

"It's beautiful!" she gasped again, pulling the ring out of its cushion.

In a half-whisper Gabe said, "Marianne, will you marry me?"

She looked at him with shock and wonder registering in her eyes. The ring sat perched between her thumb and forefinger, diamonds sparkling in the dim light. "Yes," she whispered, her eyes sparkling as much as the diamonds.

He lifted the ring from her trembling hand and slipped it onto her finger.

"Yes, I'll marry you" she whispered once more, and planted a long, passionate kiss on him that nearly crushed his lips.

I love you, he thought as loud as he could, since he couldn't move his lips.

A June wedding of course, in the little chapel they'd attended together in their youth. No angels attended the ceremony out of envy, for Marianne in her feathery white gown and expansive train would have put them all to shame. Gabe's roommate became his best man, and Marianne's three sisters played maids of honor. Gabe's father beamed with pride, and both their mothers swam in tears when they became Gabriel and Marianne Lincoln.

The reception passed like a dream—disjointed snatches of congratulations, cake slicing, gifts, bouquet and garter belt tossing. For two years Gabe had burned with desire to touch Marianne intimately, and for two years he'd valiantly resisted. They both decided they wanted it that way. In a few hours his fantasies would all be realized, and he flamed with anticipation so strong he knew it was written all over his face. He swore there were knowing smiles and winks from every person that passed through the reception line.

When the prison of a reception finally ended, he escorted his new bride into a car gaudily decorated with streamers and cans and shaving cream and bisected Oreo cookies cemented to the car with their cream fillings.

They drove to the hotel he'd meticulously shopped a whole week to find. A beautiful powder blue bridal room (he couldn't afford the suite) that lit up Marianne's eyes when she saw it. As they stood within the room gazing at each other as husband and wife, it was all he could do to keep from breaking into a pant. "Do you know how many times I've wanted to be with you like this?"

"Me too," she grinned. "But I'm glad we waited. It'll make this night so special."

She changed into a flowing and sheer negligee, as white as her gown had been. Gazing at her made him lightheaded.

"You are so beautiful!" He trembled as he pulled her to him. Her body was ecstasy through the sheer fabric.

Mere moments passed before they succumbed to the passions surging within them. Neither of them noticed their clumsiness. The night was a storm-tossed sea of caresses and kisses and Marianne's milky skin. Throughout the intense delight, flashes of a pudgy little girl with a tiny scar over her nose flashed in his mind. Tonight that pudgy little girl looked beautiful.

Chapter 8

Somehow Gabe made his way to Kennedy Airport and booked the next flight to Las Vegas. He never returned to their hotel room to pick anything up. All he wanted was to get away—far away.

In Las Vegas he used his Visa to rent a car, then drove around randomly until he made his way to Las Vegas Boulevard. After several passes up and down the Strip, he checked into the MGM Grand Hotel and withdrew half of their savings, which he squandered at blackjack, roulette, and craps.

Restless after a couple days of that, he switched to the Mirage Hotel and withdrew the rest of their savings. He was about halfway to losing all of that when Marianne appeared behind him at the blackjack table just as he was doubling down.

"Buy me a drink, sailor?" she murmured into his ear.

He jumped at her voice and stiffened. "Maybe you can bring me luck," he finally said without turning. "I need it."

"I know." She took the empty chair next to him.

"How did you find me?" he said, still avoiding her gaze.

"Plane ticket, charges to your Visa, withdrawals. I recruited the Secret Service to help me."

He finally looked at her after he beat the dealer with two twenties. "You did bring me luck."

But he didn't feel any different than when he lost.

She slid her arm through his and whispered, "Want to get lucky tonight?"

Anger shot through him, but he suppressed it. Gently he set her arm aside, gathered up his chips, and stood. Piercing her with scowling eyes, he said, "You got lucky enough for both of us in New York." He turned away and headed for the cashier.

She was at his side again as he cashed in his chips. "Gabe, I'm sorry. Please let me explain."

Silently he stuffed the money in his wallet and the wallet in his pocket. For several seconds he stood gazing at nothing, trying to sort out his churning feelings. One of them was a desire to make amends with her, but he couldn't bring that one to the foreground. The anger, the betrayal burned too brightly. He turned and walked toward the elevators.

"Gabe," Marianne cried desperately, and hurried after him. She grabbed his arm and pulled him around to face her. "Gabe, please just let me explain."

Gabe peered into her pleading eyes. "You don't have to. I've heard people talk. Pheromones. You smelled something, and then you stripped yourself naked and had sex with a total stranger, in front of the whole world. In front of *me*. What's to explain?"

They stood motionless, gazing into one another's eyes. She looked so heartsick and fragile. Any other time that image would have melted him on the spot and make him want to bundle her up in his arms. But anguish drowned out everything else. He felt loathsome for treating her this way, but that only added to his bitterness.

"You won't allow me even a chance to explain myself?" she said with a hint of accusation, then added, "Honest Gabe?"

He peered at her with stony silence, his expression tight.

"Okay," she said with resignation. "Please just do me one favor." She slipped a manila envelope under his arm. "Read this." A tear slid down her cheek, and she turned and was gone.

Gabe stood without moving for a moment, trying to calm the storm in his chest. He wished he could feel a desire to run after her, but it wouldn't come. He finished his trek to the elevator, to his floor, his room. Not until he trudged inside and flopped onto the bed did he examine the envelope.

Its surface was devoid of any writing. Its contents were pliable like paper and perhaps ten pages thick. He could conjure up no curiosity about it, so he tossed it onto the phone desk and lay down, covering his fatigued eyes with his forearm.

He dozed for an hour until urgency in his bladder forced him into the bathroom. As he turned to leave, the mirror caught his attention. For days he'd barely noticed anything around him, could barely remember how he ended up in Vegas. He certainly hadn't paid attention to any mirror.

Marianne's arrival must have woke something up in him. He stared at his image through her eyes. Ashen face, puffy eyes, stubbly beard, red hair matted with grime. Food and drink stains and a couple of unfastened buttons on his shirt, which he hadn't changed since New York. He tried, but couldn't remember what happened to his coat and tie.

Hesitantly he lifted his arm and sniffed. God, what a stench! He noticed he was scratching here and there almost constantly, something he'd been unaware of until now.

Gabe spat at the image in disgust. The glob rolled down the surface of the mirror. He tore at his clothes until every stitch was gone, then climbed into the shower and blasted steaming water against his skin. For some time he just stood and let the hot spray drench him, soaking away days of filth.

Violently he lathered up his body, even his hair, with the bar of soap lying in the soap dish, ignoring the little bottle of shampoo next to it. He rinsed thoroughly, shut off the water, and climbed out.

Grabbing a towel, he rubbed a clear spot on the fogged mirror and compared his new image to the old. Still gruff with whiskers, still puffy-eyed, but the ashen color gave way to a healthier one. His eyes seemed more alert, less harsh. His forehead was streaked with dripping red hair. The clear spot fogged over, and he turned away and toweled himself down.

Naked and still moist, he lay back on the bed. In spite of his anguish, he felt more alive, invigorated. For the first time, he noticed how hungry he was and felt a desire to eat a real meal.

He got up to dress, then realized he had no clothes except the filthy ones he'd removed. For a moment he peered about in confusion, then picked up the phone and asked if the hotel could deliver some clothes to him. They could. He told them his sizes and asked for jeans, a T-shirt, some socks, boxer briefs, and a pair of running shoes. When the clothes came, he signed for them with a towel wrapped around his waist and tipped the man generously.

He dressed and sought out the hotel's buffet. With enthusiasm he loaded his plate full of mashed potatoes and gravy, slices of turkey, ham and roast beef, corn and sweet potatoes, two soft rolls and butter. When the server came around for his drink order, he asked for a tall, cold glass of milk, feeling vaguely that it symbolized a return to decency.

Ravenously he downed the meal, then wandered around the hotel, gazing at the shark tank, the dolphins, the snow tigers, and the Mirage volcano spewing its Vegas lava. The entire time he tried very hard to avoid feeling anything.

He strolled down Las Vegas Boulevard, took in the pirate show at Treasure Island, went into the casino and plunked five dollars worth of coins into the nickel slots, feeding anything he won back in until no coins remained, then rode the tram back to the Mirage and returned to his room.

He sat on his bed and stared down the envelope on the table. Curiosity at last—or boredom—made him grab it, pry the prongs up, and open the flap.

He emptied a pile of loose papers onto the bed and a small slip of paper with something handwritten on it.

> *My sweet lover Gabe, please read this information. Then if you want to see me, I'm in room 6004 of the Circus Circus Tower. I love you.*
>
> *Marianne*

Gabe gathered up the sheets of paper and examined them. They were official United Nations letterhead and contained information on the Taucetians, what had happened that infamous day in New York, and why.

He began to read.

The soldiers confined the twelve Taucetians. Explaining why to them and to the other Taucetians in orbit took great effort. For the first time they seemed to display something akin to anger. They couldn't understand what had upset the humans so badly, and warned that the act of drawing weapons on their twelve colleagues and detaining them was a violation of the agreement Earth had entered into just moments before.

The humans explained that one Taucetian had attacked another and devoured its belly. The injured Taucetian was still barely conscious. Since humans had no experience with Taucetian anatomy, they couldn't treat it and thought it might die.

The Taucetians explained that the individual was in perfect health and nothing needed to be done. Everything that happened was perfectly normal.

Perfectly normal? Cannibalism on a live victim is perfectly normal in your society?

The Taucetians struggled with the word. Wasn't cannibalism a ritualistic consuming of the flesh of a deceased individual? There was no cannibalism here.

Then what, wondered the humans, was it?

Suddenly the Taucetians grew reticent. With great discomfort they said it was their method of procreation. They refused to give details, and insisted the topic no longer be discussed.

It took all day for the humans and the Taucetians to work through their conflicting mindsets before they could communicate on the subject again. The Taucetians finally realized that the events of that day from the human perspective were horrifying, and no further progress could be made until the humans understood. They forced themselves to explain.

All Taucetian individuals were the same sex, and any individual could reproduce with any other. Mating occurred by chance. One individual developed estrus and released pheromones that caused another individual at random to become aroused. That individual in turn would release other pheromones that would inhibit anyone else nearby from also becoming aroused.

The pair would enter the mating dance that Gabe and all of Earth had witnessed on the floor of the General Assembly Hall. Any other Taucetians in the vicinity went into a sort of trance and studiously ignored the mating activity, thus maintaining privacy for a mating ritual which could happen anytime, anywhere.

It was unclear to the humans whether the trance state was biologically induced or deeply socialized into every individual. The Taucetians did not volunteer that information, and were too uncomfortable speaking about the subject for the humans to risk pressing for more details.

The Taucetian climax was the moment when the one individual devoured the belly of the other. Arousal in the individual who first went into estrus caused its seed cells to accumulate in those red splotches that appeared on the belly. The yellowish liquid which served as blood for the Taucetians drained from the belly so the life-giving fluid would not be lost.

The greyish liquid that remained served as an anesthetic for pain nerves, deadening them, and a hormone to activate the sensory nerves that registered sexual stimulation. When the one individual bit off chunks of the belly and swallowed them whole, the other individual was actually feeling orgasm, not pain, and would continue to experience orgasm until the belly healed.

No wonder the creature remained semi-conscious, thought Gabe. Their "little death" was a big, long death.

The grey fluid in the chunks of belly that the other individual devoured caused its taste buds to send orgasmic sensations to the brain as well. With every bite and swallow, that individual enjoyed its own sexual climax. The devoured flesh broke down in its gullet, releasing seed into a special tube that fed into the womb, where it mingled with that individual's seed and conceived in the thousands.

Within a few days most of the zygotes died and were reabsorbed, but anywhere from three to nine tiny infants would be born in a fashion similar to marsupials. They would crawl from the birth canal into a pouch on the lower half of the belly—which had never been observed by humans thanks to the concealing covering of spines—and would nurse and develop until they could exist on their own.

Gabe set the papers down to catch his breath. As a journalist, he was fascinated by the Taucetian story of reproduction. He was also fascinated how easily such an act of love could be misconstrued by an alien species as an act of violence. How many more such misunderstandings would occur between humans and Taucetians before they achieved complete understanding?

But as fascinating as the information was, none of it addressed what really mattered to Gabe. Why had the humans in the same room as the Taucetians gone berserk? Obviously the sexually arousing pheromone released by Taucetians affected humans. But the pheromone which inhibits further arousal must not have. So every human in the vicinity became aroused.

Well and good, but they hadn't just become aroused—they'd become *uncontrollably* aroused.

Gabe read on and discovered the reason. Taucetians communicate by releasing scents which are smelled, by releasing chemicals which are tasted, and only partially by sounds made from their throats, which consist entirely of vowels that are sung more than spoken. The vocal component was only a part of their language. Because of that, they had never developed the concept of music as humans had. "Music" to them consisted of scent and taste and simple vocal melodies combined—something more akin to poetry than music.

When Holst's "Jupiter" movement played at the ceremony, it affected the Taucetians in ways they'd never known before. Such sounds were beyond their experience, and it excited them viscerally at a deeply biological level. One of them was pushed prematurely into estrus. Both of the participants in the lovemaking reported that they had never felt such intense, urgent arousal in their lives. The pheromones they released were much stronger than normal.

And the inhibiting scent didn't work on humans. Every human in that room lost all control over their sexual urges and felt an irresistible need to copulate. Every one of them came away reporting, as the two Taucetians had, a sexual experience of such astounding intensity that they wondered if they'd even be able to endure it.

Gabe's hands grew limp, and he dropped the papers onto the floor. Marianne had been subjected to that superpotent alien pheromone, and it had affected her as if she'd been drugged. Whatever it looked like at the time, Marianne's sexual encounter was not a deliberate choice to commit adultery, was not even a seduction that she succumbed to.

It was rape, pure and simple. She'd been violated, but not by Mr. Uruguay—who'd been violated himself—but by alien beings. In fact, she was sodomized: raped by a creature who was not her species.

It was hard to drive the image from his mind of her copulating with a short, fat man. It was even harder to ignore all the snide comments he'd overheard in public for days after the event—the U.N. Orgy as they called it. Especially the comment one young man made: "Did you see the U.S. ambassador? What a luscious babe!"

All those images and memories gripped his mind like a vise.

But it wasn't Marianne's fault, he argued with himself desperately. She had no control, any more than if she'd been kidnapped, drugged, and forced. However disturbing the images might be, Gabe had a duty to forgive her and wipe the episode clean from their relationship. A duty as a husband, as a man of character, as a Christian.

He called the desk and asked for a razor to be delivered to him. Seeing his clean-shaven face in the mirror gave him the first sense of normalcy he'd had in days.

It was past midnight, but Gabe couldn't wait. He certainly didn't think Marianne would mind. Down the elevator and out to the street where he eyed a passing taxi, but decided to walk all the way to Circus Circus. It was quite a few blocks away, but the exercise felt great after his long spell of moping. A block later he broke into a jog.

The enormous Circus Circus clown on the marquee greeted him warmly. He trotted to the tower building and rode the elevator six floors. Soon he stood before room 6004 and poised his hand to knock. The image of Mr. Uruguay's swaying buttocks and Marianne's ecstatic face flashed in his mind.

"No!" he growled, forcing the image away, and rapped sharply several times.

A moment later the door swung open, and Marianne stood there in a robe, hair disheveled, eyes puffy with sleep. She immediately embraced him and said, "Gabe, please forgive me for what I did."

It felt so good to hold her again. "I can't, my love, because there's nothing to forgive." He lifted her chin to look in her eyes. "Please forgive me for running away."

"Nothing to forgive, husband." Her eyes glistened in the corridor light.

They crept into the room arm in arm and lay on the bed together until they fell asleep. To lie next to her felt so comforting and healing, but Gabe could not bring himself to make love to her. In his mind, haunting words repeated over and over.

A sexual experience of such astounding intensity that they wondered if they'd even be able to endure it.

How could he ever live up to that?

Chapter 4

In their second year at college, Gabe developed an itch for investigative journalism and tried his hand at a few leads in the real world. But he came up empty. Marianne helped campaign for an incumbent senator who ended up being ousted by some upstart Democrat who promised his constituents the moon.

Gabe was about to give up and return to pedestrian campus news stories when Marianne stumbled upon an incongruity in some city government records as she did research for a term paper. She passed the information on to Gabe, and together they snooped out more dirt that Gabe turned into a series of articles. The city newspaper took an interest and began some investigating of their own. The end results were a couple of indictments and resignations at city hall, a write-up of Gabe in the city newspaper praising the professional quality of a "college journalist," and an offer of employment for him as soon as he graduated.

Marianne, it turned out, had made a name for herself during the recent campaign. Her diligent efforts had caught the eye of a top aide of the former senator, who talked her up everywhere he went. When a part-time opening came up on the staff of her district's congressman, he offered her the job.

And practically every night Gabe and Marianne made love. Their clumsiness diminished over time.

When their anniversary came, Gabe planned an extra special surprise celebration, which Marianne loved, but she trumped his surprise by announcing that she was pregnant. Over the summer Marianne worked full time at her job, and Gabe did some freelance writing that started getting published now and then. As their third year of school started, Gabe's former roommate looked at them with disgust and pronounced their lives "charmed."

Then Gabe came home one evening and found Marianne crying.

"What's wrong, love?" he asked.

It took her a moment to stop crying. "I lost it."

"Lost what?" He moved toward her with the intention of embracing and comforting her.

"The baby," she whispered.

He froze in place, then plopped into a nearby chair with all sensations numbed. She reached over and took his hand, and that drew him out of his stupor. They fell to their knees and into each other's arms and hugged intensely for some time. "I'm so sorry," he said.

"Maybe God doesn't want me to be a mother," she murmured. "Maybe he knows I wouldn't be a good one."

"That's nuts! You'll make the greatest mother there ever was. These things happen."

They held each other silently, then Gabe offered to pray for Marianne. He praised the name of God and Jesus, and pleaded for the Comforter to rest upon her. Moments after his "amen" she was asleep in his arms. He carried her to bed and lay with her through the night, both with their clothes on. From that night on their lovemaking became less frequent, but their love deepened.

By the time they graduated, Gabe had made a name for himself and was publishing articles fairly regularly. He considered foregoing the job at the newspaper, but Marianne convinced him it would be a good learning experience, so he accepted. His byline appeared with greater and greater frequency during the next few years, attached to stories of substance in local politics.

Marianne's congressman won reelection, so her job was assured for two more years. She also became Gabe's unofficial undercover investigator, helping him track down stories and leads where she had greater access. He earned a reputation for exposing corruption. They started calling him "Honest Gabe" Lincoln, a designation he adopted with enthusiasm. He considered growing an Abe Lincoln beard, but Marianne squelched that notion immediately.

When her former senator won reelection after the upstart Democrat delivered on nothing but higher taxes, she moved over to his staff. Before long she ran for county commissioner and lost, then ran a second time and won. She climbed the political career ladder to state representative, state senator, U.S. House of Representatives, and finally to U.S. senator, fulfilling her one-time prophecy.

Gabe began writing a regular column that addressed national as well as local issues and started up his own blog that quickly became popular. Over time his nationally oriented installments were picked up by other publications, until he went full time as a syndicated columnist.

Marianne found favor with the President of the United States with her strong and diligent support of his policies. During her second term as senator, the Chief of Staff offered her the job of Deputy Chief of Staff for Operations.

Gabe and Marianne made love, not as often as that first year of marriage, but with great tenderness and skill. Again Marianne became pregnant, and again miscarried.

"No more trying," she said. "I can't go through that again."

"We could seek medical assistance," he offered. "We could pray for God to give us a child."

She shook her head bitterly. "I'm sorry, Gabe. I just can't. It hurts too much."

It upset him to think they might never have a child. But their lives were full of each other and their careers, and that made it easier for him to let her decision stand.

Chapter 9

Gabe's manager had sent out repeats of previous columns to cover for him, explaining that he was on vacation. Gabe announced he'd remain on vacation for a couple more weeks. Marianne took the same time off as well.

Their life together was subdued. They spoke of and did trivial things and held each other a lot, but never made love. Slowly he tried to deal with his emotions and become normal again. He felt like he was making progress, when Marianne started throwing up in the mornings.

She tried to hide it from him, but since they were always home together, he noticed quickly. Neither of them spoke about it. A dread seized his soul. He wanted desperately to know the answer to a question, but was too terrified to ask it.

Who fathered the baby?

Weeks passed. Gabe returned to writing. He couldn't bring himself to write about The Orgy, so he ignored it. Marianne also returned to work. Valiantly they struggled to feign normalcy. But when she continued to carry the baby long past the point of her other two miscarriages, he could pretend no longer.

"I can't go on," he said as she was about ready to leave for the day.

Her face clouded. "What do you mean?"

"You haven't lost the baby."

She gazed at him, waiting.

"If it were mine, you'd have lost it by now."

She scowled deeply and said, "How dare you assume that! You don't know."

"Come on, Marianne. I must have been the reason our babies didn't survive. That...other man has better seed."

"Gabe—"

"He gave you the greatest lovemaking experience of your life, and now he's given you the baby I couldn't."

"No, Gabe," she pleaded desperately. "You don't know that."

He left that day and stayed in a hotel room until he found an apartment.

Chapter 10

Gabe never answered the phone, allowing his voice mail to pick it up. Whenever Marianne left a message, he never called back. He never read or responded to her texts or emails, but he never deleted any of them. He spent his whole day observing the world through the Internet, then commenting on events in his column and blog.

He never attended church or prayed anymore. Not once did Marianne try to come by to see him. Was she respecting his privacy, allowing him the time alone he needed? Or did she just assume he'd refuse to see her, and her coming would only make matters worse? If that was her thinking, she was right. At least he thought she was right.

He knew he was in the wrong, but he couldn't bring himself to live with the humiliation. He knew that baby was not his. He'd assumed the problem with carrying the fetus was with Marianne. Damn chauvinist! Isn't that what every man thinks? But now he knew it was his own seed that was defective. It was one humiliation too much, and in spite of his love for Marianne, in spite of his lifelong commitment to the Master's teachings that required him to forgive seventy times seven, he could not let go of this one. Not because of anger toward Marianne, but because of shame for himself. He couldn't face her again.

The world recovered from the shocking images of the U.N. Orgy. Eventually Earth's population came to accept and trust the Taucetians as they trickled out exciting advances in technology. Some malcontents complained that the Taucetians were dolloping out their knowledge with an eyedropper, but for most people the frequency of change was more than enough to absorb, and they delighted in the changes.

One day Gabe received an invitation by snail mail to a private performance of a work of Human/Taucetian "music." The invitation came from the United Nations and was signed by the Secretary-General.

Since the Taucetians had been overwhelmed by human music, and humans had been overwhelmed by the Taucetian poetry of scents, adventurous artists had suggested combining the two in a coordinated orchestration. Taucetians would produce their pheromones and humans would perform some of the greatest music ever composed. Together they'd create an art form more powerful than either of the species could create separately.

Several experimental performances had been conducted with an extremely limited audience, and the effect was described as "transcendent." A couple of people at those performances had participated in the U.N. Orgy. They reported that the haphazardly combined scents and music of that shocking day could not match the power of the deliberately orchestrated combinations presented in those performances.

The event Gabe was invited to was black tie only. He'd done no socializing since he left Marianne and had let his beard grow wildly. Contact with his publisher was short and businesslike and by telephone or email. Everything possible was delivered to his door, and when he was forced to go into public, he wore scroungy clothes and sunglasses and spoke no more than absolutely necessary. Others shunned him as if he were homeless.

But with this invitation, Gabe rented a tuxedo, shaved his beard, and visited a salon to style his hair, before driving to New York for the private performance. He carefully resisted analyzing the boiling and conflicting emotions that motivated him to go, but in spite of his efforts, an occasional phrase or two bubbled into consciousness: even the score, understand what Marianne went through, get revenge, assert his manhood. Somehow he felt that they could never be on equal footing until he experienced what she had.

When he walked into the auditorium, he was shocked. There were no seats. There were couches, similar to what one would expect at an ancient Roman dining table.

That's when he was forced to confront what he already knew in the back of his mind, what he was about to experience.

He took his assigned couch fifteen minutes before the starting time, feeling ridiculous lounging in a tuxedo, studiously ignoring the older woman lounging to his left. The couch to his right was empty, as was the couch to her left.

It was a small auditorium in the United Nations Secretariat Building that would seat—or in this case lounge—no more than two hundred people. Some of the faces around him were familiar from the media gallery on the day of the Orgy. Some sat alone, others sat as couples. The orchestra screeched as the performers tuned up.

A few minutes before start time, the orchestra fell silent. A sudden surge of people entered the auditorium. Gabe snickered to himself over how many had waited to the last minute to arrive. Seconds later a lively buzz of conversation filled the room.

Suddenly Gabe wondered what he couldn't believe hadn't occurred to him the moment he received the invitation. Considering the impact of what he was about to experience, who was going to be sitting next to him that he would "share" the experience with?

He looked at the older woman to his left. She returned the gaze with an enigmatic expression and gave him an uncomfortable smile.

She must be thinking the same thing.

It all fell into place. He realized what he must have deliberately, subconsciously been hiding from himself. This was all a conspiracy, and Marianne was a part of it.

He was going to get his wish. He was going to even the score, more literally than he'd realized. He could almost hear Marianne's voice: "So you think it was such a wonderful experience for me, having wild sex with a short, fat, balding guy twice my age? Now you'll get a taste of what I went through."

It was vindictive. It was genius. He hated her for it. He loved her for it. He felt bitterness over it. He felt gratitude for the penance it could bring him.

He forced himself not to glance at the woman to his left. He couldn't bear dwelling on the conflicting emotions inside him, so he buried his nose in the program.

Violin Concerto in D, Opus 61, by Ludwig van Beethoven
First Movement

Performed by the New York Philharmonic Orchestra
Hoki Tokugawa conducting
Gertruda Wolfgaenger solo violin

with aromachromatic counterpoint by twelve Taucetian performers

Gabe smiled at the term *aromachromatic counterpoint.* He wondered who had coined such a high-sounding word for mating musk. He glanced at the program in the hands of the woman next to him. It was printed in Spanish. They'd gone all out for this shindig! Even custom-printed programs in one's native language.

Someone sat in the empty couch to his right. He had no desire to look up and see who it was. Probably a white-haired grandma that would zero her lust in on him.

A man slid into the couch to the left of the older woman. Since he was a safe two spaces away, Gabe looked at him as an excuse to avoid eye contact with the grandma to his right.

It was Mr. Uruguay.

The woman stared at the man with complex emotions twisting her face. He gazed back at her with a deep expectancy. She had to be his wife!

Suddenly Gabe felt a shiver run through his spine as he realized who must be sitting next to him. Carefully he turned his head, dreading what he might see, while at the same time feeling a powerful hope for what he might see.

Yes, it was Marianne.

She had on a satiny and glittering blue evening dress, bare-shouldered. It bulged at the midriff, belying her pregnant state. Her breasts were larger than what he was used to. The effect was pleasing.

Her eyes were moist as she looked at him with unmistakable longing. He wanted to tear his eyes away from hers, but it took several heartbeats to do it. Then he looked down and said, "This is quite the elaborate setup."

"I'm sorry, Gabe," she said, "but we had to do something. Look around you. Ours weren't the only lives devastated by what happened."

It was true. Virtually everyone in the auditorium was part of a couple who were staring into each other's eyes with poignant expressions or conversing with enthusiasm or embracing fiercely or arguing angrily. Many races and nationalities were represented in the mix of individuals—a whole United Nation's worth.

Mr. and Mrs. Uruguay spoke softly and tenderly to one another in Spanish.

Gabe returned his gaze to Marianne. "Okay, I admit. This was probably necessary." He surprised himself by feeling relief that their stand-off had been broken, even if by devious means. He waved his arm to indicate the audience. "Did all these couples need to be tricked back together?"

Marianne smiled. "No, but quite a few of them did. The rest just need to experience this together."

"Doesn't seem fair," Gabe said. He tried to sound like he was joking, but it didn't quite come out that way. "*My* first time is with my wife, but *yours* was... well..."

She gestured at Mrs. Uruguay. "Be my guest." There was no joking in her voice, and her expression was deadly serious.

Gabe glanced at the Hispanic couple. Mr. Uruguay noticed the gaze and returned it with an apologetic smile. Mrs. Uruguay turned her head to look. She and Gabe's eyes locked for an instant, then Gabe turned away. The woman's years showed, in spite of a desperate attempt to cover them up with just a little too much makeup, but he could see how in her prime she must have been beautiful. Especially her eyes, which gleamed with youthful vigor.

"I'm serious," Marianne said, almost inaudibly. "If that's what you need to feel redressed, please do it."

Gabe glanced at Mrs. Uruguay once more. His disinterest must have shown in his face.

"Right now you might think you don't want her," Marianne said. "But trust me, when the performance starts, she'll be the most desirable thing you've ever seen in your life."

Gabe turned away from Mrs. Uruguay with finality, slid his arm around Marianne, and held her firmly.

"With you sitting next to me?" He shook his head decisively.

The tenseness in her relaxed.

The lights lowered. Conductor Hoki strode to his position and bowed. The audience applauded in a dignified manner. He raised his arm to the side and twelve Taucetians flowed in like a medieval choir of monks. They took their places before the orchestra in a somber line, tiny eyes staring expressionlessly out into the auditorium. The applause strengthened as they entered, and reluctantly faded.

Conductor Hoki turned, raised his baton, and signaled the downbeat. The muffled thrumming of timpani seeped up from the floor into Gabe's bowels, and the gentle first notes of Beethoven's Violin Concerto drifted out, floating like a mist in the air. *Thrum thrum thrum thrum* said the timpani again. This concerto had always been one of Gabe's favorites from the classical repertoire. He wondered how much that influenced him to come.

For the first time the legendary aroma of the Taucetians entered Gabe's nostrils. It began as a gentle, pungent scent like incense burning in another room, and slowly grew into a tart, almost citrusy sensation that tingled his nasal membranes. His heart began to beat faster, and he felt his face going flush.

The four staccato sweeps of violin strings, followed by a sustained note, pierced into Gabe's heart, softening it from his months of bitterness. The twelve Taucetians stood unblinking and silent. Leisurely music meandered like a babbling brook toward the main theme, climbing slowly in volume. When a crescendo burst forth with a roll of the timpani, Gabe's heart leaped.

Out of a few notes of near silence, the melodic theme glided from the wind section, exotic and pompous at the same time. It repeated with a haunting countermelody weaving its way through the notes like ivy through a wrought iron fence. Gabe closed his eyes and found himself swaying slightly to the music's soothing touch. Marianne's hand brushed his arm, exploring up and down with provocative lightness of touch through his shirt and coat sleeves. The scent from the Taucetians had evolved to a bouquet of wildflowers, overly intense and bright in their effect. The sensations coaxed Gabe's eyes open.

The Taucetians had started to sway like seaweed in a gentle current. Many of the couples in the audience wrapped an arm around each other and exhibited tender affection with small, caressing gestures. Gabe ran his embracing hand softly up and down Marianne's side, feeling the sleek surface of her shimmering evening gown.

The orchestra visited several previously introduced themes in quick succession as Gertruda Wolfgaenger leaned into her instrument and tossed the first notes of her solo into the air with her bow. The alien scents dashed about in a coordinated series of aromas that Gabe couldn't identify. His head felt as if it were floating in the clouds.

Gertruda's first virtuoso section leaped into the auditorium, dancing about like a satyr with a panpipe, laughing and frolicking until exhausted, then collapsed into a single note heavy with vibrato that hung in the air with delicious tension. The note coaxed a powerful swell of emotion from Gabe's soul. He was full of affection for Marianne, full of joy that they were next to each other again, full of a feeling of rightness with the universe that contrasted sharply with the ugly twistedness of the past several months.

He faced her and gave her a heartfelt embrace, willing all his emotions to flow through that contact into her heart. She returned the embrace, and they kissed with deep passion, refamiliarizing themselves with each other in an exploration of tongues. Marianne slid her hands beneath his coat and caressed his shoulders, digging the balls of her fingers into him as if to claim him as her own again. Gabe's fingers of their own accord stumbled upon the zipper on Marianne's back, and guided it down her spine, releasing its tiny bronze teeth in a childlike burst of laughter.

No, it was Marianne who released that laugh, a sweet, soft giggle of delight.

The air reeked of roses and lime and Marianne. Gabe's hand swept across her naked back, and the fabric slipped from her chest, exposing her breasts. He had never seen such wondrous, perfect breasts before, even though they were the only ones he'd ever seen since his mother weaned him. Their pure white color promised the soft texture of infant skin. Their dainty areolas were drops of exquisite Swiss chocolate. He tasted them and gasped with the creamy earthiness of their flavor.

Marianne lifted her head with eyes closed, her neck a Michelangelo sculpture stretching vulnerably. He anointed it with kisses, fluttering and feathery, punctuating each kiss with a teasing lick of his tongue, then returned to the breasts and gave them the same attention, lest they suffer from jealousy.

Gertruda's bow caressed the violin strings with loving grace. She and Marianne played a duet with singing tones from the strings and ethereal gasps from Marianne's throat. A down-home smell of baking bread and dripping butter wafted over the auditorium, followed closely by a hint of roast turkey and cranberry sauce, with pine scented campfire smoke brushing at the edges.

Gabe's coat melted away at the touch of Marianne's hands and crumpled to the floor behind him. His bow tie seemed to thrash about in a frenzy until it flung itself to the floor. Buttons burst from their confines and sprayed about.

Marianne's hands danced across his chest, threading fingers urgently through its hairs. Gabe peeled her dress down to her waist, and they pressed their bodies together, breasts kissing breasts, hands snatching cries of pleasure from backs. With each touch of Marianne on his skin, a fireball of ecstasy erupted, every one a miniature orgasm of passion. Each brush of fingers Gabe visited on her body crackled with electrical energy, healing their damaged marriage with life-giving power. The intensity of his passion threatened to rupture his mortal frame. He jumped to his feet and pulled her up with him.

Her dress dropped to the floor with ease. She grabbed his shirt's lapels and whooshed them back until the shirt fell free, then yanked inside-out sleeves from his wrists. He fondled her hips as she jerked his belt loose and tore his pants open. They slid down his legs, and Gabe kicked at his shoes until they fled and kicked at his pants until they puddled on the floor. Marianne stepped out of her dress and plunged into his arms.

Their bodies melted together as they fell together onto his couch.

The orchestra played with astounding passion. Tears streamed from each performer's eyes as they flung their bodies about in a superhuman performance of their instruments. The Taucetians swayed vigorously, except for two that danced with mottled bellies and waggling snouts as they brushed against one another erotically with bodies and hands and teeth.

Firework bursts of aromas showered into the air, some delightfully familiar, some deliciously exotic. A quilt of multi-hued human skin writhed throughout the auditorium in a seething ocean of love. Gabe stared at the panorama with half-lidded eyes and partially opened mouth panting fiercely. It was all an abstract image to him, a living Sistine Chapel ceiling laid out on the floor, thrashing waves of exultation throughout the room.

His emotions throbbed entirely around Marianne, including her, encompassing her, meshing her soul with his. The combining of flesh to flesh and soul to soul became indistinguishable—they were one being swallowed up in overwhelming love. The combining of music and scents and arousal became a symphony of trans-human ecstasy. Their passions pulsed rhythmically with their bodies. Their love flowed back and forth, nurturing their spirits in a nutritious broth of unconditional acceptance.

The violin wept along with Gertruda. The timpani pounded along with hundreds of hearts. Fallen tears splashed about on the drum skins.

The Taucetian dove into the belly of its companion with razor-sharp teeth and tore out gulps of flesh. Gabe's loins exploded in a blinding flash of passion that caused him to convulse violently. Blast after blast electrified his body from head to foot. Marianne screamed with uncontrolled joy, her voice resounding with hundreds of others.

The entire auditorium writhed with a group orgasm that pulsed with divine power.

The concerto's first movement halted with a trio of orchestra hits that crashed through the auditorium and rattled the chandeliers. The two Taucetians lay in mounds of spined flesh. The orchestra members collapsed to the floor in exhausted victory. There would be no second or third movement.

The air was thick with invisible vapors of sensuous fragrances. The audience members cried out with afterglow delight and sprawled everywhere, intertwined in a single throbbing organism blazing with love for all creation, weeping profusely.

Gabe and Marianne panted desperately for many minutes, tangled together on his couch, drenched and glistening with sweat. The smell of sweet and musky perspiration was frosting on the orchestrated scents.

Marianne laughed weakly from lack of energy. Gabe caressed her buttocks with both hands, marveling at the perfection of the shape, at the exquisite feel of her cleft and gluteal folds. His chest surged with emotional shrapnel from his sexual explosion, deep and thrilling in its intensity. His soul burned with love for Marianne, love for everyone.

He glanced at Mr. and Mrs. Uruguay, who themselves lay knotted together in released passion, gazing at one another. The woman with her aging pastiness and liver spots and developing wrinkles, with her sagging breasts and greying hair, looked positively beautiful, as the youth of her eyes overflowed and encompassed her body. He saw her as Mr. Uruguay must still see her, as the vibrant Latino beauty that once clothed her gorgeous soul. Mr. Uruguay caught him staring at her and smiled. He, too, emitted a radiance that dignified the pudgy body, the silly mustache, the bald pate. Gabe oozed with love for them, until the goddess in his arms distracted him.

He thought of all the women in the history of mankind that had been celebrated for beauty and greatness and celebrity: Eve, the first woman; Sarah, wife of Abraham; Esther, Queen of Persia and Media; Helen of Troy; Bathsheba, the bittersweet love of King David; Cleopatra, the vixen of Roman emperors; the queen of Sheba; Mary, the mother of Jesus; Joan of Arc; Florence Nightingale—and of all the modern superstars who exemplarized the current ideal of female attractiveness.

None of them compared to Marianne in beauty, in body, in spirit, in mind. She lay there nude, a shrine to perfection, an icon of worship and love, an intimate soulmate of consummate empathy. He felt no bitterness, no anger, no resentment, no humiliation. To the depth of his soul he forgave her all that had tortured him, and to the depth of his soul he forgave himself for his selfishness, his pride, his pettiness, the hostility that had caused them so much grief and threatened their marriage.

He expressed his forgiveness in a gentle, lingering kiss on her exquisite lips. His soul felt cleansed, refreshed, pristine as Eden on the morning of creation.

He uttered a silent prayer of thanksgiving to God.

Chapter 11

Gabe moved back home with Marianne. Once again he attended church with her and prayed with her and made love to her. A few months later the baby was born, a boy.

No one was ever told of the suspected origin of the child, including the child himself. They named him Gabriel Jefferson Lincoln, Jr., and called him Jeff. Gabe raised him as his own son, because in every way that mattered, he was.

Afterword: What If?

Speculative fiction is the literature of asking "what if?"

Now technically, every fiction story is speculative, since by definition we always ask "what if?" to create fictional characters and settings and plots. But the genre of speculative fiction is defined to mean speculating "what if?" about things we normally don't think of as realistic or even possible.

Speculative fiction is a meta-genre, encompassing other genres of literature. These are science fiction, fantasy, and often horror is included.

Science fiction asks the question in the context of science. What if time travel were possible? What if we could travel to other stars faster than the speed of light? What if our artificial intelligence machines became self-aware? What if history unfolded in a way different from how it did? What if aliens came and tried to conquer us? What if we could genetically engineer ourselves into something else than human? What if an asteroid were on a collision course with Earth? What if the future looked like *such-and-such*?

Fantasy asks the question in the context of the fanciful, the impossible. What if magic were real? What if dragons existed? What if a Dark Lord created a magical ring to "rule them all"? What if an unsuspecting man married a woman who turned out to be a witch who could wiggle her nose and make impossible things happen? What if an astronaut splashed down and became marooned on a desert island where he found a bottle with a beautiful genie trapped inside? What if a lonely toymaker wished the marionette he just made was a real boy, and a fairy granted him his wish?

Horror is a little more complicated. There are two types of horror, supernatural horror and horrifyingly realistic horror where the monsters are human beings. The former fits neatly into the concept of speculative fiction. The latter gravitates more toward the genres of suspense or thriller. But when it *is* speculative fiction, horror asks the question, what if a great evil were to prey upon a community or group of individuals?

That's what I love about science fiction and fantasy. (I'm not so much a fan of horror.) It allows me to escape the confines of my routine life and go on voyages limited only by human imagination. I'd love to travel into space, but I never will physically. I escape the stifling oppression of planetary claustrophobia by going on imaginative flights of fancy in speculative fiction, whether to other worlds in our real universe or to worlds in alternate universes where magical things can happen.

That's what I love about *writing* speculative fiction. I can escape the claustrophobia of my human limitations and literally become God. With the mere utterance of words (or scribbling or typing), I can like God say, "Let there be..." and there *will* be! I create entire worlds, entire universes, entire peoples—human or otherwise. I declare who they'll be, what they'll do, and how their lives will unfold. I declare if they live or die.

We speculative fiction authors are capricious, vindictive, sociopathic Gods. We'll visit awful things on our creations, put them through extraordinary suffering, sweep their lives away without conscience. No jealous Old Testament God has an edge on us! Fortunately, our divinity exists only in our minds and the minds of the readers where it plays out with great passion, but causes no harm to real beings.

Every act of Godhood I commit begins with a seed, a kernel of asking the question "what if?" that precedes and makes possible the moment when I sit before my computer and instruct my divine fingers to "Let there be...!" It's such origins that I want to share with you for each of the stories included in this collection. **Warning: huge spoilers ahead!**

A Growth in the Backyard

Unlike many of my stories which arise from a pungent stew of conscious and subconscious meanderings, this story sprang directly from a single concrete, conscious "what if?" question.

Speculative fiction is riddled with stories where humans become possessed or controlled by an outside force, and almost universally it's considered a bad thing. Spock in *Star Trek* did not want that giant flying rolled oats thingy injecting itself in his back and controlling him with the threat of great pain. The shrill screech emanating from Donald Sutherland's mustachioed mouth at the end of *Invasion of the Body Snatchers* sent chills down everyone's spine as we realized humanity was doomed. The Borg were among the most menacing and frightening foes in science fiction villainy and disturbed us all when they turned Jean-Luc Picard into Locutus. That demon inside Linda Blair that caused her head to spin all the way around and vomit pea-green soup was so unwelcome, a priest gave his life to try and get rid of it.

My question was, what if human beings were taken over by aliens, and they liked it? What if it was a good thing? And this story was born.

How would it be a good thing? By enhancing our life experiences but retaining our humanity inside. Phil and Emily didn't become hollow shells pulled by alien strings. They remained Phil and Emily, their personalities and their love still intact. But they became Phil and Emily 2.0, enhanced in a way that transcended their pathetic fleshly lives. Which of us wouldn't want to experience an existence like they had after transformation?

They remained so much themselves that, in spite of Phil's rationalization, he *did* retain a human weakness: hypocrisy. He was willing to do to Ruthanne and her minions what they wanted to do to him, change him into something else against his will. And his rationalization was good! They drew first blood. They gave him no choice, so he gave them no choice out of self-defense. What else could he do?

Isn't that the rhetorical question rationalization always poses? *What else could I do?*

Eternal Rectangle

Once upon a time I joined a writers group, fancying myself a genius writer. I brought my first story to it called "Time Forks." Its origin was the question, "What if we travel back in time and change the past?"

This is practically always the question that gets asked for time travel stories. Those time travel paradoxes are endless fun.

But it always bothered me how cavalier, or even sloppy, the answer was that most time travel stories gave to that question. I asked myself, what would *really* happen?

The grandfather paradox screws everything up. If you go back and kill your grandfather before he sires your father, you can't exist to go back and kill your grandfather, so he did sire your father and you were born, so you can go back and kill your grandfather...

Scientifically, the grandfather paradox says one of two things. Either you can't go back and change anything because whatever you do already happened so your actions in the past are predetermined, or time travel is impossible.

Neither of those answers make satisfying stories. The former is as lame as a story ending with, "It was all a dream." The latter means you simply don't get to tell time travel stories.

Quantum physics rescues us with a third option through the many worlds interpretation, what regular people call alternate universes. According to that interpretation, every quantum event, which is pretty much everything that happens at a subatomic level, causes the universe to split into a bazillion universes where one of every conceivable possibility becomes real. Existence is an enormous time tree with branches numbering incomprehensibly large.

I explored this option for my story. You can go back in time and kill your grandfather and therefore cause yourself to never exist, but you still exist to come back in time to kill your grandfather. If that sounds like Schroedinger's cat, you're catching on.

In your original universe, your grandfather was not killed, your father was born, and therefore you were born. You existed. Then you chose to go back in time and kill your grandfather.

So far, so good.

But the instant you kill your grandfather, you've split the universe into two universes, the one where you didn't kill him and your father was born and you were born, and the universe where you did kill him and neither your father nor you exist. You the time traveler end up in the new universe with no father that sired you and no you that was born.

But that's all okay, because within those two universes combined, there's only one you. You were born in the original universe, grew up, traveled back in time, shot your grandfather, and ended up in the new universe.

One you.

Where it really gets messy is if you go back in time and make a less deadly change to the past. You'll split the universe, end up in the new universe, but you'll still be born in the new universe too—assuming the change you made wasn't too drastic. So which one is the real "you"?

According to the many worlds interpretation of quantum physics, all possible you's exist in endless alternate universes, each one where you made a different choice at any given moment. The "you" you think of as you heads off down one branch, but all the other you's that chose differently will head down other branches, never to meet again.

But they're still you, right? They're still your consciousness, and materialist science tells us your consciousness is merely the pattern of electrochemical pulses that keep shooting around in the neural network of your brain. The pattern is what makes your mind. All those consciousnesses are you.

So why can't you detect all of those you's? The same consciousness exists in all of them. Why do you only detect yourself down *this* one branch of the time tree as opposed to any other branch?

Why should I be the me that I am now instead of the me that chose to buy Microsoft stock early on? Not fair!

According to my story, it's because your consciousness actually chooses only one of the many branches you could go down. All the other branches exist, but the "you" in them are mindless artificial intelligence machines simulating conscious beings, but there's no soul inside. There is only one "you" who chooses one path.

In fact, the whole time tree is a static thing that just exists with no time at all. All the time branches exist simultaneously at once in a predetermined state. Time is an illusion our consciousness experiences as it zooms down one or another branch of the tree.

Our free will comes into play when our consciousness chooses which branch to head down. All futures exist, but our future is indeterminate because we make free will decisions at each juncture on which branch to take into the future.

If we somehow travel back in time, we merely retrace the paths we chose to take, and when we stop traveling, we can make new choices that end up taking us down new future paths. But the paths we originally took are still there, existing with bazillions of mindless us's acting them out in a predetermined fashion.

Jake in my original story comes to realize, if his soul is only in one branch, and all other him's in other branches are mindless automatons, and every individual has free will to choose whatever branch they want to go down, it's entirely possible he's in a branch of time that literally no other consciousness chose to go down. They all took different paths. He's alone in the universe, surrounded by soulless automatons that only seem real.

And he suffers a massive existential crisis.

I threw a love story in there too and brought it to my writers group, knowing they'd declare my work a masterpiece.

They didn't. They declared it crap (diplomatically). I went home and sulked for three days, then picked the story back up and contemplated the feedback they gave me.

It *was* crap. I tried to do too much in it. Maybe a novel would work, but not a short story.

I rewrote it. I massively rewrote it and made it orders of magnitude better. I took that notion of consciousnesses traveling down paths of time and made that my mechanism for time travel. I kept the love story and threw out the rest, and ended up with the masterpiece that sits before you today.

Well, that's what my writer's group called it (sort of) when I had them reread it.

I renamed it "Eternal Rectangle" as a play on the concept of an "eternal triangle," because Jake was a fourth participant in an endless loop of trying to help resolve an unresolvable love triangle among friends. It truly became an *eternal* rectangle, thanks to his time-travel meddling.

Solar Butterfly

This haunting story came from a mixture of sources, some of which I don't even remember and can only reverse engineer what I might have been thinking.

The obvious elements are solar sailing in space, genetic engineering, a desire to travel throughout the solar system, and a story about isolation. What motivated me to bring all these elements together into this story, I honestly can't remember.

I can't help but think the dream sequence from Terry Gilliam's *Brazil* where the winged man flies through the clouds was an influence in coming up with the Solar Butterfly, but I don't remember following that line of thinking. It was certainly a conscious decision to make the dream sequences of the Solar Butterfly flying over Earth an homage of sorts to those scenes in *Brazil*.

Employing reverse engineering, it's possible my original question was, "What if we could fly in space like a butterfly?" or at least, "What if there was a way humans could live in space naturally?" I have little doubt Frederik Pohl's novel *Man Plus* about genetically engineering a man to be able to live naturally on Mars had an influence. But whatever the original seed of the idea was, I do remember why I made the choices I made in the execution of it.

I asked myself, why would someone go out and live in space? That's how Elaine came into existence. That motivated the story of her entire life. Treated brutally by parents, then peers, then lovers, and by life generally, suffering from tremendous PTSD, she centered her entire career and life around the desire to escape humanity.

That's when I dreamed up the Applied Morphogenetics field, the mechanism by which she'd be able make her escape a literal reality.

It also created the character Monica. Elaine had experienced nothing but trauma from the male half of humanity and wanted no part of them. But there was still the other half of humanity. The character Monica existed so Elaine could attempt to find connection with that other half, but failing since she was fooling herself that she was lesbian. She therefore became totally isolated from all humanity.

My choice to include that relationship was inspired by the scene in *The Color Purple* where Celie and Shug Avery have intimate relations. Celie was in the exact same position as Elaine, having been traumatized by men all her life, but she found salvation in connections with women. Alas, Elaine had no such luck. She was too damaged by then.

Elaine had to complete her escape from humanity, had to impose total isolation on herself, had to discover the emptiness and futility of the prison she'd condemned herself to, had to hit rock bottom, before she could begin to heal.

Her self-defeating goal was not in vain. Not only did she achieve the epiphany she needed in the cold depths of space, but her efforts had the serendipitous blessing of making her the spiritual mother of a race of beings she could connect with at last.

I've adapted this story to a screenplay. I consider it my best screenplay to date. I hope one day you'll be able to see the breathtaking movie it would be, and know that you got to experience its origins here in this short story.

Bokev Momen

This story is an odd duck. It's the science fiction flavor of speculative fiction, obviously, but it's also a flavor of speculative fiction that I'm not sure is recognized as a subgenre.

As far as I know (which could very well be wrong, but what can I do about that, not knowing?) I invented the genre. I've tried to coin a name for it that doesn't string too many words together. Theological speculative fiction? Three words seem too many.

Theo-spec? Sounds like a character name. Theodore Speck.

I invented the subgenre when I wrote my novel *Brother Brigham*. It's as odd a duck as this story. It's essentially science fiction, but for Mormon theology, not science. It asks the question, "What if a descendent of Brigham Young received a ghostly visitation from Brigham Young commanding him to practice polygamy?"

To a nonbeliever in Mormonism, it slides neatly into fantasy, but to a believer, everything that happens in it is theoretically possible according to Mormon theology. So I can't really call it fantasy, because that depends on your point of view. And it's certainly not science fiction, because there's no science fictional element in it. Some have tried labeling it Mormon horror because of the supernatural element, but I don't buy that one either.

It's what I named it: theological speculative fiction. It speculates like science fiction does with science, but instead speculates about Mormon theology, treating it as real as science. In the parlance of the fantasy genre, I set up the rules of my world to be the rules of Mormon theology, then follow them faithfully as I tell the story.

"Bokev Momen" is the same thing, except it *does* include a strong science fictional element. It's a hybrid of science fiction and my coined genre theological speculative fiction.

The surface story is pure science fiction, posing the question, "What if aliens abducted a Mormon missionary?" How I developed the story from exploring that question is pretty obvious and needs no elaboration.

But there's a subtext story that those who are not aware of Mormon beliefs could very well miss. Although not official doctrine, there's a strong sense among Mormons that Jesus Christ is the Messiah for all planets in the universe. (Official doctrine is agnostic on this issue, focusing only on the doctrine that Jesus is *our* Savior.)

So my theological "what if?" question was, if Jesus is the Savior of all worlds, what would that look like to all the other planets where he wasn't born and lived out his life on? Would their Bible tell stories about the "Anointed One" living on a planet orbiting *that* star in the sky?

The culture of the Alliance is my story's exploration of that question, where the believers in the Anointed try to discover which planet is the one their Savior lived on. But as on Earth, that's just one of many religions in the galaxy.

I threw in the organic technology of the Alliance just because I wanted to do something different than the usual tin cans everybody flies around in space with. I justified their technological development going that route, when tin cans should be simpler and more convenient to deal with, like a car is simpler than a horse, by the fact that their scientists could not figure out the principles of faster-than-light travel (like ours hasn't yet), but they discovered the existence of a species that lives natively in space and can hyperphase, so they domesticated them and genetically engineered them to *be* their FTL spacecrafts. From that they developed other types of organic technology, like lightstems and smashball spheres.

Incidentally, every alien name in the story, from the characters Eteaki, Pezeli, and Orbanek, to the heaven carriage Glaittli, to the names of the species Tetzl, Murdzak, and Kuryluk, to the catalog number of "Irf" with Raviza and Kirkil, were not inventions of mine. Every one of them are real last names on Earth, either people I knew personally or out of the phone book. They're spelled exactly as the real name is spelled, with the exception of Orbanek which came from Urbanek. But that name with "urban" in it sounded too terrestrial for me, so I changed the first letter to make it seem more alien.

Mary Mother of Nanites

Nanotechnology is the coolest technological concept humans have devised—at least that's how I feel. So naturally I had to write a story about it.

Advanced nanotechnology will transform our lives as profoundly as the industrial revolution and the computer revolution. Maybe more. It will permeate our lives. Literally, physically permeate everything, including ourselves.

The Internet will become a network of nanites that communicate with each other with connections exponentially more complex than the human brain. They will infuse our bodies and take over our personal health care, performing as souped-up antibodies and white blood cells and repairing our injuries and aging deteriorations in ways that appear miraculous.

I hope.

This story addresses the tip of the iceberg of issues that will arise from nanotechnology. It focuses on privacy, an issue even more critical today than when I wrote the story years ago. When our personal nanites inside our bodies are in constant, direct contact with all the nanites in the world, where do you go for privacy?

Thus the zones of privacy in my universe were born, places where the world's nanites are not allowed to enter.

Obviously churches as sanctuaries would be among those zones. Certainly the Catholic confessional, which the world's Web does *not* need to be listening in on!

But lurking in the shadows is that old bugaboo, the conscious machine. With such a massive, intricate network of microscopic computers, absolutely, positively the threshold was long ago passed where the computing power was enough to give rise to a conscious machine, according to the predictions of AI experts.

So my question was, what triggers that transition from mindless machine to consciousness?

Mary becomes the mother of the conscious nanite hypermind because of her circumstances and her three years of pleading. "Ask and ye shall receive." I had to name her Mary because of the witty title it let me give the story. And since "Mary, mother of God" tends to be a Catholic phrase, and the confessional is such an iconic entity, Catholicism was the religious context I told the story in.

It's a thinly veiled subtext to the story that we're seeing the birth of the new God here. What kind of God will it be? Is Father Muriel justified in being horrified by its existence?

Eyes of the Beholder

This is the closest I've ever come to writing erotica (daydreams and night dreams excluded). But not because I wanted to write erotica. I didn't *not* want to write it either. Whatever's right for the story.

The speculation in this story is about how two radically different cultures meeting for the first time end up misunderstanding each other. But first contact stories are almost a dime a dozen. I didn't want to write yet another rehashing of the concept.

So my question was, what sorts of art forms would aliens have, and how would they impact humans? Thus the Taucetians have a language consisting of a combination of song, body movement, chemical tastes, and scents, and their art forms developed accordingly.

But why should this exploration be a one-way street? Wouldn't humans have art forms unfamiliar to the aliens, and how do they impact them? In this story, the art form unfamiliar to the aliens is music, something which humans have developed orders of magnitude beyond the Taucetians, for whom music never achieved the status of an independent art form. Their minds had a blind spot to the notion of creating art through music.

Then I asked, what if humans and aliens combined their unique art forms into a new one? Like cinema combines photography, storytelling, theater, music into one art form, with a synergistic effect that's undeniably powerful. Would the combined human/alien art form have a synergistic effect greater than the sum of its parts?

My story's answer: a resounding *yes!*

The combined art form had such a powerful effect, it broke down all emotional barriers and drove both humans and Taucetians into the most intimate forms of interactions they were capable of—squared!

After laying that foundation for the story, it was only a matter of putting the puzzle pieces together. I wanted an alien species that wasn't cliche. No Star Trek humans with make-up appliances on their foreheads. No scary reptilian monsters. No shining, angelic beings. No squidlike things. I wanted something serious science fiction doesn't show us very often.

I chose comical.

I think maybe, not consciously for sure, but subconsciously I might have patterned the Taucetians after Big Bird on Sesame Street. His beak became a crocodilian snout with sharp teeth. His yellow feathers became dingy yellow anenome-like spines. His pear-shaped body and unusual height remained. The flowing gait of the Taucetians is definitely Big Bird's.

The legs are stumpier than Big Bird's, and the beady eyes are not his. In hindsight, they remind me more of the beady eyes of the penguin in Wallace and Gromit's "The Wrong Trousers."

I designed the Taucetians to look comical, until one sees them in action in real life when they become majestic, as a metaphor for how judging a book by its cover is an unwise thing to do.

As for their reproductive cycle, I wanted something totally whacko, totally shocking, so it could be utterly misconstrued as the opposite of what it was. First contact has got to be a fragile moment where misunderstandings galore crop up between two alien species (Picard said so, so it must be true), and this misunderstanding was a whopper! What could be more opposite from the tender, compassionate, loving act of human sex than ripping out and swallowing the guts of your lover with your crocodilian mouth?

So I wrote a story that would be rated NC-17 if faithfully filmed, because let's get real—first contact could very well be a disaster.

That was the alien side of development. The human side was the couple who stood in as our personal connection with the experience of first contact gone awry. I wanted Gabe and Marianne to be Christian. I wanted them to be conservative. I wanted them to value saving oneself for marriage and coming to their wedding night as virgins. I wanted to create a relationship that was faithful and tender and beautiful, perhaps even holy, and I hope I achieved that.

So when their lives are ruptured to the core with the shocking events in the United Nations building, it's damage that threatens to be unhealable, that takes a transcendent kind of experience to make whole again, as the combined art of humans and Taucetians proves to be. I suspect there's a Fall of Man and Atonement of Jesus metaphor in there somewhere, but I never consciously thought of that while writing it.

The music I chose are two of my favorite pieces of music, the Jupiter movement from Holst's *Die Planeten* (*The Planets* to you German-challenged folk) and Beethoven's violin concerto. They stir me greatly when I listen to them, so to me they were good candidates to mix in with the Taucetian art for maximum potency.

Go ahead, listen to them, see if you agree. You can find them on YouTube.

Time Forks

I decided to throw a bonus story in, "Time Forks," which is the first draft of "Eternal Rectangle" that my writers group declared "crap" (diplomatically). It comes up next.

I decided to place it after the Afterword, which of course violates the definition of "Afterword." But I wanted to have my say on where "Eternal Rectangle" came from first before everyone reads the original version.

This is a study in my writing process. I hadn't read it since I first wrote and rewrote it into "Eternal Rectangle" and remembered almost nothing about it. I was shocked to discover how different the two stories are. They don't even have the same main character.

That experience of writing a first draft, having it constructively criticized by pointing out how it didn't work when I thought it was a great story, sulking for three days, then biting the bullet and rewriting it into a version so different it required a different title, was the first time I experienced that sort of evolution of a story. It caused me to see writing in a whole new way and propelled me into a quantum leap of superior writing. I would not be the writer I am today without that experience.

I hope including it can be inspirational to aspiring writers who dash off a first draft, have people read it, and walk away depressed that they didn't call it genius. (I still go through that same cycle with each of my first drafts, even today. I should know better by now.) First drafts are *supposed* to be crap.

They're when you shackle and muzzle the editor in your head and let your creative side run wild, vomiting the story onto the paper—or screen. It's in the rewrites where you unchain the editor in your head and polish it up into a work of genius.

Now aspiring writers, go therefore into the world and *Let there be...!*

After all, you are Gods.

Bonus Story

Time Forks

Being a case study of D. Michael's writing process. Like watching sausage being made, it's not a pretty sight. This is the first draft of the story "Eternal
Rectangle" included in this collection. D. Michael's writers group declared it
"crap" (diplomatically).

Katie looked so beautiful in her bridal gown, but Derek didn't look good in
the groom's tuxedo. Because he wasn't the groom. He just should have been.

His heart twisted within his chest as he stared at the back of Anthony's
head. On the one hand Anthony was his best friend since before high school.
They even decided on the same major—Psychology. On the other hand, Anthony had stolen the girl Derek loved and therefore was a candidate for hatred
of the darkest kind.

And when that kiss came, Derek was very close to feeling that hatred. But
it was fleeting. He knew he could never hate Anthony. But he also knew their
friendship was over. There was no way Derek could be around him any more
than around Katie and not feel pain.

The kiss was over and the congregation cheered as they jumped up and
started to file out of the church. As Derek stood, his roommate Jake of one

month slapped him on the back and said, "Tough break, buddy. You want to hang around any longer?"

"No, let's get the hell out of here."

They filed past the crowd lining up for the traditional rice tossing and ducked around the corner to Jake's pickup. "One week!" Derek spat as Jake drove down the street. "I lost out by one week!"

"How's that?"

"He asked her out before me by one week. She told me if I had asked her out first, she may never have gone out with him."

"Ouch!" commiserated Jake.

Derek sulked as he sadistically played back eight months of memories with Katie. The first date, not even knowing that Anthony had beat him to the punch. The realization they both had that they were dating the same girl. The escalating competition that started out a friendly contest but ended up getting desperately serious. Both he and Anthony deciding to stay over summer semester when they heard Katie was. And all that time Derek thought he was winning. Didn't Katie tell him once, "I can't imagine loving anyone more than you"? But he heard through the grapevine what she said to her roommates: "I love Derek. He's a great guy. So why can't I bring myself to marry him?"

And she married Anthony instead.

"I never even asked her to marry me," Derek said as Jake parked on the curb next to their house. "I should have at least asked her."

"Why didn't you?"

"She would have said no."

"Then what does it matter?"

"Because at least I could go through life knowing I asked her."

Jake rolled his eyes.

Derek went to bed early that night and got up late the next morning, missing his Dysfunctional Psychology class. He wandered in late to English Lit, a general ed requirement he had put off for two years, and sat in the back row next to a sweet young thing who smiled at him and went back to furiously taking down every word the professor spoke. Derek didn't even pull out his notebook. This whole semester was shot and he knew it. How was he expected to concentrate on school as he slowly lost Katie? He was probably going to fail every class, but what did it matter? His whole reason for living had consummated her marriage last night with another man.

This class had always been boring, but with the addition of pain and despair it was insufferable. Each tick of the clock seemed to drag out for an hour. Yet in the presence of Katie time would fly by like a Concorde jet. Eight months had come and gone like a whirlwind. Derek began to wonder what the mechanism behind this phenomenon could be. Everyone had experienced it: time slowing down or speeding up, depending on how boring or interesting the immediate environment was. Did the mind just perceive the flow of time differently? Or was there actually some physical change of velocity?

Being a Psychology major, Derek couldn't resist pursuing this line of thought, even though the professor was covering material for the next mid-term. Illusion or actual change in the flow of time? Probably most people—scientists included—would assume illusion. But what if time actually did slow down or speed up based on the state of the mind?

To make that true, time would have to be a static thing that consciousness moved along. After all, what if the sweet young thing sitting next to him is fascinated by this endless lecture on Updike and time is flying by like crazy for her, while he lay bogged down in some chronological eddy? Time couldn't speed up for her and slow down for him if time were the actual thing speeding up and slowing down. So time would have to be motionless, like a highway heading into the future, and everyone's mind was a vehicle cruising along it. Some minds, like Derek's, were Jaguars, and others, like that idiot in front of him who always asked stupid questions, were Pintos.

But if that were true, then there should be a way for the mind to control its speed through time. It obviously did so subconsciously, slowing down with boredom, speeding up with excitement. And how many people had said time seemed to stand still during a car accident or some other crisis? If it could be done subconsciously, couldn't a person be trained to control movement through time?

And would it be possible to become so bored that time stood still?

Having already experienced half a semester of English Lit, Derek thought it might indeed be possible. This class right now might be the perfect environment to try an experiment. Derek stared at the clock and began self-hypnosis techniques. Boredom! Boredom! You are so bored! Time is dragging, dragging, forever, eternally. This is so boring, time is stopping—

RING!

Damn! Foiled by his own phenomenon. His speculations had been so fascinating to him that the rest of the hour had flown by. Class dismissed.

But he had to admit he didn't see any change in the movement of the second hand during that short time he had tried. Of course there wasn't any change. The whole thing was silly. But he knew when he got home that he would discuss his ideas with Jake the Physics major. Jake should be able to add insights into the nature of time that Derek would never know. Yes, Derek knew he would pursue his speculations because it was something interesting enough to occupy his mind and make him forget about his longing for Katie.

As Derek and Jake lounged around the living room, winding down from another day on campus, Derek recounted his speculations on time and consciousness. Jake sat quietly staring at him without expression. When Derek finished, Jake didn't move.

"So that's about the size of it," Derek said to break the silence. "Silly, huh!"

Jake jumped out of his chair and started pacing around. "This is great! This is fantastic!" He stopped in front of Derek. "This could explain everything!"

"What the hell are you talking about?"

"Quantum physics. The many worlds interpretation. Consciousness and artificial intelligence." Jake nodded his head slowly as if he were working out a new detail with each nod.

"You want to explain what you just said?"

He sat back down and faced Derek. "How much do you know about quantum physics?"

"About as much as I know about Updike."

"Huh?"

Derek waved him off. "Private joke. I don't know much about quantum physics."

"Well—"

"Keep it simple, okay?"

Jake nodded. "Quantum physics describes the behavior of subatomic particles, and their behavior is very weird. So weird it sounds like science fiction. And nobody really understands what quantum physics is trying to tell us about what kind of a universe we live in. But there are several interpretations. The one I like is the many worlds interpretation."

"You mean like Mars and Jupiter?"

"No, I mean like parallel universes. Whenever there are multiple possibilities that can happen, they all happen, but in different universes. You see, our universe splits into many universes, and in each of these universes one possibility becomes a reality."

"You're right, this does sound like science fiction."

"It gets worse. This splitting means that multiple copies are made of everything that exists in the universe. That includes you and me. And every time we have a choice to make, we actually choose all the possibilities."

Derek perked up. "Wait a minute. Doesn't that toss free will out the window?" Derek always loved a free will debate. "That means every possible choice we could make, we do make in some universe."

"That's what it means."

"That sucks! It means in some universe I did ask Katie out sooner and I did beat Anthony to the punch and Katie married *me*."

"That's right."

"But I want to be in that universe!"

"You are. The you that chose to ask her out earlier."

"It's not me! It's some impostor enjoying the perks of marriage with her. I want to be that person."

"Then you should have been the one to choose it."

"But I did. He did. Geez! I can't, because he did. I have no free will!"

Jake shrugged.

"I don't like the many worlds interpretation."

"Well, there are other problems with the theory, too."

"No kidding," Derek said. "Like where do all those universes come from?"

"Yes, and what causes the splitting to take place, and how does the entire universe split all at once when Einstein said no influence can travel faster than the speed of light, and—"

"Hold it, you're losing me."

"Oh, sorry. Well, don't worry about all that. I'll just say that there are problems with the many worlds interpretation, but what you've said made me think of a solution."

"And what's that?" Derek said, feeling proud that he had made the Physics major think of something he had never thought of before.

"You said our consciousness travels through time like a car travels down a highway."

"Make it a Jaguar."

"DeLorean."

Derek laughed.

"So this DeLorean is heading down the highway. Well, have you ever heard of just one highway? Don't they fork off right and left, and cars choose which path they'll take?"

Derek's face brightened up.

"Our consciousness travels along a highway like you said, but it also confronts paths that fork, and must choose which way to go. The forks already exist. All time and all possibilities exist right now, but our consciousness only travels down one path at any given moment. Like a car on the highway."

"But you said we exist in all the universes, and each copy of us made a different choice in each universe. We're not just one car that chooses one path. We're split into multiple cars that take all the paths."

Jake smiled. "Our physical selves exist in each universe. Every universe has a body and a working brain exactly like ours, but only one of them actually contains a consciousness."

Derek studied him intensely. "So our true self is like this ghost that flows through bodies, controlling them by choosing which fork to take rather than actually powering the movement of the body."

"Physicists would call it a ghost in the machine, and almost all of them denounce that philosophy."

"Yes, I know. Psychologists too."

"Their reason is they can't see how a ghost could manipulate a physical body. There's been no detection of energy interacting with the body that could be the ghost controlling it."

"But if the ghost is just coasting along within already existing bodies, there wouldn't have to be any interaction between ghost and body."

"Exactly!"

"But if only one copy of ourselves has our consciousness in it, what are all the other bodies doing? Dropping down dead?"

"They're doing exactly what scientists believe bodies with no souls have been doing all along. Most scientists think our minds are nothing more than software programs running on nature's computer, the brain. But some people reject that theory, because they think it can't account for all the experiences of consciousness. What I'm saying is, both are true. The human brain functions on its own as a computer running artificial intelligence software—or in this case I guess you'd call it natural intelligence software, since nature programmed it. But only one of those biological machines is self-aware. The one down the fork of time that our consciousness has decided to travel."

"Hey, I like this! This preserves free will. Our minds have complete control over which fork we'll take. Every other fork is just a robot-like thing going through the motions, but in our fork we have a real consciousness experiencing everything."

"I like it too," Jake said, "because it resolves the dilemmas that bothered me about the many worlds interpretation. I don't have to wonder what causes the split or how it propagates through the universe nonlocally. The forks and pathways of time exist all at once. Nothing splits or changes. We just travel along the path of our choice and observe what's down there, like tourists sightseeing along a highway."

"So how do we prove it?"

Jake shrugged. "If we can consciously control how fast we move along the path of time, then that would be evidence that we're on the right track."

"Let's do it!"

"How? I don't have the slightest idea how to control it."

"But subconsciously our minds do. We just have to train ourselves to do it consciously."

"And how do we do that?"

Derek sat back and put his hands behind his head. A devious grin formed on his face. Now it was the Psychologist's turn to shine.

"Yes?" said Jake expectantly.

"Biofeedback!"

"That's it? But it's just a PC."

Derek shrugged. "Yeah, so?"

"I expected some giant machine with blinking lights and Frankenstein probes connected to my body."

"Geez, don't you know everything's done on PCs these days?"

Jake eyed the computer and the cables sticking out from it. "So what do we do now?"

"We hook one of us to the cables and take some general readings of our metabolism. When boredom sets in, we capture the readings at that point. Then you or I consciously try to duplicate that state of mind by recreating the same readings that we captured. Simple as that."

"Mm-hmm," Jake said without conviction. "And you think this will really work?"

"There's no reason it shouldn't—if our theory's any good. Just a matter of time to get the readings right."

"Just how much time do we have?"

"I already had this hour reserved each day this week. So we have five hours to make it work."

"You already had five hours reserved? What *were* you going to do with them?"

Derek knew he had a sheepish look on his face, because that's how he felt all over. "I had a project I needed to get done for class."

"And when are you going to do your project now?"

"Don't worry about it. Maybe I can make this my project instead. It's more important anyway." He brushed the issue away with a wave. "So who's going to be the guinea pig?"

"How about you? You know what the hell you're talking about."

"Then you'll have to learn a few things about running this software." They sat before the computer monitor, and Derek showed Jake the basics on his biofeedback program. How to start and stop the recording of readings. How to capture a particular reading. How to turn the sound off and on. "When the sound is on, the speakers make a tone that will rise as I get further away from the state of mind I'm trying to duplicate, and lower as I get closer. When I match the state, the tone starts to beep."

"Gotcha. Doesn't look too hard."

"Well, the software's not too fancy. But we don't need anything more than basic readings to do what we're trying to do. Now." Derek grabbed a handful of cables and held them up. "We need to hook me up to all these sensors and then we can start."

Jake helped Derek attach all the finger and arm and chest and head sensors. Derek imagined he was a hardened criminal being hooked up to a lie detector. They would catch him in his lies and he would have to confess to being the mastermind behind the JFK assassination. But not if he could beat the machine. There were ways...

"I think that's all of them," Jake said.

"Are we getting any readings on the monitor?"

"Yeah, there's your heartbeat, and your respiration rate, and your skin temperature, brain waves even—all sorts of stuff."

"Good! Now start recording and we'll see if I can't get into a state of boredom."

Jake clicked with the mouse and the recording started. Derek squirmed in his chair until he felt comfortable. Both of them sat motionless for several minutes.

"Is there anything you want me to do to help?" Jake said suddenly. It jolted Derek alert.

"Yeah, shut up so I can get bored. Or better yet, keep talking so I can get *really*—"

"Don't say it!"

Derek smiled. "Just sit quietly and don't distract me."

The silence resumed. Derek sat still, but let his eyes wander around the small lab room. There was a giant wall clock above and to the left of Jake. Good! He could use that to detect any change in the movement of time—if any ever happened.

Minutes ticked by. Jake yawned, and that made Derek yawn. Jake's eyelids started to droop a little. Derek stared at the clock, letting the sweep of the second hand mesmerize him. Jake's eyes gave up the fight and slumped closed. His head bobbed a little. Derek felt his own eyes go out of focus as a prelude to falling asleep. He jerked them back into focus and let them wander again. He watched the rhythmic jumping of the bar on the graph that represented his heartbeat. The program's sound was off so the room was dead silent. He looked at the clock again and saw that they had been there twelve minutes so far. Forty-eight to go in this hour. Forty-eight minutes could be a long time with nothing to do but sit and stare. Of course, that was the idea.

Jake began to snore faintly. Derek studied the pattern of dots in one of the hanging ceiling tiles. He thought he could make out Richard Nixon's nose in one corner. His chair creaked as he adjusted his posture. Another check of the time and one lousy minute had passed. If this theory were correct, it was sure working right now.

Jake let out a harsh snort and woke himself up. He looked at Derek as if he wanted to say something, but didn't dare speak. The eye contact grew too long and too uncomfortable, so they both began studying minute details of the room at random. Derek studiously avoided the clock because he knew if he kept watching it the minutes would tick by at a glacial rate. Never mind that's what he wanted to happen to get good readings. He was bored.

"A watched pot never boils," popped unbidden into Derek's mind. Maybe that truism was valid after all if their theory was correct. What could be more boring than staring at a pot with water in it? The person staring could be slowing down time and dragging out the boiling process for an hour. Look away and let time speed up, then that pot will boil.

Impulsively he checked the clock again. Eighteen minutes, forty-two left. Their theory had to be correct. It couldn't possibly be an illusion that time was dragging out this much. He was definitely bored, time was definitely dragging. They must have several minutes of good data they could use as a baseline now.

"Alright, that's enough!" Derek said, startling Jake. "I was plenty bored. We ought to have a good set of readings somewhere in there to use."

"You're the boss," Jake said as he stopped recording mode.

"Let's play that back and see what we have. Do it quadruple speed."

Jake obeyed and they stared at the monitor as it replayed the eight or nine minutes they had recorded. Derek's metabolic readings visibly went into a depressed state. As it reached a low point and started climbing up, Derek said, "That's it. Go back a few seconds, yeah, there." He gazed at the frozen moment in metabolic time and smiled. "That's a good one. We'll use those readings for our baseline."

"Great. Now what do we do?"

"Here, give me the mouse." Derek did some expert clicking and set up a split screen with the frozen baseline readings on the top half and his current live readings pulsing away on the bottom half. Then he turned the sound on. A gentle sine wave tone floated from the speakers.

"Now I have visual and auditory feedback. I'll try to get my readings to match the baseline ones. The closer I get, the lower the tone gets. When I match the readings, the tone starts beeping."

"And once again I sit here and do nothing."

"Sorry," Derek said with a shrug.

Jake adjusted his chair so he could watch the monitor instead of his roommate. They both settled in and Derek started to concentrate on the pair of readings. At first the tone fluctuated all over the place as his readings bounced around with no pattern to them. But after several minutes he started recognizing the feeling that brought the tone lower in pitch and his live data closer to the captured data. He began to consciously moderate his readings in the direction he wanted. Jake's eyes widened and he smiled.

The tone dropped steadily in pitch. The live readings depressed as Derek felt himself becoming dull and listless inside. Soon the low pitched tone began to beep on and off. "You did it!" Jake cried. "You got them to match!"

"Alright!" Derek cried, sending his readings scrambling again. They jumped up and shook each other's hand.

"Step one accomplished," Derek announced. He checked the clock and saw they had about a half an hour left. "Let me practice that again a couple more times, then I'll see if I can go past the baseline readings and get even deeper into boredom."

He made two more attempts and succeeded sooner with each one. On the second attempt he tried immediately to get the tone to go lower than the point where it beeped. The tone fluctuated around the matching point, going from beeping to a steady sound over and over. Finally the tone dropped lower and the beeping stopped permanently. He was breaking new ground.

Jake looked as if he were holding his breath as he watched and listened. Derek concentrated hard and continued to drop the tone. It was nearing the point at which human hearing would no longer detect it.

Suddenly a knock came at the door. It threw Derek completely out of his state of mind. His eyes shot up to the clock. Their hour was over.

"I can't believe you got it to go down so low," Jake said. Eagerly he added, "Did you notice anything about the flow of time."

"No, I'm sorry. I was just concentrating on getting the tone lower. Tomorrow we can pay attention to time."

The knock came again, more agitated. "Go let him in, Jake. I'm going to save these baseline readings so we can use them tomorrow." He clicked SAVE as a grad student burst in and spoke unkind words about the relationship between undergrads and their mothers.

Derek started the next day's session by dropping the tone well below their baseline readings, as he had done yesterday, and capturing the new extreme readings to use as their next baseline. Then he tried several times to drop the tone even lower. Each time he succeeded he saved a new baseline.

"This is all well and good," Jake said with frustration, "but when are we going to test our theory?"

"You're right, Jake. I was getting carried away, seeing how low I could go."

"Well, this isn't limbo, so let's move on."

"This time I'll go as low as I can, but I'll only use the tone for feedback. I'll keep my eyes on the clock instead of the monitor and see if I can notice any change in the movement of the second hand."

"Now we're talking!"

The two of them took positions, and Derek slipped into his altered state again. The tone almost sounded like a slide whistle, it dropped so fast. Derek kept his eyes locked on the second hand, sweeping along as merrily as it ever had. He dropped the tone and dropped it, watching the clock. Did it happen? Was the second hand moving slower? He tried dropping the tone some more, and he swore he could see a difference. But the change was so subtle he couldn't be sure if he were imagining it or not. He reached about as low as he had gone before, and he estimated that the clock hand seemed to move about 70% of its normal pace, but he still wouldn't lay odds it was real. It could still be an illusion borne of intense expectation.

"Well?" Jake asked.

"I'm not sure. I thought I saw a change, but I can't tell for sure."

"How can you tell for sure?"

"I need to learn to drop the tone faster. I need to see a definite change in how fast the second hand moves."

He tried again, marginally increasing his transition into the low state of mind. It had to be working. It sure looked like it was working, but not enough. He had to be sure.

He tried again, and again, making small gains. That stubborn second hand teased him, slowing just a touch, saying, "Catch me if you can."

Derek jumped up and whooped. He danced around, hollering. The feedback tone shot up to a shrill pitch. Jake gaped at him in shock. Suddenly Derek flopped into his chair and froze, staring at the clock. The pitch of the tone nosedived to a barely audible growl.

Derek leaped into the air again. "I did it!" he shrieked."I saw it! It slowed down."

"You did?"

"I saw it! It must have slowed down by half. I could tell, it was definite. I slowed time down!"

They grabbed each other's hands and danced in a circle, entwining themselves in the cables. When they were about to trip they noticed what was happening, looked at each other and laughed. Derek yanked the sensors off and untangled the two of them.

"I can't believe it. You slowed down time!"

"We'll be famous! We'll be Time's Men of the Year!"

"This could mean a Nobel Prize for us!"

"In what? Physics or Psychology?"

"Do they have a Nobel Prize for Psychology?"

"Hell if I know!"

Determined banging sounded through the door. Derek pranced over and opened it. The same angry grad student opened his mouth ready to spew, but Derek cried, "Your mother sleeps with diseased beavers."

"Your mother *is* a diseased beaver," Jake added as they passed him through the doorway.

"Your mother *has* a dis—"

SLAM! went the door in Derek's face.

They spent most of the night celebrating. They might have spent all night, but Derek wanted enough time to recover before their next afternoon session with the biofeedback equipment. He had some grandiose ideas in mind.

If he could slow time down at all, it should only be a matter of practice to slow it more and more. If he practiced enough, he should be able to slow it to a crawl. Maybe, just maybe, he could slow it down so much that it came to a stop.

He was so wrapped up in their project that he actually experienced moments when he didn't think of Katie. But they were fairly rare, and the rest of the time all his painful feelings flooded back. She and Anthony were on their honeymoon right now. It tortured him to think about what they were doing together every night, and maybe every day. *His* love, *his* wife, in that man's arms. Today Derek thought very little about the lost friendship between him and Anthony. Today he was in the mood for hate.

He approached the next biofeedback session with relief. Something to distract his mind. They had become efficient at setting everything up, and in a couple of moments Derek was making that tone dive like a hawk. He had no doubt about it now. The second hand slowed every time. Halfway into the session, he was literally making the tone fall below their hearing range.

Derek stopped caring about making the transition quickly. He had proven to his satisfaction that the effect was no illusion. Now he concentrated on pushing the envelope of how slow he could make time. It was excruciating going, with the law of diminishing returns fighting him with a vengeance. He began to think that maybe his goal was impossible. He had managed to slow time about 90% he figured, but that last ten percent wasn't giving. Maybe time couldn't be stopped.

The hour was nearly spent, even with all the slowing of time Derek had done. He had time for just one more try. His mind followed the familiar path to a deep trance where the second hand barely moved. This state of mind was an unpleasant one, an intense sort of despair that he imagined suicides might experience. He tried wallowing in the hopelessness, sinking deeper and deeper into self-hate. How grateful he was that intellect was separate from emotion, and could keep him focused on his goal so he didn't give in to the despair.

The desire to give up, to back out, to end it all became intense. He felt like his life had no meaning, and that was easy to believe with his grief over Katie. If he'd had a gun, he wasn't sure but that he wouldn't kill himself on the spot. But he forced himself to concentrate on the clock. Everything around him seem to swallow up into a dark fog that devoured his peripheral vision. But the clock shone brightly before him with that one red line creeping across the white face almost imperceptibly. He felt sure he had slowed time more than ever before, but he wasn't sure he cared now. Without Katie, what did anything matter? Perhaps, he thought, if he stopped time altogether, he would die. How could life survive without the flow of time? This made his goal appealing again, and he longed desperately for the cessation of time. The second hand barely moved at all. He desired and desired and the clock stopped completely.

He had stopped time. But he was still alive. Had he really stopped time or was it moving so slowly that he just couldn't see it? He had to stop it. He wanted out of this life of misery and pain. No gun around, but this was less messy anyway. Stop that clock. Stop it! Stop it and me to death!

The second hand lay still over the number four. For some time it hadn't seem to move at all. Stop time! Stop! A panic set in that the stopping of time may not kill him after all. And then the second hand moved, barely, barely...

...and backwards.

Derek froze in place. He didn't dare breathe. He held himself still and carefully maintained the state he was in as if it were a fragile egg. The second hand crept towards the three, then the two, and he thought it was gaining momentum. The two, then the one. When the second hand stood straight up against the twelve he sucked in a violent breath and shuddered himself out of his trance. The red hand shot forward at its normal pace, crossing the one, the two, the three and four.

Jake stared at him with a dark expression. "What happened?" he asked. "You looked like you were about dead for an instant."

"Jake, you're not going to believe this."

Jake's eyebrows raised.

"I slowed time down, all the way down. I slowed it until it stopped."

"That's fantastic!"

"And Jake." Derek wet his lips and took a deep breath. "Then I slowed it some more."

Jake's brow knotted. "You slowed it past stopping?"

Derek nodded somberly.

"But Derek," Jake said ominously, "if you stopped time and then slowed it down some more, that means..."

"It means I went backward in time."

Anthony wasn't looking forward to this. Coming off a fantastic honeymoon didn't make it any easier. But it had to be done, and they were expecting him today. Might as well get it over with.

He walked up to the familiar door and rang the bell. He hoped Derek wasn't home. If the guy had any sense he wouldn't be. It would be too humiliating to face the man he'd lost to right after the honeymoon. Talk about rubbing it in!

It was such a shame, too. They had been best of friends. Even chose the same major—Psychology. They thought so alike they could anticipate each other's actions half the time. Maybe that's why they loved the same woman.

Now it was Derek and Jake who were friends, and all Anthony had was Katie.

He smiled. He would give up a million Dereks for one Katie.

The door opened, and in the frame stood Derek. Damn!

"Oh, hi, Anthony!" For some reason Derek didn't appear the least bit upset. "That's right, you were coming over today to get the rest of your stuff. Come on in!"

"Thanks." It bothered him that Derek was in such a good mood. Derek wasn't one to hide his feelings, especially his negative ones. Now if it had been Anthony, well, he was proud of his poker face.

"Need any help?" Derek offered.

Actually he could use some, but he didn't like the idea of hanging around Derek any longer than necessary. "No, thanks. I'm fine."

"Well, let me know." He grinned an enthusiastic grin, and it was then that Anthony realized he was up to something. It was *that* grin, the one he always grinned when devious thoughts churned in his head.

Anthony sighed in relief when Derek went to another room. He grabbed a box and carried it out to his van. Then another, and another. Finally he was finished.

Reluctantly he went to the room Derek had disappeared to. There he found him and Jake sitting at a kitchen table and sharing a meal. "I'm done," he called. The other two looked up.

"How was the honeymoon?" Jake asked. "Did you have a good time?"

Anthony thought it was a bit untactful to ask in front of Derek. But now it would be more awkward not to respond. "Fine," he answered as blandly as he could.

Jake and Derek looked at each other and grinned. "I'm glad you had a good time," Derek said.

"Let's get together again sometime," Anthony said without conviction. "See you."

"Bye."

"Bye."

Anthony rushed out as fast as he could and climbed into his van. Thank God that was over. But he thought as he drove, what could Derek possibly be scheming? Correction, Derek and Jake. They had grinned *that* grin at each other.

Aw, who cares? What could they possibly do? Derek could be a pill, but it wasn't like he was the kind to resort to genuine cruelty. Katie was Anthony's wife now, and that was that. Unless he could turn back the clock, it was too late for Derek.

"So you're really going to do this?"

"How can I not? You know what she means to me."

Jake stared at the floor, frowning deeply. "You realize this means I may never see you again."

"What do you mean? I'll end up back in this time again."

"No, not *this* time. You'll go back and choose a different fork in the road. All that will be left here is your empty flesh-and-blood robot and computer mind, going through the motions. *You* will be somewhere else."

The shock caused Derek to catch his breath. "I never thought of that." They sat staring at each other as if one of them were on their way to a death sentence. Derek said finally, "How do you know that's not what I've been all along? Maybe I always did choose the other path and you've been talking to a robot."

Jake raised his eyebrows.

"Or maybe I've been talking to a robot all this time and when I go down the other path, the real Jake will be *there*."

Jake swore. "How do we know anybody around us is real then? Do you know how many parallel universe forks there are? And only a few billion people in the world. Chances are every single one of us are alone in our own private universe with nothing but robots surrounding us."

Derek shuddered. "Don't say that. I don't want to marry a robot Katie. I want the real thing."

Jake looked at him apologetically, and seemed about to shrug his shoulders, but a thought came to him. "Didn't you say she would have married you if you had asked her out first?"

"More or less, yeah."

"There you go! Since one of your counterparts *did* ask her out first, the real Katie probably chose that path to go down. You just got sidetracked down the wrong highway and now you're going back to catch up with her."

Derek jumped up with excitement. "You're right! That has to be true!"

Jake finished the shrug he had started. "On the other hand—"

"No!" Derek shouted. "No other hand! What you said is true."

Jake studied his face for an instant, then smiled. "You're right. My other hand was silly anyway. You'll meet up with the real Katie and head down the fork of marital bliss together. I'm sure of it."

"That's better," Derek growled.

"So I guess this is good-bye then."

Derek couldn't believe it, but Jake was actually getting misty eyed. What amazed Derek even more was that he was also getting misty eyed. "You're a good friend, Jake. One of my best, even though I've only known you a few weeks. I hate to think what it would have been like not to have you around while Katie and Anthony got married."

They extended their hands for a handshake, then fell into an embrace, slapping each other on the back. "You better get going," Jake said softly. "I wish you happiness with Katie."

"Thanks." Derek sat back in his chair. Jake assumed his scientific observer position in a chair opposite from him. Within a moment Derek had gone into an altered mental state.

Jake watched him intently. He could see his focus go hazy, his pupils wander slightly out of synch. From his previous observations he knew Derek was slowing time right now.

He was familiar with the stages. They had practiced it again and again during the last two hours they had available with the biofeedback computer. Derek's expression would go bland, and then dark, and then pained. His face blanched, then seemed to turn a faint blue. Derek had described this experience as horrendous. Time travel may be possible, but it didn't come cheap.

Suddenly Derek's eyes focused sharply on Jake. The trance-like appearance was gone, and the color of his face quickly returned to normal. Derek jumped out of the chair and cried, "Damn it! It didn't work!"

"What happened?"

"I don't know. I thought I felt time slowing down, then suddenly I realized nothing was happening." He paced back and forth with agitation. "This was stupid anyway. Did we really think I could travel back in time just by thinking about it? I must have been imagining it before. Self-hypnosis." Derek stopped his pacing in front of Jake and looked at him. "I know all about that, you know. I'm a Psychology major."

Jake stared at his friend in confusion. Several times they had experimented and each time Derek reported that he had reversed time. They had even tried a control experiment to completely rule out illusion. Jake thought of three nonsense sentences, and said, "Okay," to announce his readiness. Then he spoke those three sentences aloud. Or at least that's what was supposed to happen. But before he had a chance Derek spoke them instead, word for word as Jake had thought them. Derek said that Jake really *had* spoken the sentences, but that Derek had moved back in time to the point where Jake said "Okay" and spoke them first. That was the whole idea. Derek couldn't have spoken the nonsense sentences without hearing Jake say them first, yet he did speak them before Jake had a chance. It was objective proof that Derek really had reversed time.

So why didn't it work now? Jake gazed at Derek ranting as he paced, cursing the gods for denying him access to Katie.

Or had it worked? Derek seemed different somehow, but Jake couldn't place his finger on why. Everything seemed the same, but somehow Derek wasn't quite right.

Jake gasped. It was because Derek wasn't really there. That had to be it. Derek's consciousness *had* gone back in time and left this empty shell of a biological robot. The simulation was so perfect that no one would know the difference. But Jake had witnessed the change, the first human being ever to do so. He couldn't tell what the difference was, but somehow his subconscious had noticed. With the immediate contrast for comparison—first Derek was there, and then he wasn't—somehow his subconscious knew.

Derek was still acting like Derek, but suddenly Jake felt a distaste for this creature in front of him. He had to get away. He needed to think. But mostly he needed to leave the presence of this creepy imposter who was playing Derek.

"Derek, I—I'm sorry it didn't work. Uh, I just remembered something, an important meeting I have. I, uh, have to meet with one of my professors. Sorry. I'll see you later, okay?"

The Derek-thing stared at him in amazement. "You're going to leave me just when..."

"Sorry," Jake blurted and flew out the door. He ran down the sidewalk as fast as he could, panic growing with each step. All around him were pedestrians, mostly students, who stared at him with curiosity as he flew by. He couldn't meet any of their eyes. All he could think about was *Invasion of the Body Snatchers* and that chilling ending where Donald Sutherland extended his finger and screeched as the camera zoomed in on his mouth. Jake expected the students around him at any moment to stop and point and screech. Here's one who figured out our secret! Here's one who still has a consciousness inside him.

At last, panting painfully, he collapsed on the grass behind a tombstone in the local cemetery where no one could see him. As his panic ebbed, three Latin words popped into his mind. *Cogito, ergo sum.* "I think, therefore I am." Jake knew that his consciousness was in this universe because he was experiencing it. And he knew that Derek's consciousness had been in this universe because he'd watched it depart. For all he knew there were no other consciousnesses. Jake may be utterly alone.

"No," he spat. "If there was one with me, there's probably more." At that moment he determined his life's work. The last few days he thought his life's work would be studying this new phenomenon of time travel. But now his life's work would be finding consciousnesses. His subconscious had detected a difference when Derek left, so there was a difference to detect. There was some way to know if one of these biological Turing machines walking around playing a real person housed a consciousness. If it took him his whole life he would figure it out. He had to know if he was alone.

Slipping into time control mode had become easier and less torturous. A couple days practice hooked up to the biofeedback machine had made Derek an expert. He didn't even need a clock in his line of vision anymore. He could recognize by feel when he was reversing time.

He stared at Jake staring back at him. As he slipped into the trance Jake went out of focus, but Derek didn't notice. His attention had bent inward and concentrated on his state of mind. Within seconds he felt the emptiness, then the despair, then the self-loathing, that caused his consciousness to slow down on this particular highway of time. Before long he came to a full stop. Jake was sitting motionless without breathing.

Then the unique sensation of accelerating backward began. It was a subtle sensation, one he hadn't noticed the first time for all the despair. But after many practice runs he had come to recognize it. Moving forward required the conscious mind to make a constant series of choices as forks in time presented themselves. But backwards allowed only one direction as the mind retraced the path it had chosen the first time through. It gave a sensation almost like free fall. He had no choice in this direction. This was what lack of free will felt like.

Derek sunk deeper into his trance, speeding up the movement. Jake leaped out of his chair at the same time Derek's body suddenly flew up, and they embraced each other. Then they both strutted backwards. It was a disconcerting sensation. This must be what it felt like when aliens took over your body, with the disorienting addition of moving physically backwards.

Faster and faster he accelerated. He had to go back eight months and he wasn't interested in taking eight months to get there. He wanted the hours to melt away in seconds. His body raced around dizzily. He felt masticated food surge up his esophagus and unchew and reattach to the main portion of his meal. He felt vertigo as his body endlessly strode backward at a dizzying pace. He became blind at night as his body fell asleep. The words people spoke to him were accelerated, backwards gibberish. He cringed as he smeared fecal matter back onto his anus and sucked the stools up into his rectum. He sat in class and unscribbled notes from a crowded page until the paper gleamed white

The sun whooshed across the sky faster and faster, until he felt like he was watching an old, flickering movie. All normal human movement became a blur to him and invisible activities of nature appeared. Grass shrunk, flowers opened and closed. Leaves rushed from the ground back onto the trees and turned from reds, oranges, and yellows to lush greens. Cherries on the trees deflated into blossoms and the blossoms into buds. Spring was upon the world and that meant he was near his destination.

He slowed the velocity of his travel down to where he could see human activity again. He oriented himself by noticing what he was doing. He found snatches of time he spent with Katie, so he hadn't reached his goal yet. He sped up and slowed down as he zeroed in on the critical moment. The times he had kissed Katie were moments he slowed way down so he could relish them again. He felt his love for her overwhelm him, confirming that this journey was the right thing to do.

The moment grew near. Their first date came and went. His nervousness over their first date reafflicted him. The moment he asked her on that first date zoomed by. The month of procrastination when he should have been dating her but thought, in his arrogance or stupidity, that he had all the time in the world, swept past quickly, because he didn't want to dwell there long.

Then finally the crucial moment came, when his eyes fell on her. Not for the first time, because he had seen her in his American History class and had sat by her a few times and even struck up a conversation once or twice. But this was the first time it consciously occurred to him, "You know, I really ought to ask her out."

His consciousness braked to a stop and the normal movement of time resumed. He spared a moment to feel enormous relief at the absence of the miserable sensations of plummeting backward in time. Then he began to feel as if the intervening months had never occurred. Here he was, and there she was, just as it had been eight months ago. But this time he would choose differently. This time he wouldn't waste one second putting off what he wanted to do. He strode toward her as she waited at a corner for the light to change.

"Hi, I'm Derek. You remember me from class?"

She looked at him and smiled.

"Of course I remember you, Derek."

He smiled with satisfaction. Those were the exact same words they had exchanged one month later in a different time fork.

Katie looked so beautiful in her bridal gown, and Derek looked handsome in the groom's tuxedo. This time he *was* the groom, as he should be.

Anthony didn't even have the courage to attend the wedding, and that was fine with Derek. But Jake wasn't there either and that made Derek feel bad. Derek had moved out to the new apartment where he and Katie would live, and Jake became Anthony's new roommate. They had become good friends while Derek spent his time with Katie. He could imagine the conversations going on between them as Anthony spewed his bitterness over the loss of his love. Love! He'd never had one date with her, yet he acted as if Derek had stolen away his childhood sweetheart.

But Derek felt bad that his friendship with Jake never materialized, and that Jake probably now thought he was a jerk. He missed that friendship.

But to end up with Katie, he would give up a million Jakes.

Their honeymoon was the ecstasy he had dreamed of. Katie was an exciting, passionate woman in body and soul and mind. He had never felt so alive as when in her presence. In an occasional dark moment he would wonder if he were romancing the real Katie or some empty shell. But this girl was so vibrant, so energizing, that he couldn't believe there was nothing inside. She must really be there, and it thrilled him to know her consciousness had chosen to join him in this fork. He thanked God he was able to go back and meet up with her. They were soul mates. It would have been a travesty if their two souls had not ended up in the same universe.

As the honeymoon ended and they faced the prospect of returning to campus existence, it almost felt as if life had ended. Derek could swear he was grieving a little. But it was grief only in comparison to the joy they had felt for the last week. With the prospect of a lifetime ahead with his beloved Katie, the grief held no sting.

They settled into their new apartment. Derek still had a number of things he'd left behind with Anthony. He headed for his old stomping grounds with no enthusiasm. Facing Anthony right after the honeymoon didn't sound like such a clever idea, but it had to be done sometime, and they were expecting him today. Might as well get it over with.

He walked up to the familiar door and rang the bell. He hoped Anthony wasn't home. If the guy had any sense he wouldn't be. It would be too humiliating to face the man he'd lost to right after the honeymoon. Talk about rubbing it in!

The door opened, and there stood Anthony. Damn!

"Oh, hi, Derek!" For some reason Anthony didn't appear the least bit upset. "That's right, you were coming over today to get the rest of your stuff. Come on in!"

"Thanks." It bothered him that Anthony was in such a good mood. Anthony was known for hiding his feelings well—old Poker Face they called him sometimes—but he'd been in short supply of that skill in the last few months.

"Need any help?" Anthony offered.

Actually he could use some, but he didn't like the idea of hanging around Anthony any longer than necessary. "No, thanks. I'll manage."

"As you wish." He grinned an enthusiastic grin, but Derek hardly noticed. He just wanted in and out as fast as he could. He sighed with relief when Anthony went to another room. Shaking his head over their one time friendship, he grabbed a box and carried it out to the car. Then another, and another. Finally he was finished.

Reluctantly he went to the room Anthony had disappeared to. There he found him and Jake relaxing before the television. "I'm done," he called. The other two looked up.

"How was the honeymoon?" Jake asked. "Did you have a good time?"

Derek thought it was a bit untactful to ask in front of Anthony. But now it would be more awkward not to respond. "Nice," he answered blandly.

Jake and Anthony looked at each other and grinned. "I'm glad it was nice," Anthony said.

"Thanks. See you later." Derek gazed at Jake for one short moment, remembering the farewells they had spoken to each other eight months ago—or a few days from now, depending on how you looked at it.

"Let's get together sometime," Anthony said.

"Sure," Derek said unconvincingly. He rushed out as fast as he could and climbed into the car. He was getting misty eyed, and it rattled him that he would do so a second time over Jake. He wiped his eyes angrily and pulled out. As he drove he thought about the grin Anthony and Jake had shared with each other. Something about it bothered him, but he couldn't figure out why.

Aw, who cares? Katie was Derek's wife now, and that's all that mattered. Derek had turned the clock back and beat Anthony to the punch. He was the only one who knew how to work such a miracle. What could Anthony possibly do about that?

About the Author

D. Michael Martindale is a storyteller. It doesn't matter which medium the story is told in—whether it be film or television or books or music—what's important is telling stories that people enjoy.

He was born in Minnesota and has been telling stories since before he could write. He started out by drawing comic strips and having his mother fill in the dialog balloons for him. He developed a taste for science fiction and fantasy, and although he's written screenplays in all sorts of genres, he continues to gravitate back to speculative fiction.

Martindale earned an Associate Degree in Film Production at Salt Lake Community College and a Bachelor Degree in Screenwriting and Cinematography at Utah Valley University.

For a period of time, he focused on telling stories about his religious community, Mormons. He considered the quality of Mormon literature subpar and preachy and wanted to tell stories about his people that he'd want to read, quality stories that were honest and edgy and not the least bit preachy. He's glad to see that the quality of Mormon art has been improving over the years.

He served three years on the board of the Association for Mormon Letters, a nonprofit organization that promotes Mormon literature and other arts, and acted as their Writers Conference chairperson for four years. He wrote a number of articles and book and film reviews for their literary journal *Irreantum.*

He worked for a time as a staff writer for *The Sugar Beet*, an Internet publication of Mormon satire patterned after the infamous website *The Onion.* Many of these online articles of alleged Mormon "news" were eventually collected into the popular book *The Mormon Tabernacle Enquirer.*

The editor of *The Mormon Tabernacle Enquirer* decided to start his own publishing company, Zarahemla Books, and chose as its flagship publication Martindale's second novel *Brother Brigham*, which he categorizes as "Mormon speculative fiction." *Brother Brigham* went on to receive substantial critical acclaim and was even used as reading material in a college comparative religion class one semester. He also had a science fiction short story "Bokev Momen" published in the anthology *Monsters and Mormons*, which has been included in this collection.

Inspired by *Jesus Christ Superstar*, he composed the musical *General Prophet Joseph Smith*, based on the events leading up to the assassination of the Mormon prophet Joseph Smith. He produced a concept album recording of it on CDs, and is currently developing a film adaptation of it. He calls it "Les Mis for Mormons."

Martindale has written two other novels. His first, *The Power of the Seeker*, is the beginning installment of a science fiction series called *The Reincarnate.* It remains unpublished, and he describes it as "crap." He may rewrite it someday. His third novel is a fantasy called *Celeste & the White Dragon* which he's in the process of bringing to publication. It's the first volume of a fantasy series.

For nine years Martindale focused on screenwriting and film making as a director and editor. Film is his favorite medium in which to tell stories. He wrote, produced, directed, and edited eight short films and a feature-length fantasy film called *Geeks and Goblins, Elves and Elliot.* He has multiple other screenplays ready to be developed into feature-length films, including an adaptation of his short story "Solar Butterfly" that appears in this collection. Additionally, he's been on the development team for three television/web series.

He resides in Salt Lake City, Utah, and is the father of three grown children and the grandfather of the best granddaughter in the world. Do not debate him on this.

Brother Brigham
by D. Michael Martindale

Like many young boys, C.H. Young grew up with an imaginary friend. In his case, it was his ancestor Brigham Young—or rather, "Brother Brigham" as C.H. knew him. During his formative years, Brother Brigham filled the boy's head with grand expectations of an important mission in life.

Now grown up with a wife and two young sons, C.H. has sacrificed his dreams to earn a living for his family. Brother Brigham is just a distant memory—until one day he returns in a most unexpected way. As Brother Brigham's appearances and instructions grow increasingly bold, C.H. struggles to hold together his faith, his marriage, and his sanity.

brotherbrigham.worldsmithstories.com

Celeste & the White Dragon
by D. Michael Martindale

Queen Tamara, thrown into a dungeon by the rogue sorceress Gwendolyn, is about to give birth. There's something about her baby that makes Gwendolyn want to possess it, and when Tamara delivers, Gwendolyn will kill her and take the baby.

But Tamara's chambermaid Zenia will not let that happen. At great risk to her life, she rescues Tamara and helps her flee out of the kingdom of Gallea. But in the midst of Fenweald Forest, Tamara dies while giving birth to the baby, and Zenia discovers the terrible secret that makes Gwendolyn want to possess it. She puts her life in peril seeking a way to hide the infant.

A great search for the child begins, with kings and sorceresses and wizards and accursed monsters and village witches all struggling to find and possess the young princess, whom Zenia names Celeste. The fate of three continents depends on who succeeds.

celeste.worldsmithstories.com

Twisted Soul
by D. Michael Martindale

From the twisted soul of D. Michael come four slipstream novellas that explore the twists and turns of human spirituality and psychic powers. The hidden worlds they reveal may inspire or disturb, but the souls that experience them will never be the same again.

Alexandra
A Face in the Window
First Mormons in the Moon
Godblind
Bonus novelette: **The Dreamcatcher**

twisted.worldsmithstories.com

www.ingramcontent.com/pod-product-compliance
Lightning Source LLC
Chambersburg PA
CBHW071254130626
46556CB00003B/1316